8·2022

FIRST PERSON SINGULAR

Books By

W. SOMERSET MAUGHAM

FIRST PERSON SINGULAR
CAKES AND ALE
or The Skeleton in the Cupboard
THE GENTLEMAN IN THE PARLOUR
ASHENDEN: OR THE BRITISH AGENT
THE CASUARINA TREE
THE PAINTED VEIL
ON A CHINESE SCREEN
OF HUMAN BONDAGE
THE MOON AND SIXPENCE
THE TREMBLING OF A LEAF
LIZA OF LAMBETH
MRS. CRADDOCK
THE EXPLORER
THE MAGICIAN
THE MERRY-GO-ROUND
THE LAND OF THE BLESSED VIRGIN
(Sketches and Impressions in Andalusia)

PLAYS

THE SACRED FLAME
THE LETTER
THE CONSTANT WIFE
THE CIRCLE
THE EXPLORER
MRS. DOT
A MAN OF HONOUR
PENELOPE
JACK STRAW
LADY FREDERICK
THE TENTH MAN
LANDED GENTRY
THE UNKNOWN
SMITH

SIX STORIES WRITTEN IN THE FIRST PERSON SINGULAR

W. Somerset Maugham

MCMXXXI

DOUBLEDAY, DORAN & COMPANY, INC.
GARDEN CITY, NEW YORK

PRINTED AT THE *Country Life Press*, GARDEN CITY, N. Y., U. S. A.

CONTENTS

INTRODUCTION

I VENTURE to trouble the reader of these pages with a little explanation. It is usual nowadays, owing to the law of libel which enables, for instance, a lawyer called Smith at least to threaten an action if a lawyer in a novel is called Smith, for an author to preface his book with the declaration that no character in it represents a living person, and I can honestly make the same statement about all the characters in these stories save one. It is because there is an exception that I feel it my duty to write these lines. I am a little sensitive on the point, since I have at one time or another been charged with portraying certain persons so exactly that it was impossible not to know them. I have been accused of bad taste. This has disturbed me, not so much for my own sake (since I am used to the slings and arrows of outrageous fortune) as for the sake of criticism in general. We authors of course try to be gentlemen, but we often fail and we must console ourselves by reflecting that few writers of any consequence have been devoid of a certain streak of vulgarity. Life is vulgar. I have long known that journalists, in private free in their speech and fond enough of bawdry, are in print great sticklers for purity, and I have no doubt that this is as it should be; but I fear that if they become *too* refined there will be so few points of contact between them and the writers whom it is their pleasant duty to appraise that criticism will become almost impossible.

I have known authors who declared that none of their characters was ever even remotely suggested by anyone they had known and I have unhesitatingly accepted their assertion. But I have ceased to wonder why they never managed to create a character that was not wooden and lifeless. It is certain that many excellent writers have founded the persons of their stories on persons they have known in real life. Anyone who reads the notes of Henri Beyle, the letters of Flaubert or the Journal of Jules Renard, will see with what care these authors observed their acquaintance when they might be useful for the creation of such and such a personage and the callous deliberation with which they jotted down typical and characteristic traits. I think indeed that most novelists, and surely the best, have worked from life. But though they have had in mind a particular person this is not to say that they have copied him nor that the character they have devised is to be taken for a portrait. In the first place they have seen him through their own temperament and if they are writers of originality this means that what they have seen is somewhat different from the fact. They have taken only what they wanted of him. They have used him as a convenient peg on which to hang their own fancies. To suit their purpose they have given him traits which the model did not possess. They have made him coherent and substantial. A real person, however eminent, is for the most part too insignificant for the purposes of fiction.

The complete character, the result of elaboration rather than of invention, is art, and life in the raw, as we know, is only its material. It is unjust then for the critics to blame an author because he draws a character in whom they detect a likeness to someone they know and wholly unreasonable of them to expect him never to take one trait or another from living creatures. The odd thing is that when these charges are made, emphasis is laid only on the less laudable characteristics of the individual. If you say of a character in a book that he is kind to his mother, but beats his wife, everyone will cry: Ah, that is Brown, how beastly to say he beats his wife; and no one thinks for a moment of Jones and Robinson who are notoriously kind to their mothers. I draw from this the somewhat surprising conclusion that we know our friends by their defects and not by their merits.

Nothing is so unsafe as to put into a novel a person drawn line by line from life. His values are all wrong, and, strangely enough, he does not make the other characters of the book seem false, but himself. He never convinces. That is why the many writers who have been attracted by the singular and powerful figure of the late Lord Northcliffe have never succeeded in presenting a credible personage. It is with diffidence then that I draw the reader's attention to Mortimer Ellis in the story called 'The Round Dozen.' I have, of course, given him a false name and considerably toned him down, for otherwise, as real persons always do, he would have burst the bounds of my story. I do not admit that it is a photograph, but it is certainly a portrait. I confess the crime. But a painter will sometimes wilfully distort a form, either for his own amusement or to exasperate the philistine, and a writer may be forgiven if on occasion he takes undue liberties with his medium. He is after all but human, and so long as he knows that he is committing an error in art, there is no great harm if he indulges now and then in his own private little bit of fun.

Mortimer Ellis has now passed to a sphere where there is neither marrying nor giving in marriage and cannot be affected by my portrait of him. By the circumstances of the case he left no children to mourn him, but he must have had a good many relations by marriage and I should not like to hurt their feelings. Of an affable nature, he doubtless made a host of friends on the Isle of Wight during the two periods he spent there, when, engaged in manual labour, he ate the bread of King George the Fifth, and if I have said anything to affront them I sincerely tender them my apologies. My justification is that he was a humorous character. The man of action expresses himself in deeds and they may well be left to speak for him, but such a man as he whom I have here called Mortimer Ellis demands the chronicler. It may be said that his celebrity should have protected him from my pen, but even the most celebrated of us are human and therefore the author's fit material. When nature produces a buffoon he is fair game and he has no just cause for complaint if the novelist to the best of his ability presents him as he is for the entertainment of his generation. He thus surely fulfils his purpose. We must not be too squeamish. The average life of a novel is ninety days and we should not mind if for three short months we afford others a little amusement.

VIRTUE

VIRTUE

THERE are few things better than a good Havana. When I was young and very poor and smoked a cigar only when somebody gave me one, I determined that if ever I had money I would smoke a cigar every day after luncheon and after dinner. This is the only resolution of my youth that I have kept. It is the only ambition I have achieved that has never been embittered by disillusion. I like a cigar that is mild, but full-flavoured, neither so small that it is finished before you have become aware of it nor so large as to be irksome, rolled so that it draws without consciousness of effort on your part, with a leaf so firm that it doesn't become messy on your lips and in such condition that it keeps its savour to the very end. But when you have taken the last pull and put down the shapeless stump and watched the final cloud of smoke dwindle blue in the surrounding air it is impossible, if you have a sensitive nature, not to feel a certain melancholy at the thought of all the labour, the care and pains that have gone, the thought, the trouble, the complicated organization that have been required, to provide you with half an hour's delight. For this men have sweltered long years under tropical suns and ships have scoured the seven seas.

These reflections become more poignant still when you are eating a dozen oysters (with half a bottle of dry white wine) and they become almost unbearable when it comes to a lamb cutlet. For these are animals, and there is something that inspires awe in the thought that since the surface of the earth became capable of supporting life from generation to generation for millions upon millions of years creatures have come into existence, to end at last upon a plate of crushed ice or on a silver grill. It may be that a sluggish fancy cannot grasp the dreadful solemnity of eating an oyster and evolution has taught us that the bivalve has through the ages kept itself to itself in a manner that inevitably alienates sympathy. There is an aloofness in it that is offensive to the aspiring spirit of man, and a self-complacency that is obnoxious to his vanity. But I do not know how anyone can look upon a lamb cutlet without thoughts too deep for tears: here man himself has taken a hand, and the history of the race is bound up with the tender morsel on your plate.

And sometimes even the fate of human beings is curious to consider. It is strange to look upon this man or that, the quiet ordinary persons of every day, the bank clerk, the dustman, the middle-aged girl in the second row of the chorus, and think of the interminable history behind them and of the long, long series of hazards by which from the primeval slime the course of events has brought them at this moment to such and such a place. When such tremendous vicissitudes have been needed to get them here at all, one would have thought some huge significance must be attached to them; one would have thought that what befell them must matter a little to the Life Spirit or whatever else it is that has produced them. An accident befalls them. The thread is broken. The story that began with the world is finished abruptly, and it looks as though it meant nothing at all. A tale told by an idiot. And is it not odd that this event, of an importance so dramatic, may be brought about by a cause so trivial?

An incident of no moment, that might easily not have happened, has consequences that are incalculable. It looks as though blind chance ruled all things. Our smallest actions may affect profoundly the whole lives of people who have nothing to do with us. The story I have to tell would never have happened if one day I had not walked across the street. Life is really very fantastic, and one has to have a peculiar sense of humour to see the fun of it.

I was strolling down Bond Street one spring morning and, having nothing much to do till lunch time, thought I would look in at Sotheby's, the auction rooms, to see whether there was anything on show that interested me. There was a block in the traffic and I threaded my way through the cars. When I reached the other side I ran into a man I had known in Borneo coming out of a hatter's.

"Hullo, Morton," I said. "When did you come home?"

"I've been back about a week."

He was a District Officer. The Governor had given me a letter of introduction to him, and I wrote and told him I meant to spend a week at the place he lived at and should like to put up at the government rest-house. He met me on the ship when I arrived and asked me to stay with him. I demurred. I did not see how I could spend a week with a total stranger, I did not want to put him to the expense of my board, and besides I thought I should have more freedom if I were on my own. He would not listen to me.

"I've got plenty of room," he said, "and the rest-house is beastly. I haven't spoken to a white man for six months and I'm fed to the teeth with my own company."

But when Morton had got me and his launch had landed us at the bungalow and he had offered me a drink, he did not in the least know what to do with me. He was seized on a sudden with shyness, and his conversation, which had been fluent and ready, ran dry. I did my best to make him feel at home (it was the least I could do, considering that it was his own house) and asked him if he had any new records. He turned on the gramophone, and the sound of ragtime gave him confidence.

His bungalow overlooked the river, and his living-room was a large verandah. It was furnished in the impersonal fashion that characterized the dwellings of government officials who were moved here and there at little notice according to the exigencies of the service. There were native hats as ornaments on the walls and the horns of animals, blow-pipes and spears. In the book-shelf were detective novels and old magazines. There was a cottage piano with yellow keys. It was very untidy, but not uncomfortable.

Unfortunately I cannot very well remember what he looked like. He was young, twenty-eight, I learnt later, and he had a boyish and attractive smile. I spent an agreeable week with him. We went up and down the river and we climbed a mountain. We had tiffin one day with some planters who lived twenty miles away, and every evening we went to the club. The only members were the manager of a kutch factory and his assistants, but they were not on speaking terms with one another and it was only on Morton's representations that they must not let him down when he had a visitor that we could get up a rubber of bridge. The atmosphere was strained. We came back to dinner, listened to the gramophone and went to bed. Morton had little office work, and one would have thought the time hung heavy on his hands, but he had energy and high spirits; it was his first post of the sort and he was happy to be independent. His only anxiety was lest he should be transferred before he had finished a road he was building. This was the joy of his heart. It was his own idea and he had wheedled the government into giving him the money to make it; he had surveyed the country himself and traced the path. He had solved unaided the technical problems that presented themselves. Every morning, before he went to his office, he drove out in a rickety old Ford to where the coolies were working and watched the progress that had been made since the day before. He thought of nothing else. He dreamt of it at night. He reckoned that it would be finished in a year and he did not want to take his leave till then. He could not have worked with more zest if he had been a painter or a sculptor creating a work of art. I think it was this eagerness that made me take a fancy to him. I liked his zeal. I liked his ingenuousness. And I was impressed by the passion for achievement that made him indifferent to the solitariness of his life, to promotion and even to the thought of going home. I forget how long the road was, fifteen or twenty miles, I think, and I forget what purpose it was to serve. I don't believe Morton cared very much. His passion was the artist's and his triumph was the triumph of man over nature. He learnt as he went along. He had the jungle to contend against, torrential rains that destroyed the labour of weeks, accidents of topography; he had to collect his labour and hold it together; he had inadequate funds. His imagination sustained him. His labours gained a sort of epic quality, and the vicissitudes of the work were a great saga that unrolled itself with an infinity of episodes.

His only complaint was that the day was too short. He had office duties, he was judge and tax collector, father and mother (at twenty-eight) of the people in his district; he had now and then to make tours that took him away from home. Unless he were on the spot nothing was done. He would have liked to be there twenty-four hours a day driving the reluctant coolies to further effort. It so happened that shortly before I arrived an incident had occurred that filled him with jubilation. He had offered a contract to a Chinese to make a certain section of the road, and the Chinese had asked more than Morton could afford to pay. Notwithstanding interminable discussions they had been unable to arrive at an agreement, and Morton with rage in his heart saw his work held up. He was at his wits' end. Then, going down to his office one morning, he heard that there had been a row in one of the Chinese gambling houses the night before. A coolie had been badly wounded and his assailant was under arrest. This assailant was the contractor. He was brought into court, the evidence was clear and Morton sentenced him to eighteen months' hard labour.

"Now he'll have to build the blasted road for nothing," said Morton, his eyes glistening when he told me the story.

We saw the fellow at work one morning, in the prison sarong, unconcerned. He was taking his misfortunes in good part.

"I've told him I'll remit the rest of his sentence when the road's finished," said Morton, "and he's as pleased as Punch. Bit of a snip for me, eh, what?"

When I left Morton I asked him to let me know when he came to England, and he promised to write to me as soon as he landed. On the spur of the moment one gives these invitations and one is perfectly sincere about them. But when one is taken at one's word a slight dismay seizes one. People are so different at home from what they are abroad. There they are easy, cordial and natural. They have interesting things to tell you. They are immensely kind. You are anxious, when your turn comes, to do something in return for the hospitality you have received. But it is not easy. The persons who were so entertaining in their own surroundings are very dull in yours. They are constrained and shy. You introduce them to your friends, and your friends find them a crashing bore. They do their best to be civil, but sigh with relief when the strangers go and the conversation can once more run easily in its accustomed channels. I think the residents in far places early in their careers understand the situation pretty well, as the result maybe of bitter and humiliating experiences, for I have found that they seldom take advantage of the invitation which on some outstation on the edge of the jungle has been so cordially extended to them and by them as cordially accepted. But Morton was different. He was a young man and single. It is generally the wives that are the difficulty; other women look at their drab clothes, in a glance take in their provincial air, and freeze them with their indifference. But a man can play bridge and tennis, and dance. Morton had charm. I had no doubt that in a day or two he would find his feet.

"Why didn't you let me know you were back?" I asked him.

"I thought you wouldn't want to be bothered with me," he smiled.

"What nonsense!"

Of course now as we stood in Bond Street on the curb and chatted for a minute he looked strange to me. I had never seen him in anything but khaki shorts and a tennis shirt, except when we got back from the club at night and he put on a pajama jacket and a sarong for dinner. It is as comfortable a form of evening dress as has ever been devised. He looked a bit awkward in his blue serge suit. His face against a white collar was very brown.

"How about the road?" I asked him.

"Finished. I was afraid I'd have to postpone my leave. We struck one or two snags towards the end, but I made 'em hustle and the day before I left I drove the Ford to the end and back without stopping."

I laughed. His pleasure was charming.

"What have you been doing with yourself in London?"

"Buying clothes."

"Been having a good time?"

"Marvellous. A bit lonely, you know, but I don't mind that. I've been to a show every night. The Palmers, you know—I think you met them in Sarawak—were going to be in town and we were going to do the plays together, but they had to go to Scotland because her mother's ill."

His words, said so breezily, cut me to the quick. His was the common experience. It was heart-breaking. For months, for long months before it was due, these people planned their leave, and when they got off the ship they were in such spirits they could hardly contain themselves. London. Shops and clubs and theatres and restaurants. London. They were going to have the time of their lives. London. It swallowed them. A strange, turbulent city, not hostile but indifferent, and they were lost in it. They had no friends. They had nothing in common with the acquaintances they made. They were more lonely than in the jungle. It was a relief when at a theatre they ran across someone they had known in the East (and perhaps been bored stiff by or disliked) and they could fix up an evening together and have a good laugh and tell one another what a grand time they were having and talk of common friends and at last confide to one another a little shyly that they would not be sorry when their leave was up and they were once again in harness. They went to see their families and of course they were glad to see them, but it wasn't the same as it had been; they did feel a bit out of it, and when you came down to brass tacks the life people led in England was deadly. It was grand fun to come home, but you couldn't live there any more, and sometimes you thought of your bungalow overlooking the river and your tours of the district and what a lark it was to run over once in a blue moon to Sandakan or Kuching or Singapore.

And because I remembered what Morton had looked forward to when, the road finished and off his chest, he went on leave, I could not but feel a pang when I thought of him dining by himself in a dismal club where he knew nobody, or alone in a restaurant in Soho and then going off to see a play with no one by his side with whom he could enjoy it, and no one to have a drink with during the interval. And at the same time I reflected that even if I had known he was in London I could have done nothing much for him, for during the last week I had not had a moment free. That very evening I was dining with friends and going to a play, and the next day I was going abroad.

"What are you doing to-night?" I asked him.

"I'm going to the Pavilion. It's packed jammed full, but there's a fellow over the road who's wonderful and he's got me a ticket that had been returned. You can often get one seat, you know, when you can't get two."

"Why don't you come and have supper with me? I'm taking some people to the Haymarket and we're going on to Ciro's afterwards."

"I'd love to."

We arranged to meet at eleven, and I left him to keep an engagement.

I was afraid the friends I had asked him to meet would not amuse Morton very much, for they were distinctly middle-aged, but I could not think of anyone young that at this season of the year I should be likely to get hold of at the last moment. None of the girls I knew would thank me for asking her to supper to dance with a shy young man from Malaya. I could trust the Bishops to do their best for him, and after all it must be jollier for him to have supper in a club with a good band where he could see pretty women dancing than to go home to bed at eleven because he had nowhere else in the world to go. I had known Charlie Bishop first when I was a medical student. He was then a thin little fellow with sandy hair and blunt features; he had fine eyes, dark and gleaming, but he wore spectacles. He had a round, merry, red face. He was very fond of the girls. I suppose he had a way with him, for with no money and no looks, he managed to pick up a succession of young persons who gratified his roving desires. He was clever and bumptious, argumentative and quick-tempered. He had a caustic tongue. Looking back, I should say he was a rather disagreeable young man, but

I do not think he was a bore. Now, halfway through the fifties, he was inclined to be stout and he was very bald, but his eyes behind the gold-rimmed spectacles were still bright and alert. He was dogmatic and somewhat conceited, argumentative still and caustic, but he was good-natured and amusing. After you have known a person so long his idiosyncrasies cease to trouble you. You accept them as you accept your own physical defects. He was by profession a pathologist, and now and then he sent me a slim book he had just published. It was severe and extremely technical and grimly illustrated with photographs of bacteria. I did not read it. I gathered from what I sometimes heard that Charlie's views on the subjects with which he dealt were unsound. I do not believe that he was very popular with the other members of his profession—he made no secret of the fact that he looked upon them as a set of incompetent idiots—but he had his job, it brought him in six or eight hundred a year, I think, and he was completely indifferent to other people's opinion of him.

I liked Charlie Bishop because I had known him for thirty years, but I liked Margery, his wife, because she was very nice. I was extremely surprised when he told me he was going to be married. He was hard on forty at the time, and so fickle in his affections that I had made up my mind he would remain single. He was very fond of women, but he was not in the least sentimental, and his aims were loose. His views on the female sex would in these idealistic days be thought crude. He knew what he wanted and he asked for it, and if he couldn't get it for love or money he shrugged his shoulders and went

VIRTUE 15

his way. To be brief, he did not look to women to gratify
his ideal but to provide him with fornication. It was
odd that, though small and plain, he found so many
who were prepared to grant his wishes. For his spiritual
needs he found satisfaction in unicellular organisms.
He had always been a man who spoke to the point, and
when he told me he was going to marry a young woman
called Margery Hobson I did not hesitate to ask him
why. He grinned.

"Three reasons. First, she won't let me go to bed
with her without. Second, she makes me laugh like a
hyena. And third, she's alone in the world, without a
single relation, and she must have someone to take care
of her."

"The first reason is just swank and the second is
eyewash. The third is the real one and it means that
she's got you by the short hairs."

His eyes gleamed softly behind his large spectacles.

"I shouldn't be surprised if you weren't dead right."

"She's not only got you by the short hairs but you're
as pleased as Punch that she has."

"Come and lunch to-morrow and have a look at her.
She's easy on the eye."

Charlie was a member of a cock-and-hen club which
at that time I used a good deal, and we arranged to
lunch there. I found Margery a very attractive young
woman. She was then just under thirty. She was a lady.
I noticed the fact with satisfaction, but with a certain
astonishment, for it had not escaped my notice that
Charlie was attracted as a rule by women whose breeding left something to be desired. She was not beautiful,

but comely, with fine dark hair and fine eyes, a good colour and a look of health. She had a pleasant frankness and an air of candour that was very taking. She looked honest, simple and dependable. I took an immediate liking to her. She was easy to talk to, and though she did not say anything very brilliant she understood what other people were talking about; she was quick to see a joke and she was not shy. She gave you the impression of being competent and businesslike. She had a happy placidity that suggested a good temper and an excellent digestion.

They seemed extremely pleased with one another. I had asked myself when I first saw her why Margery was marrying this irritable little man, baldish already and by no means young, but I discovered very soon that it was because she was in love with him. They chaffed one another a good deal and laughed a lot, and every now and then their eyes met more signifi-cantly and they seemed to exchange a little private message. It was really rather touching.

A week later they were married at a registrar's office. It was a very successful marriage. Looking back now after sixteen years I could not but chuckle sympatheti-cally at the thought of the lark they had made of their life together. I had never known a more devoted couple. They had never had very much money. They never seemed to want any. They had no ambitions. Their life was a picnic that never came to an end. They lived in the smallest flat I ever saw, in Panton Street, a small bedroom, a small sitting-room and a bathroom that served also as a kitchen. But they had no sense of home,

they ate their meals in restaurants, and only had breakfast in the flat. It was merely a place to sleep in. It was
comfortable, though a third person coming in for a
whisky and soda crowded it, and Margery with the help
of a charwoman kept it as neat as Charlie's untidiness
permitted, but there was not a single thing in it that
had a personal note. They had a tiny car, and whenever
Charlie had a holiday they took it across the Channel
and started off, with a bag each for all their luggage, to
drive wherever the fancy took them. Breakdowns never
disturbed them, bad weather was part of the fun, a
puncture was no end of a joke, and if they lost their
way and had to sleep out in the open they thought they
were having the time of their lives.

Charlie continued to be irascible and contentious,
but nothing he did ever disturbed Margery's lovely
placidity. She could calm him with a word. She still
made him laugh. She typed his monographs on obscure
bacteria and corrected the proofs of his articles in the
scientific magazines. Once I asked them if they ever
quarrelled.

"No," she said, "we never seem to have anything
to quarrel about. Charlie has the temper of an angel."

"Nonsense," I said, "he's an overbearing, aggressive
and cantankerous fellow. He always has been."

She looked at him and giggled, and I saw that she
thought I was being funny.

"Let him rave," said Charlie. "He's an ignorant fool
and he uses words of whose meaning he hasn't the
smallest idea."

They were sweet together. They were very happy in

one another's company and were never apart if they could help it. Even after the long time they had been married Charlie used to get into the car every day at luncheon time to come west and meet Margery at a restaurant. People used to laugh at them, not unkindly, but perhaps with a little catch in the throat, because when they were asked to go and spend a week-end in the country Margery would write to the hostess and say they would like to come if they could be given a double bed. They had slept together for so many years that neither of them could sleep alone. It was often a trifle awkward. Husbands and wives as a rule not only demanded separate rooms, but were inclined to be peevish if asked to share the same bathroom. Modern houses were not arranged for domestic couples, but among their friends it became an understood thing that if you wanted the Bishops you must give them a room with a double bed. Some people of course thought it a little indecent and it was never convenient, but they were a pleasant pair to have to stay and it was worth while to put up with their crankiness. Charlie was always full of spirits and in his caustic way extremely amusing, and Margery was peaceful and easy. They were no trouble to entertain. Nothing pleased them more than to be left to go out together for a long ramble in the country.

When a man marries, his wife sooner or later estranges him from his old friends, but Margery on the contrary increased Charlie's intimacy with them. By making him more tolerant she made him a more agreeable companion. They gave you the impression not of a married couple, but, rather amusingly, of two middle-aged bachelors living together; and when Margery, as was the rule, found herself the only woman among half a dozen men, ribald, argumentative and gay, she was not a bar to good-fellowship but an asset. Whenever I was in England I saw them. They generally dined at the club of which I have spoken, and if I happened to be alone I joined them.

When we met that evening for a snack before going to the play I told them I had asked Morton to come to supper.

"I'm afraid you'll find him rather dull," I said. "But he's a very decent sort of boy and he was awfully kind to me when I was in Borneo."

"Why didn't you let me know sooner?" cried Margery. "I'd have brought a girl along."

"What do you want a girl for?" said Charlie. "There'll be you."

"I don't think it can be much fun for a young man to dance with a woman of my advanced years," said Margery.

"Rot. What's your age got to do with it?" He turned to me. "Have you ever danced with anyone who danced better?"

I had, but she certainly danced very well. She was light on her feet and she had a good sense of rhythm.

"Never," I said heartily.

Morton was waiting for us when we reached Ciro's. He looked very sunburned in his evening clothes. Perhaps it was because I knew that they had been wrapped away in a tin box with moth balls for four years that I felt he did not look quite at home in them. He was certainly more at ease in khaki shorts. Charlie Bishop was a good talker and liked to hear himself speak. Morton was shy. I gave him a cocktail and ordered some champagne. I had a feeling that he would be glad to dance, but was not quite sure whether it would occur to him to ask Margery. I was acutely conscious that we all belonged to another generation.

"I think I should tell you that Mrs. Bishop is a beautiful dancer," I said.

"Is she?" He flushed a little. "Will you dance with me?"

She got up and they took the floor. She was looking peculiarly nice that evening, not at all smart, and I do not think her plain black dress had cost more than six guineas, but she looked a lady. She had the advantage of having extremely good legs, and at that time skirts were still being worn very short. I suppose she had a little make-up on, but in contrast with the other women there she looked very natural. Shingled hair suited her; it was not even touched with white and it had an attractive sheen. She was not a pretty woman, but her kindliness, her wholesome air, her good health, gave you, if not the illusion that she was, at least the feeling that it didn't at all matter. When she came back to the table her eyes were bright and she had a heightened colour.

"How does he dance?" asked her husband.

"Divinely."

"You're very easy to dance with," said Morton.

Charlie went on with his discourse. He had a sardonic

humour and he was interesting because he was himself so interested in what he said. But he spoke of things that Morton knew nothing about, and though he listened with a civil show of interest I could see that he was too much excited by the gaiety of the scene, the music and the champagne to give his attention to conversation. When the music struck up again his eyes immediately sought Margery's. Charles caught the look and smiled.

"Dance with him, Margery. Good for my figure to see you take exercise."

They set off again, and for a moment Charlie watched her with fond eyes.

"Margery's having the time of her life. She loves dancing, and it makes me puff and blow. Not a bad youth."

My little party was quite a success, and when Morton and I, having taken leave of the Bishops, walked together towards Piccadilly Circus he thanked me warmly. He had really enjoyed himself. I said good-bye to him. Next morning I went abroad.

I was sorry not to have been able to do more for Morton, and I knew that when I returned he would be on his way back to Borneo. I gave him a passing thought now and then, but by the autumn when I got home he had slipped my memory. After I had been in London a week or so I happened to drop in one night at the club to which Charlie Bishop also belonged. He was sitting with three or four men I knew and I went up. I had not seen any of them since my return. One of them, a man

called Bill Marsh, whose wife, Janet, was a great friend
of mine, asked me to have a drink.

"Where have you sprung from?" asked Charlie.
"Haven't seen you about lately."

I noticed at once that he was drunk. I was astonished.
Charlie had always liked his liquor, but he carried it well
and never exceeded. In years gone by, when we were
very young, he got tight occasionally, but probably
more than anything to show what a great fellow he was,
and it is unfair to bring up against a man the excesses
of his youth. But I remembered that Charlie had never
been very nice when he was drunk: his natural aggres-
siveness was exaggerated then and he talked too much
and too loud; he was very apt to be quarrelsome. He
was very dogmatic now, laying down the law and refusing to listen to any of the objections his rash state-
ments called forth. The others knew he was drunk and
were struggling between the irritation his cantankerous-
ness aroused in them and the good-natured tolerance
which they felt his condition demanded. He was not an
agreeable object. A man of that age, bald and fattish,
with spectacles, is disgusting drunk. He was generally
rather dapper, but he was untidy now and there was
tobacco ash all over him. Charlie called the waiter and
ordered another whisky. The waiter had been at the
club for thirty years.

"You've got one in front of you, sir."

"Mind your own damned business," said Charlie
Bishop. "Bring me a double whisky right away or I'll
report you to the secretary for insolence."

"Very good, sir," said the waiter.

Charlie emptied his glass at a gulp, but his hand was unsteady and he spilled some of the whisky over himself.

"Well, Charlie, old boy, we'd better be toddling along," said Bill Marsh. He turned to me. "Charlie's staying with us for a bit."

I was more surprised still. But I felt that something was wrong and thought it safer not to say anything.

"I'm ready," said Charlie. "I'll just have another drink before I go. I shall have a better night if I do."

It did not look to me as though the party would break up for some time, so I got up and announced that I meant to stroll home.

"I say," said Bill, as I was about to go, "you wouldn't come and dine with us to-morrow night, would you, just me and Janet and Charlie?"

"Yes, I'll come with pleasure," I said.

It was evident that something was up.

The Marshes lived in a terrace on the east side of Regent's Park. The maid who opened the door for me asked me to go in to Mr. Marsh's study. He was waiting for me there.

"I thought I'd better have a word with you before you went upstairs," he said as he shook hands with me. "You know Margery's left Charlie?"

"No?"

"He's taken it very hard. Janet thought it was so awful for him alone in that beastly little flat that we asked him to stay here for a bit. We've done everything we could for him. He's been drinking like a fish. He hasn't slept a wink for a fortnight."

"But she hasn't left him for good?"

"Yes. She's crazy about a fellow called Morton."

I was astounded.

"Morton. Who's he?"

It never struck me it was my friend from Borneo.

"Damn it all, you introduced him, and a pretty piece of work you did. Let's go upstairs. I thought I'd better put you wise."

He opened the door and we went out. I was thoroughly confused.

"But look here——" I said.

"Ask Janet. She knows the whole thing. It beats me. I've got no patience with Margery, and he must be a mess."

He preceded me into the drawing-room. Janet Marsh rose as I entered, and came forward to greet me. Charlie was sitting at the window, reading the evening paper; he put it aside as I went up to him and shook his hand. He was quite sober and he spoke in his usual rather perky manner, but I noticed that he looked very ill. We had a glass of sherry and went down to dinner. Janet was a woman of spirit. She was tall and fair and good to look at. She kept the conversation going with alertness. When she left us to drink a glass of port it was with instructions not to stay more than ten minutes. Bill, as a rule somewhat taciturn, exerted himself now to talk. I tumbled to the game. I was hampered by my ignorance of what exactly had happened, but it was plain that the Marshes wanted to prevent Charlie from brooding, and I did my best to interest him. He seemed willing to play his part, he was always fond of holding forth, and he discussed, from the pathologist's standpoint, a murder that was just then absorbing the public. But he spoke without life. He was an empty shell, and one had the feeling that though for the sake of his host he forced himself to speak, his thoughts were elsewhere. It was a relief when a knocking on the floor above indicated to us that Janet was getting impatient. This was an occasion when a woman's presence eased the situation. We went upstairs and played family bridge. When it was time for me to go Charlie said he would walk with me as far as the Marylebone Road.

"Oh, Charlie, it's so late, you'd much better go to bed," said Janet.

"I shall sleep better if I have a stroll before turning in," he replied.

She gave him a worried look. You cannot forbid a middle-aged professor of pathology from going for a little walk if he wants to. She glanced brightly at her husband.

"I daresay it'll do Bill no harm."

I think the remark was tactless. Women are often a little too managing. Charlie gave her a sullen look.

"There's absolutely no need to drag Bill out," he said with some firmness.

"I haven't the smallest intention of coming," said Bill, smiling. "I'm tired out and I'm going to hit the hay."

I fancy we left Bill Marsh and his wife to a little argument.

"They've been frightfully kind to me," said Charlie, as we walked along by the railings. "I don't know what

I should have done without them. I haven't slept for a fortnight."

I expressed regret but did not ask the reason, and we walked for a little in silence. I presumed that he had come with me in order to talk to me of what had happened, but I felt that he must take his own time. I was anxious to show my sympathy, but afraid of saying the wrong thing; I did not want to seem eager to extract confidences from him. I did not know how to give him a lead. I was sure he did not want one. He was not a man given to beating about the bush. I imagined that he was choosing his words. We reached the corner.

"You'll be able to get a taxi at the church," he said. "I'll walk on a bit farther. Good-night."

He nodded and slouched off. I was taken aback. There was nothing for me to do but to stroll on till I found a cab. I was having my bath next morning when a telephone call dragged me out of it, and with a towel round my wet body I took up the receiver. It was Janet.

"Well, what do you think of it all?" she said. "You seem to have kept Charlie up pretty late last night. I heard him come home at three."

"He left me at the Marylebone Road," I answered. "He said nothing to me at all."

"Didn't he?"

There was something in Janet's voice that suggested that she was prepared to have a long talk with me. I suspected she had a telephone by the side of her bed.

"Look here," I said quickly, "I'm having my bath."

"Oh, have you got a telephone in your bathroom?" she answered eagerly, and I think with envy.

"No, I haven't." I was abrupt and firm. "And I'm dripping all over the carpet."

"Oh!" I felt disappointment in her tone and a trace of irritation. "Well, when can I see you? Can you come here at twelve?"

It was inconvenient, but I was not prepared to start an argument.

"Yes, good-bye."

I rang off before she could say anything more. In heaven when the blessed use the telephone they will say what they have to say and not a word besides.

I was devoted to Janet, but I knew that there was nothing that thrilled her more than the misfortunes of her friends. She was only too anxious to help them, but she wanted to be in the thick of their difficulties. She was the friend in adversity. Other people's business was meat and drink to her. You could not enter upon a love affair without finding her somehow your confidante, nor be mixed up in a divorce case without discovering that she too had a finger in the pie. Withal she was a very nice woman. I could not help, then, chuckling in my heart when at noon I was shown in to Janet's drawing-room and observed the subdued eagerness with which she received me. She was very much upset by the catastrophe that had befallen the Bishops, but it was exciting, and she was tickled to death to have someone fresh to whom she could tell all about it. Janet had just that businesslike expectancy that a mother has when she is discussing with the family doctor her married daughter's first confinement. Janet was conscious that the matter was very serious, and she would not for a moment have been thought to regard it flippantly, but she was determined to get every ounce of value out of it.

"I mean, no one could have been more horrified than I was when Margery told me she'd finally made up her mind to leave Charlie," she said, speaking with the fluency of a person who has said the same thing in the same words a dozen times at least. "They were the most devoted couple I'd ever known. It was a perfect marriage. They got on like a house on fire. Of course Bill and I are devoted to one another, but we have awful rows now and then. I mean, I could kill him sometimes."

"I don't care a hang about your relations with Bill," I said. "Tell me about the Bishops. That's what I've come here for."

"I simply felt I must see you. After all, you're the only person who can explain it."

"Oh, God, don't go on like that. Until Bill told me last night I didn't know a thing about it."

"That was my idea. It suddenly dawned on me that perhaps you didn't know and I thought you might put your foot in it too awfully."

"Supposing you began at the beginning," I said.

"Well, you're the beginning. After all you started the trouble. You introduced the young man. That's why I was so crazy to see you. You know all about him. I never saw him. All I know is what Margery has told me about him."

"At what time are you lunching?" I asked.

"Half-past one."

"So am I. Get on with the story."

But my remark had given Janet an idea.

"Look here, will you get out of your luncheon if I get out of mine? We could have a snack here. I'm sure there's some cold meat in the house, and then we needn't hurry. I don't have to be at the hair-dresser's till three."

"No, no, no," I said. "I hate the notion of that. I shall leave here at twenty minutes past one at the latest."

"Then I shall just have to race through it. What do *you* think of Gerry?"

"Who's Gerry?"

"Gerry Morton. His name's Gerald."

"How should I know that?"

"You stayed with him. Weren't there any letters lying about?"

"I daresay, but I didn't happen to read them," I answered somewhat tartly.

"Oh, don't be so stupid. I meant the envelopes. What's he like?"

"All right. Rather the Kipling type, you know. Very keen on his work. Hearty. Empire-builder and all that sort of thing."

"I don't mean that," cried Janet, not without impatience. "I mean, what does he look like?"

"More or less like everybody else, I think. Of course I should recognize him if I saw him again, but I can't picture him to myself very distinctly. He looks clean."

"Oh, my God," said Janet. "Are you a novelist or are you not? What's the colour of his eyes?"

"I don't know."

"You must know. You can't spend a week with any-

one without knowing if their eyes are blue or brown.
Is he fair or dark?"
    "Neither."
    "Is he tall or short?"
    "Average, I should say."
    "Are you trying to irritate me?"
    "No. He's just ordinary. There's nothing in him to
attract your attention. He's neither plain nor good-
looking. He looks quite decent. He looks a gentleman."
    "Margery says he has a charming smile and a lovely
figure."
    "I daresay."
    "He's absolutely crazy about her."
    "What makes you think that?" I asked dryly.
    "I've seen his letters."
    "Do you mean to say she's shown them to you?"
    "Why, of course."
    It is always difficult for a man to stomach the want
of reticence that women betray in their private affairs.
They have no shame. They will talk to one another
without embarrassment of the most intimate matters.
Modesty is a masculine virtue. But though a man may
know this theoretically, each time he is confronted with
women's lack of reserve he suffers a new shock. I wondered what Morton would think if he knew that not
only were his letters read by Janet Marsh as well as by
Margery, but that she had been kept posted from day
to day with the progress of his infatuation. According
to Janet he had fallen in love with Margery at first sight.
The morning after they had met at my little supper
party at Ciro's he had rung up and asked her to come

and have tea with him at some place where they could dance. While I listened to Janet's story I was conscious of course that she was giving me Margery's view of the circumstances, and I kept an open mind. I was interested to observe that Janet's sympathies were with Margery. It was true that when Margery left her husband it was her idea that Charlie should come to them for two or three weeks rather than stay on in miserable loneliness in the deserted flat, and she had been extraordinarily kind to him. She lunched with him almost every day, because he had been accustomed to lunch every day with Margery; she took him for walks in Regent's Park and made Bill play golf with him on Sundays. She listened with wonderful patience to the story of his unhappiness and did what she could to console him. She was terribly sorry for him. But all the same she was definitely on Margery's side, and when I expressed my disapproval of her she came down on me like a thousand of bricks. The affair thrilled her. She had been in it from the beginning, when Margery, smiling, flattered and a little doubtful, came and told her that she had a young man, to the final scene when Margery, exasperated and distraught, announced that she could not stand the strain any more and had packed her things and moved out of the flat.

"Of course, at first I couldn't believe my ears," she said. "You know how Charlie and Margery were. They simply lived in one another's pockets. One couldn't help laughing at them, they were so devoted to one another. I never thought him a very nice little man, and heaven knows he wasn't very attractive physically, but one couldn't help liking him because he was so awfully nice to Margery. I rather envied her sometimes. They had no money and they lived in a hugger-mugger sort of way, but they were frightfully happy. Of course I never thought anything would come of it. Margery was rather amused. 'Naturally I don't take it very seriously,' she told me, 'but it is rather fun to have a young man at my time of life. I haven't had any flowers sent me for years. I had to tell him not to send any more because Charlie would think it so silly. He doesn't know a soul in London and he loves dancing and he says I dance like a dream. It's miserable for him going to the theatre by himself all the time, and we've done two or three matinées together. It's pathetic to see how grateful he is when I say I'll go out with him.' 'I must say,' I said, 'he sounds rather a lamb.' 'He is,' she said. 'I knew you'd understand. You don't blame me, do you?' 'Of course not, darling,' I said, 'surely you know me better than that. I'd do just the same in your place.'"

Margery made no secret of her outings with Morton, and her husband chaffed her good-naturedly about her beau. But he thought him a very civil, pleasant-spoken young man and was glad that Margery had someone to play with while he was busy. It never occurred to him to be jealous. The three of them dined together several times and went to a show. But presently Gerry Morton begged Margery to spend an evening with him alone; she said it was impossible, but he was persuasive, he gave her no peace; and at last she went to Janet and asked her to ring up Charlie one day and ask him to come to dinner and make a fourth at bridge. Charlie would never go anywhere without his wife, but the Marshes were old friends, and Janet made a point of it. She invented some cock-and-bull story that made it seem important that he should consent. Next day Margery and she met. The evening had been wonderful. They had dined at Maidenhead and danced there and then had driven home through the summer night.

"He says he's crazy about me," Margery told her.

"Did he kiss you?" asked Janet.

"Of course," Margery chuckled. "Don't be silly, Janet. He is awfully sweet and, you know, he has such a nice nature. Of course I don't believe half the things he says to me."

"My dear, you're not going to fall in love with him."

"I have," said Margery.

"Darling, isn't it going to be rather awkward?"

"Oh, it won't last. After all, he's going back to Borneo in the autumn."

"Well, one can't deny that it's made you look years younger."

"I know, and I feel years younger."

Soon they were meeting every day. They met in the morning and walked in the park together or went to a picture gallery. They separated for Margery to lunch with her husband and after lunch met again and motored into the country or to some place on the river. Margery did not tell her husband. She very naturally thought he would not understand.

"How was it you never met Morton?" I asked Janet.

"Oh, she didn't want me to. You see, we belong to

the same generation, Margery and I. I quite understand that."

"I see."

"Of course I did everything I could. When she went out with Gerry she was always supposed to be with me."

I am a person who likes to cross a t and dot an i.

"Were they having an affair?" I asked.

"Oh, no. Margery isn't that sort of woman at all."

"How do you know?"

"She would have told me."

"I suppose she would."

"Of course I asked her. But she denied it point-blank and I'm sure she was telling me the truth. There's never been anything of that sort between them at all."

"It seems rather odd to me."

"Well, you see, Margery is a very good woman."

I shrugged my shoulders.

"She was absolutely loyal to Charlie. She wouldn't have deceived him for anything in the world. She couldn't bear the thought of having any secret from him. As soon as she knew she was in love with Gerry she wanted to tell Charlie. Of course I begged her not to. I told her it wouldn't do any good and it would only make Charlie miserable. And after all, the boy was going away in a couple of months; it didn't seem much good to make a lot of fuss about a thing that couldn't possibly last."

But Gerry's imminent departure was the cause of the crash. The Bishops had arranged to go abroad as usual and proposed to motor through Belgium, Holland and the north of Germany. Charlie was busy with maps and

guides. He collected information from friends about
hotels and roads. He looked forward to his holiday with
the bubbling excitement of a schoolboy. Margery listened to him discussing it with a sinking heart. They
were to be away four weeks, and in September Gerry
was sailing. She could not bear to lose so much of the
short time that remained to them, and the thought of
the motor tour filled her with exasperation. As the interval grew shorter and shorter she grew more and more
nervous. At last she decided that there was only one
thing to do.

"Charlie, I don't want to come on this trip," she
interrupted him suddenly, one day when he was talking
to her of some restaurant he had just heard of. "I wish
you'd get someone else to go with you."

He looked at her blankly. She was startled at what
she had said, and her lips trembled a little.

"Why, what's the matter?"

"Nothing's the matter. I don't feel like it. I want to
be by myself for a bit."

"Are you ill?"

She saw the sudden fear in his eyes. His concern drove
her beyond her endurance.

"No. I've never been better in my life. I'm in love."

"You? Who with?"

"Gerry."

He looked at her in amazement. He could not believe
his ears. She mistook his expression.

"It's no good blaming me. I can't help it. He's going
away in a few weeks. I'm not going to waste the little
time he has left."

He burst out laughing.

"Margery, how can you make such a damned fool of yourself? You're old enough to be his mother."

She flushed.

"He's just as much in love with me as I am with him."

"Has he told you so?"

"A thousand times."

"He's a bloody liar, that's all."

He chuckled. His fat stomach rippled with mirth. He thought it a huge joke. I daresay Charlie did not treat his wife in the proper way. Janet seemed to think he should have been tender and compassionate. *He should have understood.* I saw the scene that was in her mind's eye, the stiff upper lip, the silent sorrow, and the final renunciation. Women are always sensitive to the beauty of the self-sacrifice of others. Janet would have sympathized also if he had flown into a violent passion, broken one or two pieces of furniture (which he would have had to replace), or given Margery a sock in the jaw. But to laugh at her was unpardonable. I did not point out that it is very difficult for a rather stout and not very tall professor of pathology, aged fifty-five, to act all of a sudden like a caveman. Anyhow, the excursion to Holland was given up and the Bishops stayed in London through August. They were not very happy. They lunched and dined together every day because they had been in the habit of doing so for so many years, and the rest of the time Margery spent with Gerry. The hours she passed with him made up for all she had to put up with, and she had to put up with a good deal. Charlie had a ribald and sarcastic humour and he made himself very funny at her expense and at Gerry's. He persisted in refusing to take the matter seriously. He was vexed with Margery for being so silly, but apparently it never occurred to him that she might have been unfaithful to him. I commented upon this to Janet.

"He never suspected it even," she said. "He knew Margery much too well."

The weeks passed and at last Gerry sailed. He went from Tilbury and Margery saw him off. When she came back she cried for forty-eight hours. Charlie watched her with increasing exasperation. His nerves were much frayed.

"Look here, Margery," he said at last, "I've been very patient with you, but now you must pull yourself together. This is getting past a joke."

"Why can't you leave me alone?" she cried. "I've lost everything that made life lovely to me."

"Don't be such a fool," he said.

I do not know what else he said. But he was unwise enough to tell her what he thought of Gerry, and I gather that the picture he drew was virulent. It started the first violent scene they had ever had. She had borne Charlie's jibes when she knew that she would see Gerry in an hour or next day, but now that she had lost him for ever she could bear them no longer. She had held herself in for weeks: now she flung her self-control to the winds. Perhaps she never knew exactly what she said to Charlie. He had always been irascible, and at last he hit her. They were both frightened when he had. He seized a hat and flung out of the flat. During all that

miserable time they had shared the same bed, but when
he came back, in the middle of the night, he found that
she had made herself up a shake-down on the sofa in the
sitting-room.

"You can't sleep there," he said. "Don't be so silly.
Come to bed."

"No, I won't, let me alone."

For the rest of the night they wrangled, but she had
her way and now made up her bed every night on the
sofa. But in that tiny flat they could not get away from
one another; they could not even get out of sight or out
of hearing of one another. They had lived in such intimacy for so many years that it was an instinct for them
to be together. He tried to reason with her. He thought
her incredibly stupid and argued with her interminably
in the effort to show her how wrong-headed she was.
He could not leave her alone. He would not let her sleep,
and he talked half through the night till they were both
exhausted. He thought he could talk her out of love.
For two or three days at a time they would not speak
to one another. Then one day, coming home, he found
her crying bitterly; the sight of her tears distracted him;
he told her how much he loved her and sought to move
her by the recollection of all the happy years they had
spent together. He wanted to let bygones be bygones.
He promised never to refer to Gerry again. Could they
not forget the nightmare they had been through? But
the thought of all that a reconciliation implied revolted
her. She told him she had a racking headache and asked
him to give her a sleeping draught. She pretended to be
still asleep when he went out next morning, but the

moment he was gone she packed up her things and left.
She had a few trinkets that she had inherited, and by
selling them she got a little money. She took a room at
a cheap boarding-house and kept her address a secret
from Charlie.

It was when he found she had left him that he went
all to pieces. The shock of her flight broke him. He told
Janet that his loneliness was intolerable. He wrote to
Margery imploring her to come back, and asked Janet
to intercede for him; he was willing to promise anything;
he abased himself. Margery was obdurate.

"Do you think she'll ever go back?" I asked Janet.

"She says not."

I had to leave then, for it was nearly half-past one
and I was bound for the other end of London.

Two or three days later I got a telephone message
from Margery asking if I could see her. She suggested
coming to my rooms. I asked her to tea. I tried to be
nice to her; her affairs were no business of mine, but in
my heart I thought her a very silly woman and I daresay my manner was cold. She had never been handsome
and the passing years had changed her little. She had
still those fine dark eyes and her face was astonishingly
unlined. She was very simply dressed, and if she wore
make-up it was so cunningly put on that I did not perceive it. She had still the charm she had always had of
perfect naturalness and of a kindly humour.

"I want you to do something for me if you will," she
began without beating about the bush.

"What is it?"

"Charlie is leaving the Marshes to-day and going back to the flat. I'm afraid his first few days there will be rather difficult; it would be awfully nice of you if you'd ask him to dinner or something."

"I'll have a look at my book."

"I'm told he's been drinking heavily. It's such a pity. I wish you could give him a hint."

"I understand he's had some domestic worries of late," I said perhaps acidly.

Margery flushed. She gave me a pained look. She winced as though I had struck her.

"Of course you've known him ever so much longer than you've known me. It's natural that you should take his part."

"My dear, to tell you the truth I've known him all these years chiefly on your account. I have never very much liked him, but I thought you were awfully nice."

She smiled at me and her smile was very sweet. She knew that I meant what I said.

"Do you think I was a good wife to him?"

"Perfect."

"He used to put people's backs up. A lot of people didn't like him, but I never found him difficult."

"He was awfully fond of you."

"I know. We had a wonderful time together. For sixteen years we were perfectly happy." She paused and looked down. "I had to leave him. It became quite impossible. That cat-and-dog life we were leading was too awful."

"I never see why two persons should go on living together if they don't want to."

"You see, it was awful for us. We'd always lived in such close intimacy. We could never get away from one another. At the end I hated the sight of him."

"I don't suppose the situation was easy for either of you."

"It wasn't my fault that I fell in love. You see, it was quite a different love from the one I'd felt for Charlie. There was always something maternal in that and protective. I was so much more reasonable than he was. He was unmanageable, but I could always manage him. Gerry was different." Her voice grew soft and her face was transfigured with glory. "He gave me back my youth. I was a girl to him and I could depend on his strength and be safe in his care."

"He seemed to me a very nice lad," I said slowly. "I imagine he'll do well. He was very young for the job he had when I ran across him. He's only twenty-nine now, isn't he?"

She smiled softly. She knew quite well what I meant.

"I never made any secret of my age to him. He says it doesn't matter."

I knew this was true. She was not the woman to have lied about her age. She had found a sort of fierce delight in telling him the truth about herself.

"How old are you?"

"Forty-four."

"What are you going to do now?"

"I've written to Gerry and told him I've left Charlie. As soon as I hear from him I'm going out to join him."

I was staggered.

"You know, it's a very primitive little colony he's

living in. I'm afraid you'll find your position rather
awkward."

"He made me promise that if I found my life impossible after he left I'd go to him."

"Are you sure you're wise to attach so much importance to the things a young man says when he's in
love?"

Again that really beautiful look of exaltation came
into her face.

"Yes, when the young man happens to be Gerry."

My heart sank. I was silent for a moment. Then I
told her the story of the road Gerry Morton had built.
I dramatized it, and I think I made it rather effective.

"What did you tell me that for?" she asked when I
finished.

"I thought it rather a good story."

She shook her head and smiled.

"No, you wanted to show me that he was very young
and enthusiastic, and so keen on his work that he hadn't
much time to waste on other interests. I wouldn't interfere with his work. You don't know him as I do. He's
incredibly romantic. He looks upon himself as a pioneer.
I've caught from him something of his excitement at
the idea of taking part in the opening up of a new country. It *is* rather splendid, isn't it? It makes life here seem
very humdrum and commonplace. But of course it's
very lonely there. Even the companionship of a middle-
aged woman may be worth having."

"Are you proposing to marry him?" I asked.

"I leave myself in his hands. I want to do nothing
that he does not wish."

She spoke with so much simplicity, there was something so touching in her self-surrender, that when she left me I no longer felt angry with her. Of course I thought her very foolish, but if the folly of men made one angry one would pass one's life in a state of chronic ire. I thought all would come right. She said Gerry was romantic. He was, but the romantics in this workaday world only get away with their nonsense because they have at bottom a shrewd sense of reality: the mugs are the people who take their vapourings at their face value. The English are romantic; that is why other nations think them hypocritical; they are not: they set out in all sincerity for the Kingdom of God, but the journey is arduous and they have reason to pick up any gilt-edged investment that offers itself by the way. The British soul, like Wellington's armies, marches on its belly. I supposed that Gerry would go through a bad quarter of an hour when he received Margery's letter. My sympathies were not deeply engaged in the matter and I was only curious to see how he would extricate himself from the pass he was in. I thought Margery would suffer a bitter disappointment—well, that would do her no great harm, and then she would go back to her husband and I had no doubt the pair of them, chastened, would live in peace, quiet and happiness for the rest of their lives.

The event was different. It happened that it was quite impossible for me to make any sort of engagement with Charlie Bishop for some days, but I wrote to him and asked him to dine with me one evening in the following week. I proposed, though with misgiving, that we should go to a play; I knew he was drinking like a fish, and when tight he was noisy. I hoped he would not make a nuisance of himself in the theatre. We arranged to meet at our club and dine at seven because the piece we were going to began at a quarter past eight. I arrived. I waited. He did not come. I rang up his flat, but could get no reply, so concluded that he was on his way. I hate missing the beginning of a play and I waited impatiently in the hall so that when he came we could go straight upstairs. To save time I had ordered dinner. The clock pointed to half-past seven, then a quarter to eight; I did not see why I should wait for him any longer, so walked up to the dining-room and ate my dinner alone. He did not appear. I put a call through from the dining-room to the Marshes and presently was told by a waiter that Bill Marsh was at the end of the wire.

"I say, do you know anything about Charlie Bishop?" I said. "We were dining together and going to a play and he hasn't turned up."

"He died this afternoon."

"What?"

My exclamation was so startled that two or three people within earshot looked up. The dining-room was full and the waiters were hurrying to and fro. The telephone was on the cashier's desk, and a wine waiter came up with a bottle of hock and two long-stemmed glasses on a tray and gave the cashier a chit. The portly steward showing two men to a table jostled me.

"Where are you speaking from?" asked Bill.

I suppose he heard the clatter that surrounded me. When I told him he asked me if I could come round as

soon as I had finished my dinner. Janet wanted to speak
to me.

"I'll come at once," I said.

I found Janet and Bill sitting in the drawing-room.
He was reading the paper and she was playing patience.
She came forward swiftly when the maid showed me in.
She walked with a sort of spring, crouching a little, on
silent feet, like a panther stalking his prey. I saw at
once that she was in her element. She gave me her hand
and turned her face away to hide her eyes brimming
with tears. Her voice was low and tragic.

"I brought Margery here and put her to bed. The
doctor has given her a sedative. She's all in. Isn't it
awful?" She gave a sound that was something between
a gasp and a sob. "I don't know why these things always
happen to me."

The Bishops had never kept a servant, but a charwoman went in every morning, cleaned the flat and
washed up the breakfast things. She had her own key.
That morning she had gone in as usual and done the
sitting-room. Since his wife had left him Charlie's hours
had been irregular and she was not surprised to find
him asleep. But the time passed and she knew he had
his work to go to. She went to the bedroom door and
knocked. There was no answer. She thought she heard
him groaning. She opened the door softly. He was lying
in bed, on his back, and was breathing stertorously.
He did not wake. She called him. Something about him
frightened her. She went to the flat on the same landing.
It was occupied by a journalist. He was still in bed when
she rang, and opened the door to her in pajamas.

"Beg pardon, sir," she said, "but would you just come and 'ave a look at my gentleman? I don't think he's well."

The journalist walked across the landing and into Charlie's flat. There was an empty bottle of veronal by the bed.

"I think you'd better fetch a policeman," he said.

A policeman came and rang through to the police station for an ambulance. They took Charlie to Charing Cross Hospital. He never recovered consciousness. Margery was with him at the end.

"Of course there'll have to be an inquest," said Janet. "But it's quite obvious what happened. He'd been sleeping awfully badly for the last three or four weeks and I suppose he'd been taking veronal. He must have taken an overdose by accident."

"Is that what Margery thinks?" I asked.

"She's too upset to think anything, but I told her I was positive he hadn't committed suicide. I mean, he wasn't that sort of a man. Am I right, Bill?"

"Yes, dear," he answered.

"Did he leave any letter?"

"No, nothing. Oddly enough Margery got a letter from him this morning—well, hardly a letter, just a line. 'I'm so lonely without you, darling.' That's all. But of course that means nothing and she's promised to say nothing about it at the inquest. I mean, what is the use of putting ideas in people's heads? Everyone knows that you never can tell with veronal—I wouldn't take it myself for anything in the world—and it was quite obviously an accident. Am I right, Bill?"

"Yes, dear," he answered.

I saw that Janet was quite determined to believe that Charlie Bishop had not committed suicide, but how far in her heart she believed what she wanted to believe I was not sufficiently expert in female psychology to know. And of course it might be that she was right. It is unreasonable to suppose that a middle-aged scientist should kill himself because his middle-aged wife leaves him, and it is extremely plausible that, exasperated by sleeplessness, and in all probability far from sober, he took a larger dose of the sleeping draught than he realized. Anyhow that was the view the coroner took of the matter. It was indicated to him that of late Charles Bishop had given way to habits of intemperance which had caused his wife to leave him, and it was quite obvious that nothing was further from his thoughts than to put an end to himself. The coroner expressed his sympathy with the widow and commented very strongly on the dangers of sleeping draughts.

I hate funerals, but Janet begged me to go to Charlie's. Several of his colleagues at the hospital had intimated their desire to come, but at Margery's wish they were dissuaded; and Janet and Bill, Margery and I were the only persons who attended it. We were to fetch the hearse from the mortuary, and they offered to call for me on their way. I was on the lookout for the car, and when I saw it drive up went downstairs, but Bill got out and met me just inside the door.

"Half a minute," he said. "I've got something to say to you. Janet wants you to come back afterwards and have tea. She says it's no good Margery moping and after tea we'll play a few rubbers of bridge. Can you come?"

"Like this?" I asked.

I had a tail coat on and a black tie and my evening dress trousers.

"Oh, that's all right. It'll take Margery's mind off."

"Very well."

But we did not play bridge after all. Janet, with her fair hair, was very smart in her deep mourning and she played the part of the sympathetic friend with amazing skill. She cried a little, wiping her eyes delicately so as not to disturb the black on her eyelashes, and, when Margery sobbed broken-heartedly, put her arm tenderly through hers. She was a very present help in trouble. We returned to the house. There was a telegram for Margery. She took it and went upstairs. I presumed it was a message of condolence from one of Charlie's friends who had just heard of his death. Bill went to change and Janet and I went up to the drawing-room and got the bridge table out. She took off her hat and put it on the piano.

"It's no good being hypocritical," she said. "Of course Margery has been frightfully upset, but she must pull herself together now. A rubber of bridge will help her to get back to her normal state. Naturally I'm dreadfully sorry about poor Charlie, but as far as he was concerned I don't believe he'd ever have got over Margery's leaving him, and one can't deny that it has made things much easier for her. She wired to Gerry this morning."

"What about?"

"To tell him about poor Charlie."

At that moment the maid came to the room.

"Will you go up to Mrs. Bishop, please, ma'am. She wants to see you."

"Yes, of course."

She went out of the room quickly and I was left alone. Bill joined me presently and we had a drink. At last Janet came back. She handed a telegram to me. It read as follows:

For God's sake await letter. Gerry.

"What do you think it means?" she asked me.

"What it says," I replied.

"Idiot! Of course I've told Margery that it doesn't mean anything, but she's rather worried. It must have crossed her cable telling him that Charles was dead. I don't think she feels very much like bridge after all. I mean, it would be rather bad form to play on the very day her husband has been buried."

"Quite," I said.

"Of course he may wire in answer to the cable. He's sure to do that, isn't he? The only thing we can do now is to sit tight and wait for his letter."

I saw no object in continuing the conversation. I left. In a couple of days Janet rang me up to tell me that Margery had received a telegram of condolence from Morton. She repeated it to me:

Dreadfully distressed to hear sad news. Deeply sympathize with your great grief. Love. Gerry.

"What do you think of it?" she asked me.

"I think it's very proper."

"Of course he couldn't say he was as pleased as Punch, could he?"

"Not with any delicacy."

"And he did put in *love*."

I imagined how those women had examined the two telegrams from every point of view and scrutinized every word to press from it every possible shade of meaning. I almost heard their interminable conversations.

"I don't know what'll happen to Margery if he lets her down now," Janet went on. "Of course it remains to be seen if he's a gentleman."

"Rot," I said and rang off quickly.

In the course of the following days I dined with the Marshes a couple of times. Margery looked tired. I guessed that she awaited the letter that was on the way with sickening anxiety. Grief and fear had worn her to a shadow; she seemed very fragile now, and she had acquired a spiritual look that I had never seen in her before. She was very gentle, very grateful for every kindness shown her, and in her smile, unsure and a little timid, was an infinite pathos. Her helplessness was very appealing. But Morton was several thousand miles away. Then one morning Janet rang me up.

"The letter has come. Margery says I can show it to you. Will you come round?"

Her tense voice told me everything. When I arrived Janet gave it to me. I read it. It was a very careful letter and I guessed that Morton had written it a good many times. It was very kind and he had evidently taken great pains to avoid saying anything that could possibly wound Margery; but what transpired was his terror. It was obvious that he was shaking in his shoes. He had felt apparently that the best way to cope with the situation was to be mildly facetious, and he made very good fun of the white people in the colony. What would they say if Margery suddenly turned up? He would be given the order of the boot pretty damn quick. People thought the East was free and easy; it wasn't, it was more suburban than Clapham. He loved Margery far too much to bear the thought of those horrible women out there turning up their noses at her. And besides he had been sent to a station ten days from anywhere; she couldn't live in his bungalow exactly, and of course there wasn't a hotel, and his work took him out into the jungle for days at a time. It was no place for a woman anyhow. He told her how much she meant to him, but she mustn't bother about him and he couldn't help thinking it would be better if she went back to her husband. He would never forgive himself if he thought he had come between her and Charlie. Yes, I am quite sure it had been a difficult letter to write.

"Of course he didn't know then that Charlie was dead. I've told Margery that changes everything."

"Does she agree with you?"

"I think she's being rather unreasonable. What do you make of the letter?"

"Well, it's quite plain that he doesn't want her."

"He wanted her badly enough two months ago."

"It's astonishing what a change of air and a change of

scene will do for you. It must seem to him already like a year since he left London. He's back among his old friends and his old interests. My dear, it's no good Margery kidding herself, the life there has taken him back and there's no place for her."

"I've advised her to ignore the letter and go straight out to him."

"I hope she's too sensible to expose herself to a very terrible rebuff."

"But then what's to happen to her? Oh, it's too cruel. She's the best woman in the world. She has real goodness."

"It's funny, if you come to think of it, it's her goodness that has caused all the trouble. Why on earth didn't she have an affair with Morton? Charlie would have known nothing about it and wouldn't have been a penny the worse. She and Morton could have had a grand time, and when he went away they could have parted with the consciousness that a pleasant episode had come to a graceful end. It would have been a jolly recollection, and she could have gone back to Charlie satisfied and rested and continued to make him the excellent wife she had always been."

Janet pursed her lips. She gave me a look of disdain.

"There is such a thing as virtue, you know."

"Virtue be damned. A virtue that only causes havoc and unhappiness is worth nothing. You can call it virtue if you like. I call it cowardice."

"The thought of being unfaithful to Charlie while she was living with him revolted her. There are women like that, you know."

"Good gracious, she could have remained faithful to him in spirit while she was being unfaithful to him in the flesh. That is a feat of legerdemain that women find it easy to accomplish."

"What an odious cynic you are."

"If it's cynical to look truth in the face and exercise common-sense in the affairs of life, then certainly I'm a cynic and odious, if you like. Let's face it: Margery's a middle-aged woman, Charlie was fifty-five and they'd been married for sixteen years. It was natural enough that she should lose her head over a young man who made a fuss of her. But don't call it love. It was physiology. She was a fool to take anything he said seriously. It wasn't himself speaking, it was his starved sex; he'd suffered from sexual starvation, at least as far as white women are concerned, for four years; it's monstrous that she should seek to ruin his life by holding him to the wild promises he made then. It was an accident that Margery took his fancy; he wanted her, and because he couldn't get her wanted her more. I daresay he thought it love; believe me, it was only letch. If they'd gone to bed together Charlie would be alive to-day. It's her damned virtue that caused the whole trouble."

"How stupid you are. Don't you see that she couldn't help herself? She just doesn't happen to be a loose woman."

"I prefer a loose woman to a selfish one and a wanton to a fool."

"Oh, shut up. I didn't ask you to come here in order to make yourself absolutely beastly."

"What did you ask me to come here for?"

"Gerry is your friend. You introduced him to Margery. If she's in the soup it's on his account. But *you* are the cause of the whole trouble. It's your duty to write to him and tell him he must do the right thing by her."

"I'm damned if I will," I said.

"Then you'd better go."

I started to do so.

"Well, at all events it's a mercy that Charlie's life was insured," said Janet.

Then I turned on her.

"And you have the nerve to call me a cynic."

I will not repeat the opprobrious word I flung at her as I slammed the door behind me. But Janet is all the same a very nice woman. I often think it would be great fun to be married to her.

THE ROUND DOZEN

THE ROUND DOZEN

I LIKE Elsom. It is a seaside resort in the south of England, not very far from Brighton, and it has something of the late Georgian charm of that agreeable town. But it is neither bustling nor garish. Ten years ago, when I used to go there not infrequently, you might still see here and there an old house, solid and pretentious in no unpleasing fashion (like a decayed gentlewoman of good family whose discreet pride in her ancestry amuses rather than offends you) which was built in the reign of the First Gentleman in Europe and where a courtier of fallen fortunes may well have passed his declining years. The main street had a lackadaisical air and the doctor's motor seemed a trifle out of place. The housewives did their housekeeping in a leisurely manner. They gossiped with the butcher as they watched him cut from his great joint of South Down a piece of the best end of the neck, and they asked amiably after the grocer's wife as he put half a pound of tea and a packet of salt into their string bag. I do not know whether Elsom was ever fashionable: it certainly was not so then; but it was respectable and cheap. Elderly ladies, maiden and widowed, lived there. Indian civilians and retired soldiers: they looked forward with little shudders of dismay to August and September which would bring holiday-makers; but did not disdain to let them their houses and on the proceeds spend a few worldy weeks in a Swiss pension. I never knew Elsom at that hectic time when the lodging-houses were full and young men in blazers sauntered along the front, when Pierrots performed on the beach and in the billiard-room at the Dolphin you heard the click of balls till eleven at night. I only knew it in winter. Then in every house on the sea-front, stucco houses with bow-windows built a hundred years ago, there was a sign to inform you that apartments were to let; and the guests of the Dolphin were waited on by a single waiter and the boots. At ten o'clock the porter came into the smoking-room and looked at you in so marked a manner that you got up and went to bed. Then Elsom was a restful place and the Dolphin a very comfortable inn. It was pleasing to think that the Prince Regent drove over with Mrs. Fitzherbert more than once to drink a dish of tea in its coffee-room. In the hall was a framed letter from Mr. Thackeray ordering a sitting-room and two bedrooms overlooking the sea and giving instructions that a fly should be sent to the station to meet him.

One November, two or three years after the war, having had a bad attack of influenza, I went down to Elsom to regain my strength. I arrived in the afternoon and when I had unpacked my things went for a stroll on the front. The sky was overcast and the calm sea grey and cold. A few seagulls flew close to the shore. Sailing boats, their masts taken down for the winter, were drawn up high on the shingly beach and the bathing huts stood side by side in a long, grey and tattered row. No one was sitting on the benches that the town council had put here and there, but a few people were trudging up and down for exercise. I passed an old colonel with a red nose who stamped along in plus fours followed by a terrier, two elderly women in short skirts and stout shoes and a plain girl in a Tam o' Shanter. I had never seen the front so deserted. The lodging-houses looked like bedraggled old maids waiting for lovers who would never return, and even the friendly Dolphin seemed wan and desolate. My heart sank. Life on a sudden seemed very drab. I returned to the hotel, drew the curtains of my sitting-room, poked the fire and with a book sought to dispel my melancholy. But I was glad enough when it was time to dress for dinner. I went into the coffee-room and found the guests of the hotel already seated. I gave them a casual glance. There was one lady of middle age by herself and there were two elderly gentlemen, golfers probably, with red faces and baldish heads, who ate their food in moody silence. The only other persons in the room were a group of three who sat in the bow-window, and they immediately attracted my surprised attention. The party consisted of an old gentleman and two ladies, one of whom was old and probably his wife, while the other was younger and possibly his daughter. It was the old lady who first excited my interest. She wore a voluminous dress of black silk and a black lace cap; on her wrists were heavy gold bangles and round her neck a substantial gold chain from which hung a large gold locket; at her neck was a large gold brooch. I did not know that anyone still wore jewelry of that sort. Often, passing second-hand jewellers and pawnbrokers, I had lingered for a moment to look at these strangely old-fashioned articles, so solid, costly and hideous, and thought, with a smile in which there was a tinge of sadness, of the women long since dead who had worn them. They suggested the period when the bustle and the flounce were taking the place of the crinoline and the pork-pie hat was ousting the poke-bonnet. The British people liked things solid and good in those days. They went to church on Sunday morning and after church walked in the Park. They gave dinner parties of twelve courses where the master of the house carved the beef and the chickens, and after dinner the ladies who could play favoured the company with Mendelssohn's Songs Without Words and the gentleman with the fine baritone voice sang an old English ballad.

The younger woman had her back turned to me and at first I could see only that she had a slim and youthful figure. She had a great deal of brown hair which seemed to be elaborately arranged. She wore a grey dress. The three of them were chatting in low tones and presently she turned her head so that I saw her profile. It was astonishingly beautiful. The nose was straight and delicate, the line of the cheek exquisitely modelled; I saw then that she wore her hair after the manner of Queen Alexandra. The dinner proceeded to its close and the party got up. The old lady sailed out of the room, looking neither to the right nor to the left, and the young one followed her. Then I saw with a shock that she was old. Her frock was simple enough. The skirt was longer than was at that time worn, and there was something slightly old-fashioned in the cut. I daresay the waist was more clearly indicated than was then usual, but it was a girl's frock. She was tall, like a heroine of Tennyson's, slight, with long legs and a graceful carriage. I had seen the nose before: it was the nose of a Greek goddess; her mouth was beautiful, and her eyes were large and blue. Her skin was of course a little tight on the bones, and there were wrinkles on her forehead and about her eyes, but in youth it must have been lovely. She reminded you of those Roman ladies with features of an exquisite regularity whom Alma-Tadema used to paint, but who, notwithstanding their antique dress, were so stubbornly English. It was a type of cold perfection that one had not seen for five-and-twenty years. Now it is as dead as the epigram. I was like an archæologist who finds some long-buried statue and I was thrilled in so unexpected a manner to hit upon this survival of a past era. For no day is so dead as the day before yesterday.

The gentleman rose to his feet when the two ladies left, and then resumed his chair. A waiter brought him a glass of heavy port. He smelt it, sipped it, and rolled it round his tongue. I observed him. He was a little man, much shorter than his imposing wife, well-covered without being stout, with a fine head of curling grey hair. His face was much wrinkled and it bore a faintly humorous expression. His lips were tight and his chin was square. He was, according to our present notions, somewhat extravagantly dressed. He wore a black velvet jacket, a frilled shirt with a low collar and a large black tie, and very wide evening trousers. It gave you vaguely the effect of costume. Having drunk his port with deliberation, he got up and sauntered out of the room.

When I passed through the hall, curious to know who these singular people were, I glanced at the visitors' book. I saw, written in an angular feminine hand, the writing that was taught to young ladies in modish schools forty years or so ago, the names: Mr. and Mrs. Edwin St. Clair and Miss Porchester. Their address was given as 68, Leinster Square, Bayswater, London. These must be the names and this the address of the persons who had so much interested me. I asked the manageress who Mr. St. Clair was and she told me that she believed he was something in the City. I went into the billiard-room and knocked the balls about for a little while and then on my way upstairs passed through the lounge. The two red-faced gentlemen were reading the evening paper and the middle-aged lady was dozing over a novel. The party of three sat in a corner. Mrs. St. Clair was knitting, Miss Porchester was busy with embroidery, and Mr. St. Clair was reading aloud in a discreet but resonant tone. As I passed I discovered that he was reading *Bleak House*.

I read and wrote most of the next day, but in the afternoon I went for a walk and on my way home I sat down for a little on one of those convenient benches on the sea-front. It was not quite so cold as the day before and the air was pleasant. For want of anything better to do I watched a figure advancing towards me from a distance. It was a man and as he came nearer I saw that it was rather a shabby little man. He wore a thin

black greatcoat and a somewhat battered bowler. He
walked with his hands in his pockets and looked cold.
He gave me a glance as he passed by, went on a few
steps, hesitated, stopped and turned back. When he
came up once more to the bench on which I sat he took
a hand out of his pocket and touched his hat. I noticed
that he wore shabby black gloves, and surmised that
he was a widower in straitened circumstances. Or he
might have been a mute recovering, like myself, from
influenza.

"Excuse me, sir," he said, "but could you oblige me
with a match?"

"Certainly."

He sat down beside me and while I put my hand in
my pocket for matches he hunted in his for cigarettes.
He took out a small packet of Goldflakes and his face
fell.

"Dear, dear, how very annoying! I haven't got a
cigarette left."

"Let me offer you one," I replied, smiling.

I took out my case and he helped himself.

"Gold?" he asked, giving the case a tap as I closed it.
"Gold? That's a thing I never could keep. I've had
three. All stolen."

His eyes rested in a melancholy way on his boots,
which were sadly in need of repair. He was a wizened
little man with a long thin nose and pale blue eyes.
His skin was sallow and he was much lined. I could not
tell what his age was; he might have been five-and-
thirty or he might have been sixty. There was nothing
remarkable about him except his insignificance. But

though evidently poor he was neat and clean. He was respectable and he clung to respectability. No, I did not think he was a mute, I thought he was a solicitor's clerk who had lately buried his wife and been sent to Elsom by an indulgent employer to get over the first shock of his grief.

"Are you making a long stay, sir?" he asked me.

"Ten days or a fortnight."

"Is this your first visit to Elsom, sir?"

"I have been here before."

"I know it well, sir. I flatter myself there are very few seaside resorts that I have not been to at one time or another. Elsom is hard to beat, sir. You get a very nice class of people here. There's nothing noisy or vulgar about Elsom if you understand what I mean. Elsom has very pleasant recollections for me, sir. I knew Elsom well in bygone days. I was married in St. Martin's Church, sir."

"Really," I said feebly.

"It was a very happy marriage, sir."

"I'm very glad to hear it," I returned.

"Nine months, that one lasted," he said reflectively.

Surely the remark was a trifle singular. I had not looked forward with any enthusiasm to the probability which I so clearly foresaw that he would favour me with an account of his matrimonial experiences, but now I waited if not with eagerness at least with curiosity for a further observation. He made none. He sighed a little. At last I broke the silence.

"There don't seem to be very many people about," I remarked.

"I like it so. I'm not one for crowds. As I was saying just now I reckon I've spent a good many years at one seaside resort after the other, but I never came in the season. It's the winter I like."

"Don't you find it a little melancholy?"

He turned towards me and placed his black-gloved hand for an instant on my arm.

"It is melancholy. And because it's melancholy a little ray of sunshine is very welcome."

The remark seemed to me perfectly idiotic and I did not answer. He withdrew his hand from my arm and got up.

"Well, I mustn't keep you, sir. Pleased to have made your acquaintance."

He took off his dingy hat very politely and strolled away. It was beginning now to grow chilly and I thought I would return to the Dolphin. As I reached its broad steps a landau drove up, drawn by two scraggy horses, and from it stepped Mr. St. Clair. He wore a hat that looked like the unhappy result of a union between a bowler and a top-hat. He gave his hand to his wife and then to his niece. The porter carried in after them rugs and cushions. As Mr. St. Clair paid the driver I heard him tell him to come at the usual time next day, and I understood that the St. Clairs took a drive every afternoon in a landau. It would not have surprised me to learn that none of them had ever been in a motor-car.

The manageress told me that they kept very much to themselves and sought no acquaintance among the other persons staying at the hotel. I rode my imagination on a loose rein. I watched them eat three meals a

day. I watched Mr. and Mrs. St. Clair sit at the top
of the hotel steps in the morning. He read *The Times*
and she knitted. I suppose Mrs. St. Clair had never read
a paper in her life, for they never took anything but
The Times and Mr. St. Clair of course took it with him
every day to the City. At about twelve Miss Porchester
joined them.

"Have you enjoyed your walk, Eleanor?" asked Mrs.
St. Clair.

"It was very nice, Aunt Gertrude," answered Miss
Porchester.

And I understood that just as Mrs. St. Clair took
'her drive' every afternoon Miss Porchester took 'her
walk' every morning.

"When you have come to the end of your row, my
dear," said Mr. St. Clair, with a glance at his wife's
knitting, "we might go for a constitutional before
luncheon."

"That will be very nice," answered Mrs. St. Clair.
She folded up her work and gave it to Miss Porchester.
"If you're going upstairs, Eleanor, will you take my
work?"

"Certainly, Aunt Gertrude.'

"I daresay you're a little tired after your walk, my
dear."

"I shall have a little rest before luncheon."

Miss Porchester went into the hotel and Mr. and Mrs.
St. Clair walked slowly along the sea-front, side by side,
to a certain point, and then walked slowly back.

When I met one of them on the stairs I bowed and
received an unsmiling, polite bow in return, and in the

morning I ventured upon a good-day, but there the matter ended. It looked as though I should never have a chance to speak to any of them. But presently I thought that Mr. St. Clair gave me now and then a glance, and thinking he had heard my name I imagined, perhaps vainly, that he looked at me with curiosity. And a day or two after that I was sitting in my room when the porter came in with a message.

"Mr. St. Clair presents his compliments and could you oblige him with the loan of Whitaker's Almanack."

I was astonished.

"Why on earth should he think that I have a Whitaker's Almanack?"

"Well, sir, the manageress told him you wrote."

I could not see the connection.

"Tell Mr. St. Clair that I'm very sorry that I haven't got a Whitaker's Almanack, but if I had I would very gladly lend it to him."

Here was my opportunity. I was by now filled with eagerness to know these fantastic persons more closely. Now and then in the heart of Asia I have come upon a lonely tribe living in a little village among an alien population. No one knows how they came there or why they settled in that spot. They live their own lives, speak their own language, and have no communication with their neighbours. No one knows whether they are the descendants of a band that was left behind when their nation swept in a vast horde across the continent or whether they are the dying remnant of some great people that in that country once held empire. They are a mystery. They have no future and no history. This odd little family seemed to me to have something of the same character. They were of an era that is dead and gone. They reminded me of persons in one of those leisurely, old-fashioned novels that one's father read. They belonged to the eighties and they had not moved since then. How extraordinary it was that they could have lived through the last forty years as though the world stood still! They took me back to my childhood and I recollected people who are long since dead. I wonder if it is only distance that gives me the impression that they were more peculiar than anyone is now. When a person was described then as "quite a character," by heaven, it meant something.

So that evening after dinner I went into the lounge and boldly addressed Mr. St. Clair.

"I'm so sorry I haven't got a Whitaker's Almanack," I said, "but if I have any other book that can be of service to you I shall be delighted to lend it to you."

Mr. St. Clair was obviously startled. The two ladies kept their eyes on their work. There was an embarrassed hush.

"It does not matter at all, but I was given to understand by the manageress that you were a novelist."

I racked my brain. There was evidently some connection between my profession and Whitaker's Almanack that escaped me.

"In days gone by Mr. Trollope used often to dine with us in Leinster Square and I remember him saying that the two most useful books to a novelist were the Bible and Whitaker's Almanack."

"I see that Thackeray once stayed in this hotel," I

remarked, anxious not to let the conversation drop.

"I never very much cared for Mr. Thackeray, though he dined more than once with my wife's father, the late Mr. Sargeant Saunders. He was too cynical for me. My niece has not read *Vanity Fair* to this day."

Miss Porchester blushed slightly at this reference to herself. A waiter brought in the coffee and Mrs. St. Clair turned to her husband.

"Perhaps, my dear, this gentleman would do us the pleasure to have his coffee with us."

Although not directly addressed, I answered promptly.

"Thank you very much."

I sat down.

"Mr. Trollope was always my favourite novelist," said Mr. St. Clair. "He was so essentially a gentleman. I admire Charles Dickens. But Charles Dickens could never draw a gentleman. I am given to understand that young people nowadays find Mr. Trollope a little slow. My niece, Miss Porchester, prefers the novels of Mr. William Black."

"I'm afraid I've never read any," I said.

"Ah, I see that you are like me; you are not up-to-date. My niece once persuaded me to read a novel by a Miss Rhoda Broughton, but I could not manage more than a hundred pages of it."

"I did not say I liked it, Uncle Edwin," said Miss Porchester, defending herself, with another blush. "I told you it was rather fast, but everybody was talking about it."

"I'm quite sure it is not the sort of book your Aunt Gertrude would have wished you to read, Eleanor."

"I remember Miss Broughton telling me once that when she was young people said her books were fast and when she was old they said they were slow, and it was very hard, since she had written exactly the same sort of book for forty years."

"Oh, did you know Miss Broughton?" asked Miss Porchester, addressing me for the first time. "How very interesting! And did you know Ouida?"

"My dear Eleanor, what will you say next! I'm quite sure you've never read anything by Ouida."

"Indeed, I have, Uncle Edwin. I've read *Under Two Flags* and I liked it very much."

"You amaze and shock me. I don't know what girls are coming to nowadays."

"You always said that when I was thirty you gave me complete liberty to read anything I liked."

"There is a difference, my dear Eleanor, between liberty and license," said Mr. St. Clair, smiling a little in order not to make his reproof offensive, but with a certain gravity.

I do not know if in recounting this conversation I have managed to convey the impression it gave me of a charming and old-fashioned air. I could have listened all night to them discussing the depravity of an age that was young in the eighteen-eighties. I would have given a good deal for a glimpse of their large and roomy house in Leinster Square. I should have recognized the suite covered in red brocade that stood stiffly about the drawing-room, each piece in its appointed place; and the cabinets filled with Dresden china would have brought me back my childhood. In the dining-room, where they habitually sat, for the drawing-room was used only for parties, there was a Turkey carpet and a vast mahogany sideboard 'groaning' with silver. On the walls were the pictures that had excited the admiration of Mrs. Humphry Ward and her uncle Matthew in the Academy of eighteen-eighty.

Next morning, strolling through a pretty lane at the back of Elsom, I met Miss Porchester, who was taking 'her walk.' I should have liked to go a little way with her, but felt certain that it would embarrass this maiden of fifty to saunter alone with a man even of my respectable years. She bowed as I passed her, and blushed. Oddly enough, a few yards behind her I came upon the funny shabby little man in black gloves with whom I had spoken for a few minutes on the front. He touched his old bowler hat.

"Excuse me, sir, but could you oblige me with a match?" he said.

"Certainly," I retorted, "but I'm afraid I have no cigarettes on me."

"Allow me to offer you one of mine," he said, taking out the paper case. It was empty. "Dear, dear, I haven't got one either. What a curious coincidence!"

He went on and I had a notion that he a little hastened his steps. I was beginning to have my doubts about him. I hoped he was not going to bother Miss Porchester. For a moment I thought of walking back, but I did not. He was a civil little man and I did not believe he would make a nuisance of himself to a single lady.

I saw him again that very afternoon. I was sitting on the front. He walked towards me with little, halting steps. There was something of a wind and he looked like a dried leaf being driven before it. This time he did not hesitate, but sat down beside me.

"We meet again, sir. The world is a small place. If it will not inconvenience you perhaps you will allow me to rest a few minutes. I am a wee bit tired."

"This is a public bench, and you have just as much right to sit on it as I."

I did not wait for him to ask me for a match, but at once offered him a cigarette.

"How very kind of you, sir! I have to limit myself to so many cigarettes a day, but I enjoy those I smoke. As one grows older the pleasures of life diminish, but my experience is that one enjoys more those that remain."

"That is a very consoling thought."

"Excuse me, sir, but am I right in thinking that you are the well-known author?"

"I am an author," I replied. "But what made you think it?"

"I have seen your portrait in the illustrated papers. I suppose you don't recognize me?"

I looked at him again, a weedy little man in neat but shabby black clothes, with a long nose and watery blue eyes.

"I'm afraid I don't."

"I daresay I've changed," he sighed. "There was a time when my photograph was in every paper in the United Kingdom. Of course, those press photographs never do you justice. I give you my word, sir, that if I hadn't seen my name underneath I should never have guessed that some of them were meant for me."

He was silent for a while. The tide was out, and beyond the shingle of the beach was a strip of yellow mud.
The breakwaters were half buried in it like the back-
bones of prehistoric beasts.

"It must be a wonderfully interesting thing to be an
author, sir. I've often thought I had quite a turn for
writing myself. At one time and another I've done a
rare lot of reading. I haven't kept up with it much
lately. For one thing my eyes are not so good as they
used to be. I believe I could write a book if I tried."

"They say anybody can write one," I answered.

"Not a novel, you know. I'm not much of a one for
novels; I prefer histories and that like. But memoirs.
If anybody was to make it worth my while I wouldn't
mind writing my memoirs."

"It's very fashionable just now."

"There are not many people who've had the experiences I've had in one way and another. I did write
to one of the Sunday papers about it some little while
back, but they never answered my letter."

He gave me a long, appraising look. He had too respectable an air to be about to ask me for half a crown.

"Of course you don't know who I am, sir, do you?"

"I honestly don't."

He seemed to ponder for a moment, then he smoothed
down his black gloves on his fingers, looked for a moment at a hole in one of them, and then turned to me
not without self-consciousness.

"I am the celebrated Mortimer Ellis," he said.

"Oh?"

I did not know what other ejaculation to make, for to

the best of my belief I had never heard the name before.
I saw a look of disappointment come over his face, and
I was a trifle embarrassed.

"Mortimer Ellis," he repeated. "You're not going to
tell me you don't know."

"I'm afraid I must. I'm very often out of England."

I wondered to what he owed his celebrity. I passed
over in my mind various possibilities. He could never
have been an athlete, which alone in England gives a
man real fame, but he might have been a faith-healer or
a champion billiard-player. There is of course no one
so obscure as a cabinet minister out of office and he
might have been the President of the Board of Trade
in a defunct administration. But he had none of the
look of a politician.

"That's fame for you," he said bitterly. "Why, for
weeks I was the most talked-about man in England.
Look at me. You must have seen my photograph in the
papers. Mortimer Ellis."

"I'm sorry," I said, shaking my head.

He paused a moment to give his disclosure effective-
ness.

"I am the well-known bigamist."

Now what are you to reply when a person who is
practically a stranger to you informs you that he is a
well-known bigamist? I will confess that I have sometimes had the vanity to think that I am not as a rule at
a loss for a retort, but here I found myself speechless.

"I've had eleven wives, sir," he went on.

"Most people find one about as much as they can
manage."

"Ah, that's want of practice. When you've had eleven there's very little you don't know about women."

"But why did you stop at eleven?"

"There now, I knew you'd say that. The moment I set eyes on you I said to myself, he's got a clever face. You know, sir, that's the thing that always grizzles me. Eleven does seem a funny number, doesn't it? There's something unfinished about it. Now three anyone might have, and seven's all right, they say nine's lucky, and there's nothing wrong with ten. But eleven! That's the one thing I regret. I shouldn't have minded anything if I could have brought it up to the Round Dozen."

He unbuttoned his coat and from an inside pocket produced a bulging and very greasy pocketbook. From this he took a large bundle of newspaper cuttings; they were worn and creased and dirty. But he spread out two or three.

"Now just you look at those photographs. I ask you, are they like me? It's an outrage. Why, you'd think I was a criminal to look at them."

The cuttings were of imposing length. In the opinion of sub-editors Mortimer Ellis had obviously been a news item of value. One was headed, A Much Married Man; another, Heartless Ruffian Brought to Book; a third, Contemptible Scoundrel Meets his Waterloo.

"Not what you would call a good press," I murmured.

"I never pay any attention to what the newspapers say," he answered, with a shrug of his thin shoulders. "I've known too many journalists myself for that. No, it's the judge I blame. He treated me shocking and it did him no good, mind you; he died within the year."

I ran my eyes down the report I held.

"I see he gave you five years."

"Disgraceful, I call it, and see what it says." He pointed to a place with his forefinger. "'Three of his victims pleaded for mercy to be shown to him.' That shows what they thought of me. And after that he gave me five years. And just look what he called me, a heartless scoundrel—me, the best-hearted man that ever lived—a pest of society and a danger to the public. Said he wished he had the power to give me the cat. I don't so much mind his giving me five years, though you'll never get me to say it wasn't excessive, but I ask you, had he the right to talk to me like that? No, he hadn't, and I'll never forgive him, not if I live to be a hundred."

The bigamist's cheeks flushed and his watery eyes were filled for a moment with fire. It was a sore subject with him.

"May I read them?" I asked him.

"That's what I gave them you for. I want you to read them, sir. And if you can read them without saying that I'm a much wronged man, well, you're not the man I took you for."

As I glanced through one cutting after another I saw why Mortimer Ellis had so wide an acquaintance with the seaside resorts of England. They were his hunting-ground. His method was to go to some place when the season was over and take apartments in one of the empty lodging-houses. Apparently it did not take him long to make acquaintance with some woman or other, widow or spinster, and I noticed that their ages at the time were between thirty-five and fifty. They stated in the witness-box that they had met him first on the sea-front. He generally proposed marriage to them within a fortnight of this and they were married shortly after. He induced them in one way or another to entrust him with their savings and in a few months, on the pretext that he had to go to London on business, he left them, never to return. Only one had ever seen him again till, obliged to give evidence, they saw him in the dock. They were women of a certain respectability; one was the daughter of a doctor and another of a clergyman; there was a lodging-house keeper, there was the widow of a commercial traveller, and there was a retired dressmaker. For the most part, their fortunes ranged from five hundred to a thousand pounds, but whatever the sum the misguided women were stripped of every penny. Some of them told really pitiful stories of the destitution to which they had been reduced. But they all acknowledged that he had been a good husband to them. Not only had three actually pleaded for mercy to be shown him; but one said in the witness-box that, if he was willing to come, she was ready to take him back. He noticed that I was reading this.

"And she'd have worked for me," he said, "there's no doubt about that. But I said, better let bygones be bygones. No one likes a cut off the best end of the neck better than I do, but I'm not much of a one for cold roast mutton, I will confess."

It was only by an accident that Mortimer Ellis did not marry his twelfth wife and so achieve the Round Dozen which I understand appealed to his love of symmetry. For he was engaged to be married to a Miss

Hubbard—"two thousand pounds she had, if she had a penny, in war-loan," he confided to me—and the banns had been read, when one of his former wives saw him, made enquiries, and communicated with the police. He was arrested on the very day before his twelfth wedding.

"She was a bad one, she was," he told me. "She deceived me something cruel."

"How did she do that?"

"Well, I met her at Eastbourne, one December it was, on the pier, and she told me in course of conversation that she'd been in the millinery business and had retired. She said she'd made a tidy bit of money. She wouldn't say exactly how much it was, but she gave me to understand it was something like fifteen hundred pounds. And when I married her—would you believe it?—she hadn't got three hundred. And that's the one who gave me away. And mind you, I'd never blamed her. Many a man would have cut up rough when he found out he'd been made a fool of. I never showed her that I was disappointed even, I just went away without a word."

"But not without the three hundred pounds, I take it."

"Oh come, sir, you must be reasonable," he returned in an injured tone. "You can't expect three hundred pounds to last for ever, and I'd been married to her four months before she confessed the truth."

"Forgive my asking," I said, "and pray don't think my question suggests a disparaging view of your personal attractions, but—why did they marry you?"

"Because I asked them," he answered, evidently very much surprised at my enquiry.

"But did you never have any refusals?"

"Very seldom. Not more than four or five in the whole course of my career. Of course I didn't propose till I was pretty sure of my ground and I don't say I didn't draw a blank sometimes. You can't expect to click every time, if you know what I mean, and I've often wasted several weeks making up to a woman before I saw there was nothing doing."

I surrendered myself for a time to my reflections. But I noticed presently that a broad smile spread over the mobile features of my friend.

"I understand what you mean," he said. "It's my appearance that puzzles you. You don't know what it is they see in me. That's what comes of reading novels and going to the pictures. You think what women want is the cowboy type, or the romance-of-old-Spain touch, flashing eyes, an olive skin, and a beautiful dancer. You make me laugh."

"I'm glad," I said.

"Are you a married man, sir?"

"I am. But I only have one wife."

"You can't judge by that. You can't generalize from a single instance, if you know what I mean. Now, I ask you, what would you know about dogs if you'd never had anything but one bull-terrier?"

The question was rhetorical and I felt sure did not require an answer. He paused for an effective moment and went on.

"You're wrong, sir. You're quite wrong. They may

take a fancy to a good-looking young fellow, but they don't want to marry him. They don't really care about looks."

"Douglas Jerrold, who was as ugly as he was witty, used to say that if he was given ten minutes' start with a woman he could cut out the handsomest man in the room."

"They don't want wit. They don't want a man to be funny; they think he's not serious. They don't want a man who's too handsome; they think he's not serious either. That's what they want, they want a man who's serious. Safety first. And then—attention. I may not be handsome and I may not be amusing, but believe me, I've got what every woman wants. Poise. And the proof is, I've made every one of my wives happy."

"It certainly is much to your credit that three of them pleaded for mercy to be shown to you and that one was willing to take you back."

"You don't know what an anxiety that was to me all the time I was in prison. I thought she'd be waiting for me at the gate when I was released, and I said to the Governor, 'For God's sake, sir, smuggle me out so as no one can see me.'"

He smoothed his gloves again over his hands and his eye once more fell upon the hole in the first finger.

"That's what comes of living in lodgings, sir. How's a man to keep himself neat and tidy without a woman to look after him? I've been married too often to be able to get along without a wife. There are men who don't like being married. I can't understand them. The fact is, you can't do a thing really well unless you've got your heart in it, and I like being a married man. It's no difficulty to me to do the little things that women like and that some men can't be bothered with. As I was saying just now, it's attention a woman wants. I never went out of the house without giving my wife a kiss and I never came in without giving her another. And it was very seldom I came in without bringing her some chocolates or a few flowers. I never grudged the expense."

"After all, it was her money you were spending," I interposed.

"And what if it was? It's not the money that you've paid for a present that signifies, it's the spirit you give it in. That's what counts with women. No, I'm not one to boast, but I will say this for myself, I am a good husband."

I looked desultorily at the reports of the trial which I still held.

"I'll tell you what surprises me," I said. "All these women were very respectable, of a certain age, quiet, decent persons. And yet they married you without any enquiry after the shortest possible acquaintance."

He put his hand impressively on my arm.

"Ah, that's what you don't understand, sir. Women have got a craving to be married. It doesn't matter how young they are or how old they are, if they're short or tall, dark or fair, they've all got one thing in common: they want to be married. And mind you, I married them in church. No woman feels really safe unless she's married in church. You say I'm no beauty. Well, I never thought I was, but if I had one leg and a hump on my back I could find any number of women who'd jump at the chance of marrying me. It's not the man they care about, it's marriage. It's a mania with them. It's a disease. Why, there's hardly one of them who wouldn't have accepted me the second time I saw her only I like to make sure of my ground before I commit myself. When it all came out there was a rare to-do because I'd married eleven times. Eleven times? Why, it's nothing, it's not even a Round Dozen. I could have married thirty times if I'd wanted to. I give you my word, sir, when I consider my opportunities, I'm astounded at my moderation."

"You told me you were very fond of reading history."

"Yes, Warren Hastings said that, didn't he? It struck me at the time I read it. It seemed to fit me like a glove."

"And you never found these constant courtships a trifle monotonous?"

"Well, sir, I think I've got a logical mind, and it always gave me a rare lot of pleasure to see how the same effects followed on the same causes, if you know what I mean. Now, for instance, with a woman who'd never been married before I always passed myself off as a widower. It worked like a charm. You see, a spinster likes a man who knows a thing or two. But with a widow I always said I was a bachelor: a widow's afraid a man who's been married before knows too much."

I gave him back his cuttings; he folded them up neatly and replaced them in his greasy pocketbook.

"You know, sir, I always think I've been misjudged. Just see what they say about me: a pest of society, unscrupulous villain, contemptible scoundrel. Now just look at me. I ask you, do I look that sort of man? You know me, you're a judge of character, I've told you all about myself; do you think me a bad man?"

"My acquaintance with you is very slight," I answered with what I thought considerable tact.

"I wonder if the judge, I wonder if the jury, I wonder if the public ever thought about my side of the question. The public booed me when I was taken into court and the police had to protect me from their violence. Did any of them think what I'd done for these women?"

"You took their money."

"Of course I took their money. I had to live the same as anybody has to live. But what did I give them in exchange for their money?"

This was another rhetorical question, and though he looked at me as though he expected an answer I held my tongue. Indeed I did not know the answer. His voice was raised and he spoke with emphasis. I could see that he was serious.

"I'll tell you what I gave them in exchange for their money. Romance. Look at this place." He made a wide, circular gesture that embraced the sea and the horizon. "There are a hundred places in England like this. Look at that sea and that sky; look at these lodging-houses; look at that pier and the front. Doesn't it make your heart sink? It's dead as mutton. It's all very well for you who come down here for a week or two because you're run down. But think of all those women who live here from one year's end to another. They haven't a chance. They hardly know anyone. They've just got

enough money to live on and that's all. I wonder if you
know how terrible their lives are. Their lives are just like
the front, a long, straight, cemented walk that goes on
and on from one seaside resort to another. Even in the
season there's nothing for them. They're out of it. They
might as well be dead. And then I come along. Mind
you, I never made advances to a woman who wouldn't
have gladly acknowledged to thirty-five. And I give
them love. Why, many of them had never known what
it was to have a man do them up behind. Many of them
had never known what it was to sit on a bench in the
dark with a man's arm round their waist. I bring them
change and excitement. I give them a new pride in
themselves. They were on the shelf and I come along
quite quietly and I deliberately take them down. A little
ray of sunshine in those drab lives, that's what I was.
No wonder they jumped at me, no wonder they wanted
me to go back to them. The only one who gave me away
was the milliner. She said she was a widow. My private
opinion is that she'd never been married at all. You say
I did the dirty on them; why, I brought happiness and
glamour into eleven lives that never thought they had
even a dog's chance of it again. You say I'm a villain
and a scoundrel. You're wrong. I'm a philanthropist.
Five years, they gave me; they should have given me
the medal of the Royal Humane Society."

He took out his empty packet of Goldflakes and
looked at it with a melancholy shake of the head. When
I handed him my cigarette case he helped himself without a word. I watched the spectacle of a good man
struggling with his emotion.

"And what did I get out of it, I ask you?" he continued presently. "Board and lodging and enough to buy cigarettes. But I never was able to save, and the proof is that now, when I'm not so young as I was, I haven't got half a crown in my pocket." He gave me a sidelong glance. "It's a great come-down for me to find myself in this position. I've always paid my way and I've never asked a friend for a loan in all my life. I was wondering, sir, if you could oblige me with a trifle. It's humiliating to me to have to suggest it, but the fact is, if you could oblige me with a pound it would mean a great deal to me."

Well, I had certainly had a pound's worth of entertainment out of the bigamist and I dived for my pocketbook.

"I shall be very glad," I said.

He looked at the notes I took out.

"I suppose you couldn't make it two, sir?"

"I think I could."

I handed him a couple of pound notes and he gave a little sigh as he took them.

"You don't know what it means to a man who's used to the comforts of home life not to know where to turn for a night's lodging."

"But there is one thing I should like you to tell me," I said. "I shouldn't like you to think me cynical, but I had a notion that women on the whole take the maxim, it is more blessed to give than to receive, as applicable exclusively to our sex. How did you persuade these respectable, and no doubt thrifty, women to entrust you so confidently with all their savings?"

An amused smile spread over his undistinguished features.

"Well, sir, you know what Shakespeare said about ambition o'erleaping itself. That's the explanation. Tell a woman you'll double her capital in six months if she'll give it you to handle and she won't be able to give you the money quick enough. Greed, that's what it is. Just greed."

It was a sharp sensation, stimulating to the appetite (like hot sauce with ice cream) to go from this diverting ruffian to the respectability, all lavender bags and crinolines, of the St. Clairs and Miss Porchester. I spent every evening with them now. No sooner had the ladies left him than Mr. St. Clair sent his compliments to my table and asked me to drink a glass of port with him. When we had finished it we went into the lounge and drank coffee. Mr. St. Clair enjoyed his glass of old brandy. The hour I thus spent with them was so exquisitely boring that it had for me a singular fascination. They were told by the manageress that I had written plays.

"We used often to go to the theatre when Sir Henry Irving was at the Lyceum," said Mr. St. Clair. "I once had the pleasure of meeting him. I was taken to supper at the Garrick Club by Sir Everard Millais and I was introduced to Mr. Irving as he then was."

"Tell him what he said to you, Edwin," said Mrs. St. Clair.

Mr. St. Clair struck a dramatic attitude and gave not at all a bad imitation of Henry Irving.

"'You have the actor's face, Mr. St. Clair,' he said to me. 'If you ever think of going on the stage, come to me and I will give you a part.'" Mr. St. Clair resumed his natural manner. "It was enough to turn a young man's head."

"But it didn't turn yours," I said.

"I will not deny that if I had been otherwise situated I might have allowed myself to be tempted. But I had my family to think of. It would have broken my father's heart if I had not gone into the business."

"What is that?" I asked.

"I am a tea-merchant, sir. My firm is the oldest in the City of London. I have spent forty years of my life in combating to the best of my ability the desire of my fellow-countrymen to drink Ceylon tea instead of the China tea which was universally drunk in my youth."

I thought it charmingly characteristic of him to spend a lifetime in persuading the public to buy something they didn't want rather than something they did.

"But in his younger days my husband did a lot of amateur acting and he was thought very clever," said Mrs. St. Clair.

"Shakespeare, you know, and sometimes *The School for Scandal*. I would never consent to act trash. But that is a thing of the past. I had a gift. Perhaps it was a pity to waste it, but it's too late now. When we have a dinner-party I sometimes let the ladies persuade me to recite the great soliloquies of Hamlet. But that is all I do."

Oh! Oh! Oh! I thought with shuddering fascination

of those dinner-parties and wondered whether I should ever be asked to one of them. Mrs. St. Clair gave me a little smile, half shocked, half prim.

"My husband was very bohemian as a young man," she said.

"I sowed my wild oats. I knew quite a lot of painters and writers, Wilkie Collins, for instance, and even men who wrote for the papers. Watts painted a portrait of my wife, and I bought a picture of Millais. I knew a number of the pre-Raphaelites."

"Have you a Rossetti?" I asked.

"No. I admired Rossetti's talent, but I could not approve of his private life. I would never buy a picture by an artist whom I should not care to ask to dinner at my house."

My brain was reeling when Miss Porchester, looking at her watch, said: "Are you not going to read to us to-night, Uncle Edwin?"

I withdrew.

It was while I was drinking a glass of port with Mr. St. Clair one evening that he told me the sad story of Miss Porchester. She was engaged to be married to a nephew of Mrs. St. Clair, a barrister, when it was discovered that he had had an intrigue with the daughter of his laundress.

"It was a terrible thing," said Mr. St. Clair. "A terrible thing. But of course my niece took the only possible course. She returned him his ring, his letters and his photograph, and said that she could never marry him. She implored him to marry the young person he had wronged and said she would be a sister to her.

It broke her heart. She has never cared for anyone
since."

"And did he marry the young person?"

Mr. St. Clair shook his head and sighed.

"No, we were greatly mistaken in him. It has been
a sore grief to my dear wife to think that a nephew of
hers should behave in such a dishonourable manner.
Some time later we heard that he was engaged to a
young lady in a very good position with ten thousand
pounds of her own. I considered it my duty to write to
her father and put the facts before him. He answered
my letter in a most insolent fashion. He said he would
much rather his son-in-law had a mistress before marriage than after."

"What happened then?"

"They were married and now my wife's nephew is
one of His Majesty's Judges of the High Court, and his
wife is My Lady. But we've never consented to receive
them. When my wife's nephew was knighted Eleanor
suggested that we should ask them to dinner, but my
wife said that he should never darken our doors and I
upheld her."

"And the laundress's daughter?"

"She married in her own class of life and has a public-
house at Canterbury. My niece, who has a little money
of her own, did everything for her and is godmother to
her eldest child."

Poor Miss Porchester. She had sacrificed herself on
the altar of Victorian morality, and I am afraid the
consciousness that she had behaved beautifully was the
only benefit she had got from it.

"Miss Porchester is a woman of striking appearance," I said. "When she was younger she must have been perfectly lovely. I wonder she never married somebody else."

"Miss Porchester was considered a great beauty. Alma-Tadema admired her so much that he asked her to sit as a model for one of his pictures, but of course we couldn't very well allow that." Mr. St. Clair's tone conveyed that the suggestion had deeply outraged his sense of decency. "No, Miss Porchester never cared for anyone but her cousin. She never speaks of him and it is now thirty years since they parted, but I am convinced that she loves him still. She is a true woman, my dear sir, one life, one love, and though perhaps I regret that she has been deprived of the joys of marriage and motherhood I am bound to admire her fidelity."

But the heart of woman is incalculable, and rash is the man who thinks she will remain in one stay. Rash, Uncle Edwin. You have known Eleanor for many years, for when, her mother having fallen into a decline and died, you brought the orphan to your comfortable and even luxurious house in Leinster Square, she was but a child; but what, when it comes down to brass tacks, Uncle Edwin, do you really know of Eleanor?

It was but two days after Mr. St. Clair had confided to me the touching story which explained why Miss Porchester had remained a spinster that, coming back to the hotel in the afternoon after a round of golf, the manageress came up to me in an agitated manner.

"Mr. St. Clair's compliments and will you go up to
number twenty-seven the moment you come in."

"Certainly. But why?"

"Oh, there's a rare upset. They'll tell you."

I knocked at the door. I heard a 'come in, come in,'
which reminded me that Mr. St. Clair had played
Shakespearean parts in probably the most refined
amateur dramatic company in London. I entered and
found Mrs. St. Clair lying on the sofa with a handkerchief soaked in eau-de-Cologne on her brow and a bottle
of smelling salts in her hand. Mr. St. Clair was standing
in front of the fire in such a manner as to prevent anyone else in the room from obtaining any benefit from it.

"I must apologize for asking you to come up in this
unceremonious fashion, but we are in great distress, and
we thought you might be able to throw some light on
what has happened."

His perturbation was obvious.

"What *has* happened?"

"Our niece, Miss Porchester, has eloped. This morning she sent in a message to my wife that she had one of
her sick headaches. When she has one of her sick headaches she likes to be left absolutely alone, and it wasn't
till this afternoon that my wife went to see if there was
anything she could do for her. The room was empty.
Her trunk was packed. Her dressing-case with silver
fittings was gone. And on the pillow was a letter telling
us of her rash act."

"I'm very sorry," I said. "I don't know exactly what
I can do."

"We were under the impression that you were the

only gentleman at Elsom with whom she had any acquaintance."

His meaning flashed across me.

"I haven't eloped with her," I said. "I happen to be a married man."

"I see you haven't eloped with her. At the first moment we thought perhaps . . . but if it isn't you, who is it?"

"I'm sure I don't know."

"Show him the letter, Edwin," said Mrs. St. Clair from the sofa.

"Don't move, Gertrude. It will bring on your lumbago."

Miss Porchester had 'her' sick headaches and Mrs. St. Clair had 'her' lumbago. What had Mr. St. Clair? I was willing to bet a fiver that Mr. St. Clair had 'his' gout. He gave me the letter and I read it with an air of decent commiseration.

DEAREST UNCLE EDWIN AND AUNT GERTRUDE:
When you receive this I shall be far away. I am going to be married this morning to a gentleman who is very dear to me. I know I am doing wrong in running away like this, but I was afraid you would endeavour to set obstacles in the way of my marriage, and since nothing would induce me to change my mind I thought it would save us all much unhappiness if I did it without telling you anything about it. My fiancé is a very retiring man, owing to his long residence in tropical countries not in the best of health, and he thought it much better that we should be married quite privately. When you know how

*radiantly happy I am I hope you will forgive me. Please
send my box to the luggage office at Victoria Station.*

Your loving niece,

ELEANOR.

"I will never forgive her," said Mr. St. Clair as I
returned him the letter. "She shall never darken my
doors again. Gertrude, I forbid you ever to mention
Eleanor's name in my hearing."

Mrs. St. Clair began to sob quietly.

"Aren't you rather hard?" I said. "Is there any
reason why Miss Porchester shouldn't marry?"

"At her age?" he answered angrily. "It's ridiculous.
We shall be the laughing-stock of everyone in Leinster
Square. Do you know how old she is? She's fifty-one."

"Fifty-four," said Mrs. St. Clair through her sobs.

"She's been the apple of my eye. She's been like a
daughter to us. She's been an old maid for years. I think
it's positively improper for her to think of marriage."

"She was always a girl to us, Edwin," pleaded Mrs.
St. Clair.

"And who is this man she's married? It's the decep-
tion that rankles. She must have been carrying on with
him under our very noses. She does not even tell us his
name. I fear the very worst."

Suddenly I had an inspiration. That morning after
breakfast I had gone out to buy myself some cigarettes
and at the tobacconist's I ran across Mortimer Ellis.
I had not seen him for some days.

"You're looking very spruce," I said.

His boots had been repaired and were neatly blacked,

his hat was brushed, he was wearing a clean collar and new gloves. I thought he had laid out my two pounds to advantage.

"I have to go to London this morning on business," he said.

I nodded and left the shop.

I remembered that a fortnight before, walking in the country, I had met Miss Porchester and, a few yards behind, Mortimer Ellis. Was it possible that they had been walking together and he had fallen back as they caught sight of me? By heaven, I saw it all.

"I think you said that Miss Porchester had money of her own," I said.

"A trifle. She has three thousand pounds."

Now I was certain. I looked at them blankly. Suddenly Mrs. St. Clair, with a cry, sprang to her feet.

"Edwin, Edwin, supposing he doesn't marry her?"

Mr. St. Clair at this put his hand to his head and in a state of collapse sank into a chair.

"The disgrace would kill me," he groaned.

"Don't be alarmed," I said. "He'll marry her all right. He always does. He'll marry her in church."

They paid no attention to what I said. I suppose they thought I'd suddenly taken leave of my senses. I was quite sure now. Mortimer Ellis had achieved his ambition after all. Miss Porchester completed the Round Dozen.

THE HUMAN ELEMENT

THE HUMAN ELEMENT

I seem never to find myself in Rome but at the dead season. I pass through in August or September on my way somewhere or other and spend a couple of days revisiting places or pictures that are endeared to me by old associations. It is very hot then and the inhabitants of the city spend their day interminably strolling up and down the Corso. The Caffé Nazionale is crowded with people sitting at little tables for long hours with an empty cup of coffee in front of them and a glass of water. In the Sistine Chapel you see blond and sun-burned Germans, in knickerbockers and shirts open at the neck, who have walked down the dusty roads of Italy with knapsacks on their shoulders; and in St. Peter's little groups of the pious, tired but eager, who have come on pilgrimage (at an inclusive rate) from some distant country. They are under the charge of a priest and they speak strange tongues. The Hotel Plaza then is cool and restful. The public rooms are dark, silent and spacious. In the lounge at teatime the only persons are a young, smart officer and a woman with fine eyes, drinking iced lemonade, and they talk intimately, in low tones, with the unwearying fluency of their race. You go up to your room and read and write

97

letters and come down again two hours later and they
are still talking. Before dinner a few people saunter into
the bar, but for the rest of the day it is empty and the
barman has time to tell you of his mother in Switzerland and his experiences in New York. You discuss life
and love and the high cost of liquor.

And on this occasion too I found that I had the hotel
almost to myself. When the reception clerk took me to
my room he told me that they were pretty full, but
when, having bathed and changed, I came down again
to the hall, the liftman, an old acquaintance, informed
me that there were not more than a dozen people staying
there. I was tired after a long and hot journey down
Italy and had made up my mind to dine quietly in the
hotel and go to bed early. It was late when I went into
the dining-room, vast and brightly lit, but not more
than three or four tables were occupied. I looked round
me with satisfaction. It is very agreeable to find yourself alone in a great city which is yet not quite strange
to you and in a large empty hotel. It gives you a de-
lectable sense of freedom. I felt the wings of my spirit
give a little flutter of delight. I had paused for ten
minutes in the bar and had a dry Martini. I ordered
myself a bottle of good red wine. My limbs were weary,
but my soul responded wonderfully to food and drink
and I began to feel a singular lightness of heart. I ate
my soup and my fish and pleasant thoughts filled my
mind. Scraps of dialogue occurred to me and my fancy
played happily with the persons of a novel I was then
at work on. I rolled a phrase on my tongue and it tasted
better than the wine. I began to think of the difficulty of

describing the looks of people in such a way as to make
the reader see them as you see them. To me it has
always been one of the most difficult things in fiction.
What does the reader really get when you describe a
face feature by feature? I should think nothing. And
yet the plan some writers adopt of taking a salient
characteristic, a crooked smile or shifty eyes, and
emphasizing that, though effective, avoids rather than
solves the problem. I looked about me and wondered
how I would describe the people at the tables round
me. There was one man by himself just opposite and
for practice I asked myself in what way I should treat
him. He was a tall, spare fellow, and what I believe
is generally called loose-limbed. He wore a dinner-
jacket and a boiled shirt. He had a rather long face and
pale eyes; his hair was fairish and wavy, but it was
growing thin, and the baldness of his temples gave him
a certain nobility of brow. His features were undistinguished. His mouth and nose were like everybody
else's; he was clean-shaven; his skin was naturally pale,
but at the moment sunburned. His appearance suggested an intellectual but slightly commonplace distinction. He looked as though he might have been a
lawyer or a don who played a pretty game of golf. I
felt that he had good taste and was well-read and would
be a very agreeable guest at a luncheon party in Chelsea.
But how the devil one was to describe him so as in a few
lines to give a vivid, interesting and accurate picture
I could not imagine. Perhaps it would be better to let
all the rest go and dwell only on that rather fatigued
distinction which on the whole was the most definite

BAY TREE INN.

impression he gave. I looked at him reflectively. Suddenly he leaned forwards and gave me a stiff but courtly little bow. I have a ridiculous habit of flushing when I am taken aback and now I felt my cheeks redden. I was startled. I had been staring at him for several minutes as though he were a dummy. He must have thought me extremely rude. I nodded with a good deal of embarrassment and looked away. Fortunately at that moment the waiter was handing me a dish. To the best of my belief I had never seen the fellow before. I asked myself whether his bow was due to my insistent stare, which made him think that he had met me somewhere, or whether I had really run across him and completely forgotten. I have a bad memory for faces and I had in this case the excuse that he looked exactly like a great many other people. You saw a dozen of him at every golf course round London on a fine Sunday.

He finished his dinner before me. He got up, but on his way out stopped at my table. He stretched out his hand.

"How d'you do," he said. "I didn't recognize you when you first came in. I wasn't meaning to cut you."

He spoke in a pleasant voice with the tones cultivated at Oxford and copied by many who have never been there. It was evident that he knew me, and evident too that he had no notion that I did not also know him. I had risen, and since he was a good deal taller than I he looked down on me. He held himself with a sort of languor. He stooped a little which added to the impression he gave me of having about him an air that was vaguely apologetic. His manner was a trifle condescending and at the same time a trifle shy.

"Won't you come and have your coffee with me?" he said. "I'm quite alone."

"Yes, I shall be glad to."

He left me and I still had no notion who he was or where I had met him. I had noticed one curious thing about him. Not once during the few sentences we exchanged, when we shook hands, or when with a nod he left me, did even the suspicion of a smile cross his face. Seeing him more closely I observed that he was in his way good-looking; his features were regular, his grey eyes were handsome, he had a slim figure; but it was a way that I found uninteresting. A silly woman would say he looked romantic. He reminded you of one of the knights of Burne-Jones though he was on a larger scale and there was no suggestion that he suffered from the chronic colitis that afflicted those unfortunate creatures. He was the sort of man whom you expected to look wonderful in fancy dress till you saw him in it and then you found that he looked absurd.

Presently I finished my dinner and went into the lounge. He was sitting in a large armchair and when he saw me he called a waiter. I sat down. The waiter came up and he ordered coffee and liqueurs. He spoke Italian very well. I was wondering by what means I could find out who he was without offending him. People are always a little disconcerted when you do not recognize them; they are so important to themselves, it is a shock to discover of what small importance they are to others. The excellence of his Italian recalled him to me. I remembered who he was and remembered at the same time that I did not like him. His name was Humphrey Carruthers. He was in the Foreign Office and he had a position of some importance. He was in charge of I know not what department. He had been attached to various embassies, and I supposed that a sojourn in Rome accounted for his idiomatic Italian. It was stupid of me not to have seen at once that he was connected with the diplomatic service. He had all the marks of the profession. He had the supercilious courtesy that is so well calculated to put up the backs of the general public, and the aloofness due to the consciousness the diplomat has that he is not as other men are, joined with the shyness occasioned by his uneasy feeling that other men do not quite realize it. I had known Carruthers for a good many years, but had met him infrequently, at luncheon parties where I said no more than 'How do you do' to him, and at the opera where he gave me a cool nod. He was generally thought intelligent; he was certainly cultured. He could talk of all the right things. It was inexcusable of me not to have remembered him, for he had lately acquired a very considerable reputation as a writer of short stories. They had appeared first in one or other of those magazines that are founded now and then by well-disposed persons to give the intelligent reader something worthy of his attention, and that die when their proprietors have lost as much money as they want to; and in their discreet and handsomely printed pages had excited as much attention as an exiguous circulation permitted. Then they were published in book form. They created a sensation. I have

seldom read such unanimous praise in the weekly
papers. Most of them gave the book a column, and the
Literary Supplement of *The Times* reviewed it not
among the common ruck of novels but in a place by
itself cheek by jowl with the memoirs of a distinguished
statesman. The critics welcomed Humphrey Carruthers
as a new star in the firmament. They praised his distinction, his subtlety, his delicate irony and his insight.
They praised his style, his sense of beauty and his
atmosphere. Here at last was a writer who had raised
the short story from the depths into which in English-
speaking countries it had fallen, and here was work to
which an Englishman could point with pride; it bore
comparison with the best compositions in this manner
of Finland, Russia and Czecho-Slovakia.

Three years later Humphrey Carruthers brought out
his second book and the critics commented on the
interval with satisfaction. Here was no hack prostitut-
ing his talent for money! The praise it received was
perhaps a little cooler than that which welcomed his
first volume—the critics had had time to collect themselves—but it was enthusiastic enough to have delighted any common writer who earns his living by his
pen, and there was no doubt that his position in the
world of letters was secure and honourable. The story
that attracted most commendation was called 'The
Shaving Mop' and all the best critics pointed out with
what beauty the author in three or four pages had laid
bare the tragic soul of a barber's assistant.

But his best-known story, which was also his longest,
was called 'Week-End.' It gave its title to his first book.

It narrated the adventures of a number of people who left Paddington Station on Saturday afternoon to stay with friends at Taplow and on Monday morning returned to London. It was so delicate that it was a little difficult to know exactly what happened. A young man, parliamentary secretary to a cabinet minister, very nearly proposed to a baronet's daughter, but didn't. Two or three others went on the river in a punt. They all talked a great deal in an allusive way, but none of them ever finished a sentence, and what they meant was very subtly indicated by dots and dashes. There were a good many descriptions of flowers in the garden and a sensitive picture of the Thames under the rain. It was all seen through the eyes of the German governess, and everyone agreed that Carruthers had conveyed her outlook on the situation with quite delicious humour.

I read both Humphrey Carruthers' books. I think it part of the writer's business to make himself aware of what is being written by his contemporaries. I am very willing to learn, and I thought I might discover in them something that would be useful to me. I was disappointed. I like a story to have a beginning, a middle, and an end. I have a weakness for a point. I think atmosphere is all very well, but atmosphere without anything else is like a frame without a picture; it has not much significance. But it may be that I could not see the merit of Humphrey Carruthers on account of defects in myself, and if I have described his two most successful stories without enthusiasm the cause perhaps lies in my own wounded vanity. For I was perfectly

conscious that Humphrey Carruthers looked upon me
as a writer of no account. I am convinced that he had
never read a word I had written. The popularity I enjoyed was sufficient to persuade him that there was no
occasion for him to give me any of his attention. For a
moment, such was the stir he created, it looked as
though he might himself be faced with that ignominy,
but it soon appeared that his exquisite work was above
the heads of the public. One can never tell how large
the intelligentsia is, but one can tell fairly well how
many of its members are prepared to pay money to
patronize the arts they cherish. The plays that are of
too fine a quality to attract the patrons of the commercial
theatre can count on an audience of ten thousand,
and the books that demand from their readers more
comprehension than can be expected from the common
herd sell twelve hundred copies. For the intelligentsia,
notwithstanding their sensitiveness to beauty, prefer
to go to the theatre on the nod and to get a book from
the library.

I am sure this did not distress Carruthers. He was an
artist. He was also a clerk in the Foreign Office. His
reputation as a writer was distinguished; he was not
interested in the vulgar, and to sell well would possibly
have damaged his career. I could not surmise what had
induced him to invite me to have coffee with him. It is
true he was alone, but I should have supposed he found
his thoughts excellent company, and I could not believe
he imagined that I had anything to say that would
interest him. Nevertheless I could not but see that he
was doing his dreary best to be affable. He reminded me

of where we had last met, and we talked for a moment of
common friends in London. He asked me how I came
to be in Rome at this season, and I told him. He volun-
teered the information that he had arrived that morning
from Brindisi. Our conversation did not go easily, and I
made up my mind that as soon as I civilly could I would
get up and leave him. But presently I had an odd sensation—I hardly know what caused it—that he was
conscious of this and was desperately anxious not to give
me the opportunity. I was surprised. I gathered my
wits about me. I noticed that whenever I paused he
broke in with a new topic. He was trying to find something to interest me so that I should stay. He was
straining every nerve to be agreeable. Surely he could
not be lonely; with his diplomatic connections he must
know plenty of people with whom he could have spent
the evening. I wondered indeed that he was not dining
at the Embassy; even though it was summer there must
be someone there he knew. I noticed also that he never
smiled. He talked with a sort of harsh eagerness as
though he were afraid of a moment's silence and the
sound of his voice shut out of his mind something that
tortured him. It was very strange. Though I did not like
him, though he meant nothing to me and to be with
him irked me somewhat, I was against my will a trifle
interested. I gave him a searching glance. I wondered if
it was my fancy that I saw in those pale eyes of his the
cowed look of a hunted dog, and notwithstanding his
neat features and his expression so civilly controlled,
in his aspect something that suggested the grimace of a
soul in pain. I could not understand. A dozen absurd

notions flashed through my mind. I was not particularly sympathetic: like an old war horse scenting the
fray I roused myself. I had been feeling very tired, but
now I grew alert. My sensibilities put out tentacles. I
was suddenly alive to every expression of his face and
every gesture. I put aside the thought that had come to
me that he had written a play and wanted my advice.
These exquisite persons succumb strangely to the
glamour of the footlights, and they are not averse from
getting a few tips from the craftsman whose competence
they superciliously despise. No, it was not that. A
single man in Rome, of æsthetic leanings, is liable to get
into trouble, and I asked myself whether Carruthers
had got into some difficulty to extricate himself from
which the Embassy was the last place he could go to.
The idealist, I have noticed, is apt at times to be im-
prudent in the affairs of the flesh. He sometimes finds
love in places which the police inconveniently visit. I
tittered in my heart. Even the gods laugh when a prig
is caught in an equivocal situation.

Suddenly Carruthers said something that staggered
me.

"I'm so desperately unhappy," he muttered.

He said it without warning. He obviously meant
it. There was in his tone a sort of gasp. It might very
well have been a sob. I cannot describe what a shock
it was to me to hear him say those words. I felt as
you do when you turn a corner of the street and on a
sudden a great blast of wind meets you, takes your
breath away, and nearly blows you off your feet. It was
so unexpected. After all, I hardly knew the fellow. We

were not friends. I did not like him; he did not like me. I had never looked on him as quite human. It was amazing that a man so self-controlled, so urbane, accustomed to the usages of polite society, should break in upon a stranger with such a confession. I am naturally reticent. I should be ashamed, whatever I was suffering, to disclose my pain to another. I shivered. His weakness outraged me. For a moment I was filled with a passion of anger. How dared he thrust the anguish of his soul on me? I very nearly cried:

"What the hell do I care?"

But I didn't. He was sitting huddled up in the big armchair. The solemn nobility of his features, which reminded one of the marble statue of a Victorian statesman, had strangely crumpled and his face sagged. He looked almost as though he were going to cry. I hesitated. I faltered. I had flushed when he spoke and now I felt my face go white. He was a pitiable object.

"I'm awfully sorry," I said.

"Do you mind if I tell you about it?"

"No."

It was not the moment for many words. I suppose Carruthers was in the early forties. He was a well-made man, athletic in his way, and with a confident bearing. Now he looked twenty years older and strangely shrivelled. He reminded me of the dead soldiers I had seen during the war and how oddly small death had made them. I was embarrassed and looked away, but I felt his eyes claiming mine and I looked back.

"Do you know Betty Welldon-Burns?" he asked me.

"I used to meet her sometimes in London years ago.
I've not seen her lately."

"She lives in Rhodes now, you know. I've just
come from there. I've been staying with her."

"Oh?"

He hesitated.

"I'm afraid you'll think it awfully strange of me to
talk to you like this. I'm at the end of my tether. If I
don't talk to somebody I shall go off my head."

He had ordered double brandies with the coffee
and now, calling the waiter, he ordered himself another.
We were alone in the lounge. There was a little shaded
lamp on the table between us. Because it was a public
room he spoke in a low voice. The place gave one, oddly
enough, a sense of intimacy. I cannot repeat all that
Carruthers said to me in the words he said it; it would
be impossible for me to remember them; it is more
convenient for me to put it in my own fashion. Sometimes he could not bring himself to say a thing right out
and I had to guess at what he meant. Sometimes he had
not understood, and it seemed to me that in certain
ways I saw the truth more clearly than he. Betty
Welldon-Burns had a very keen sense of humour and he
had none. I perceived a good deal that had escaped him.

I had met her a good many times, but I knew her
chiefly from hearsay. In her day she had made a great
stir in the little world of London, and I had heard of
her often before I met her. This was at a dance in Portland Place soon after the war. She was then already at
the height of her celebrity. You could not open an illustrated paper without seeing in it a portrait of her, and

her mad pranks were a staple of conversation. She was twenty-four. Her mother was dead, her father, the Duke of St. Erth, old and none too rich, spent most of the year in his Cornish castle, and she lived in London with a widowed aunt. At the outbreak of the war she went to France. She was just eighteen. She was a nurse in a hospital at the base and then drove a car. She acted in a theatrical tour designed to amuse the troops; she posed in tableaux at home for charitable purposes, held auctions for this object and that and sold flags in Piccadilly. Every one of her activities was widely advertised and in every new rôle she was profusely photographed. I suppose that she managed to have a very good time. But now that the war was over she was having her fling with a vengeance. Just then everybody a little lost his head. The young, relieved of the burden that for five years had oppressed them, indulged in one wild escapade after another. Betty took part in them all. Sometimes, for one reason or another, an account of them found its way into the newspapers, and her name was always in the headline. At that time night clubs were in the first flush of their success, and she was to be seen at them every night. She lived a life of hectic gaiety. It can only be described in a hackneyed phrase, because it was a hackneyed thing. The British public in its odd way took her to its heart, and Lady Betty was a sufficient description of her throughout the British islands. Women mobbed her when she went to a wedding, and the gallery applauded her at first nights as though she were a popular actress. Girls copied the way she did her hair, and manufacturers of soap and face cream paid her money to use her photograph to advertise their wares.

Of course dull, stodgy people, the people who remembered and regretted the old order, disapproved of her. They sneered at her constant appearance in the limelight. They said she had an insane passion for self-advertisement. They said she was fast. They said she drank too much. They said she smoked too much. I will admit that nothing I had heard of her had predisposed me to think very well of her. I held cheap the women who seemed to look upon the war as an occasion to enjoy themselves and be talked about. I am bored by the papers in which you see photographs of persons in society walking in Cannes or playing golf at St. Andrew's. I have always found the Bright Young People extremely tedious. The gay life seems dull and stupid to the onlooker, but the moralist is unwise to judge it harshly. It is as absurd to be angry with the young things who lead it as with a litter of puppies scampering aimlessly around, rolling one another over and chasing their tails. It is well to bear it with fortitude if they cause havoc in the flower beds or break a piece of china. Some of them will be drowned because their points are not up to the mark, and the rest will grow up into well-behaved dogs. Their unruliness is due only to the vitality of youth.

And it was vitality that was Betty's most shining characteristic. The urge of life flowed through her with a radiance that dazzled you. I do not think I shall ever forget the impression she made on me at the party at which I first saw her. She was like a maenad. She danced with an abandon that made you laugh, so obvious was her intense enjoyment of the music and the movement of her young limbs. Her hair was brown, slightly disordered by the vigour of her gestures, but her eyes were deep blue, and her skin was milk and roses. She was a great beauty, but she had none of the coldness of great beauty. She laughed constantly, and when she was not laughing she smiled and her eyes danced with the joy of living. She was like a milkmaid on the farmstead of the gods. She had the strength and health of the people; and yet the independence of her bearing, a sort of noble frankness of carriage, suggested the great lady. I do not quite know how to put the feeling she gave me, that though so simple and unaffected she was not unconscious of her station. I fancied that if occasion arose she could get on her dignity and be very grand indeed. She was charming to everybody because, probably without being quite aware of it, in the depths of her heart she felt that the rest of the world was perfectly insignificant. I understood why the factory girls in the East End adored her and why half a million people who had never seen her except in a photograph looked upon her with the intimacy of personal friendship. I was introduced to her and she spent a few minutes talking to me. It was extraordinarily flattering to see the interest she showed in you; you knew she could not really be so pleased to meet you as she seemed, or so delighted with what you said, but it was very attractive. She had the gift of being able to jump over the first difficult phases of acquaintance, and you had not known her for five minutes before you felt you had known her all her life. She was snatched away from me by someone who wanted to dance with her, and she surrendered herself to her partner's arms with just the same eager happiness as she had shown when she sank into a chair by my side. I was surprised, when I met her at luncheon a fortnight later, to find that she remembered exactly what we had talked about during those noisy ten minutes at the dance. A young woman with all the social graces.

I mentioned the incident to Carruthers.

"She was no fool," he said. "Very few people knew how intelligent she was. She wrote some very good poetry. Because she was so gay, because she was so reckless and never cared a damn for anybody, people thought she was scatter-brained. Far from it. She was as clever as a monkey. You would never have thought she'd had the time to read all the things she had. I don't suppose anyone knew that side of her as well as I did. We used to take walks together, in the country at week-ends, and in London we'd drive out to Richmond Park and walk there, and talk. She loved flowers and trees and grass. She was interested in everything. She had a lot of information and a lot of sense. There was nothing she couldn't talk about. Sometimes when we'd been for a walk in the afternoon and we met at a night club and she'd had a couple of glasses of champagne— that was enough to make her completely buffy, you know—and she was the life and soul of the party, I couldn't help thinking how amazed the rest of them would be if they knew how seriously we'd been talking only a few hours before. It was an extraordinary contrast. There seemed to be two entirely different women in her."

Carruthers said all this without a smile. He spoke with the melancholy he might have used if he had been speaking of some person snatched from the pleasant company of the living by untimely death. He gave a deep sigh.

"I was madly in love with her. I proposed to her half a dozen times. Of course I knew I hadn't a chance, I was only a very junior clerk at the F. O., but I couldn't help myself. She refused me, but she was always frightfully nice about it. It never made any difference to our friendship. You see, she really liked me. I gave her something that other people didn't. I always thought that she was really fonder of me than of anybody. I was crazy about her."

"I don't suppose you were the only one," I said, having to say something.

"Far from it. She used to get dozens of love letters from men she'd never seen or heard of, farmers in Africa, miners, and policemen in Canada. All sorts of people proposed to her. She could have married anyone she liked."

"Even royalty, one heard."

"Yes, she said she couldn't stand the life. And then she married Jimmie Welldon-Burns."

"People were rather surprised, weren't they?"

"Did you ever know him?"

"No, I don't think so. I may have met him, but he left no impression on me."

"He wouldn't. He was the most insignificant fellow that ever breathed. His father was a big manufacturer up in the north. He'd made a lot of money during the war and bought a baronetcy. I believe he hadn't an aitch to his name. Jimmie was at Eton with me—they'd tried hard to make a gentleman of him—and in London after the war he was about a good deal. He was always willing to throw a party. No one ever paid any attention to him. He just paid the bill. He was the most crashing bore. You know, rather prim, terribly polite; he made you rather uncomfortable because he was so anxious not to do the wrong thing. He always wore his clothes as though he'd just put them on for the first time and they were a little too tight for him."

When Carruthers innocently opened his *Times* one morning and, casting his eyes down the fashionable intelligence of the day, saw that a marriage had been arranged between Elizabeth, only daughter of the Duke of St. Erth, and James, eldest son of Sir John Welldon-Burns, Bart., he was dumbfounded. He rang Betty up and asked if it was true.

"Of course," she said.

He was so shocked that for the moment he found nothing to say. She went on speaking.

"He's bringing his family to luncheon to-day to meet Father. I daresay it'll be a bit grim. You might stand me a cocktail at Claridge's to fortify me, will you?"

"At what time?" he asked.

"One."

"All right. I'll meet you there."

He was waiting for her when she came in. She walked with a sort of spring as though her eager feet itched to break into a dance. She was smiling. Her eyes shone with the joy that suffused her because she was alive and the world was such a pleasant place to live in. People recognizing her whispered to one another as she came in. Carruthers really felt that she brought sunshine and the scent of flowers into the sober but rather overwhelming splendour of Claridge's lounge. He did not wait to say 'How do you do' to her.

"Betty, you can't do it," he said. "It's simply out of the question."

"Why?"

"He's awful."

"I don't think he is. I think he's rather nice."

A waiter came up and took their order. Betty looked at Carruthers with those beautiful blue eyes of hers that managed to be at the same time so gay and so tender.

"He's such a frightful bounder, Betty."

"Oh, don't be so silly, Humphrey. He's just as good as anybody else. I think you're rather a snob."

"He's so dull."

"No, he's rather quiet. I don't know that I want a husband who's too brilliant. I think he'll make a very good background. He's quite good-looking and he has nice manners."

"My God, Betty."

"Oh, don't be idiotic, Humphrey."

"Are you going to pretend you're in love with him?"

"I think it would be tactful, don't you?"

"Why are you going to marry him?"

She looked at him coolly.

"He's got pots of money. I'm nearly twenty-six."

There was nothing much more to be said. He drove her back to her aunt's house. She had a very grand marriage, with dense crowds lining the approach to St. Margaret's, Westminster, presents from practically all the royal family, and the honeymoon was passed on the yacht her father-in-law had lent them. Carruthers applied for a post abroad and was sent to Rome (I was right in guessing that he had thus acquired his admirable Italian) and later to Stockholm. Here he was counsellor and here he wrote the first of his stories.

Perhaps Betty's marriage had disappointed the British public who expected much greater things of her, perhaps only that as a young married woman she no longer appealed to the popular sense of romance; the fact was plain that she soon lost her place in the public eye. You ceased to hear very much about her. Not long after her marriage it was rumoured that she was going to have a baby and a little later that she had had a miscarriage. She did not drop out of society; I suppose she continued to see her friends, but her activities were no longer spectacular. She was certainly but seldom seen any more in those raffish assemblies where the members of a tarnished aristocracy hob-nob with the hangers-on of the arts and flatter themselves that they are being at once smart and cultured. People said she was settling down. They wondered how she was getting on with her husband, and no sooner did they do this than they concluded that she was not getting on very well. Presently gossip said that Jimmie was drinking too much and then, a year or two later, one heard that

he had contracted tuberculosis. The Welldon-Burns
spent a couple of winters in Switzerland. Then the news
spread that they had separated and Betty had gone to
live in Rhodes. An odd place to choose.

"It must be deadly," her friends said.

A few of them went to stay with her now and then
and came back with reports of the beauty of the island
and the leisurely charm of the life. But of course it
was very lonely. It seemed strange that Betty, with her
brilliance and her energy, should be content to settle
there. She had bought a house. She knew no one but a
few Italian officials, there was indeed no one to know;
but she seemed perfectly happy. Her visitors could not
make it out. But the life of London is busy and memories are short. People ceased to concern themselves with
her. She was forgotten. Then, a few weeks before I met
Humphrey Carruthers in Rome, *The Times* announced
the death of Sir James Welldon-Burns, second baronet.
His younger brother succeeded him in the title. Betty
had never had a child.

Carruthers continued to see her after her marriage.
Whenever he came to London they lunched together.
She had the ability to take up a friendship after a long
separation as though no passage of time had intervened,
so that there was never any strangeness in their meet-
ings. Sometimes she asked him when he was going to
marry.

"You're getting on, you know, Humphrey. If you
don't marry soon you'll get rather old-maidish."

"D'you recommend marriage?"

It was not a very kindly thing to say, because like everyone else he had heard that she was not getting on too well with her husband, but her remark piqued him.

"On the whole. I think probably an unsatisfactory marriage is better than no marriage at all."

"You know quite well that nothing would induce me to marry and you know why."

"Oh my dear, you're not going to pretend that you're still in love with me?"

"I am."

"You are a damned fool."

"I don't care."

She smiled at him. Her eyes always had that look, partly bantering, partly tender, that gave him such a happy pain in his heart. Funny, he could almost localize it.

"You're rather sweet, Humphrey. You know I'm devoted to you, but I wouldn't marry you even if I were free."

When she left her husband and went to live in Rhodes Carruthers ceased to see her. She never came to England. They maintained an active correspondence.

"Her letters were wonderful," he said. "You seemed to hear her talking. They were just like her. Clever and witty, inconsequent and yet so shrewd."

He suggested coming to Rhodes for a few days, but she thought he had better not. He understood why. Everyone knew he had been madly in love with her. Everyone knew he was still. He did not know in what circumstances exactly the Welldon-Burns had separated. It might be that there had been a good deal of bad feeling. Betty might think that his presence on the island would compromise her.

"She wrote a charming letter to me when my first book came out. You know I dedicated it to her. She was surprised that I had done anything so good. Everyone was very nice about it, and she was delighted with that. I think her pleasure was the chief thing that pleased me. After all I'm not a professional writer, you know: I don't attach much importance to literary success."

Fool, I thought, and liar. Did he think I had not noticed the self-satisfaction that consumed him on account of the favourable reception of his books? I did not blame him for feeling that; nothing could be more pardonable; but why be at such pains to deny it? But it was doubtless true that it was mostly for Betty's sake that he relished the notoriety they had brought him. He had a positive achievement to offer her. He could lay at her feet now not only his love, but a distinguished reputation. Betty was not very young any more, she was thirty-four; her marriage, her sojourn abroad, had changed things; she was no longer surrounded by suitors; she had lost the halo with which the public admiration had surrounded her. The distance between them was no longer insuperable. He alone had remained faithful through the years. It was absurd that she should continue to bury her beauty, her wit, her social grace in an island in a corner of the Mediterranean. He knew she was fond of him. She could hardly fail to be touched by his long devotion. And the life he had to offer her now was one that he knew would appeal to her. He made up his mind to ask her once more to marry him. He was able to get away towards the end of July. He wrote and said that he was going to spend his leave in the Greek islands and if she would be glad to see him he would stop off at Rhodes for a day or two where he had heard the Italians had opened a very good hotel. He put his suggestion in this casual way out of delicacy. His training at the Foreign Office had taught him to eschew abruptness. He never willingly put himself in a position from which he could not if necessary withdraw with tact. Betty sent him a telegram in reply. She said it was too marvellous that he was coming to Rhodes and of course he must come and stay with her, for at least a fortnight, and he was to wire what boat he was coming by.

He was in a state of wild excitement when at last the ship he had taken at Brindisi steamed, soon after sunrise, into the neat and pretty harbour of Rhodes. He had hardly slept a wink all night, and getting up early had watched the island loom grandly out of the dawn and the sun rise over the summer sea. Boats came out as the ship dropped her anchor. The gangway was lowered. Humphrey, leaning over the rail, watched the doctor and the port officials and the hotel couriers swarm up it. He was the only Englishman on board. His nationality was obvious. A man came on deck and immediately walked up to him.

"Are you Mr. Carruthers?"

"Yes."

He was about to smile and put out his hand, but he

perceived in the twinkling of an eye that the person who addressed him, an Englishman like himself, was not a gentleman. Instinctively his manner, remaining exceedingly polite, became a trifle stiff. Of course Carruthers did not tell me this, but I see the scene so clearly that I have no hesitation in describing it.

"Her ladyship hopes you don't mind her not coming to meet you, but the boat got in so early and it's more than an hour's drive to where we live."

"Oh, of course. Her ladyship well?"

"Yes, thank you. Got your luggage ready?"

"Yes."

"If you'll show me where it is I'll tell one of these fellows to put it in a boat. You won't have any difficulty at the Customs. I've fixed that up all right, and then we'll get off. Have you had breakfast?"

"Yes, thank you."

The man was not quite sure of his aitches. Carruthers wondered who he was. You could not say he was uncivil, but he was certainly a little offhand. Carruthers knew that Betty had rather a large estate; perhaps he was her agent. He seemed very competent. He gave the porters instructions in fluent Greek, and when they got in the boat and the boatmen asked for more money than he gave them, he said something that made them laugh and they shrugged their shoulders, satisfied. The luggage was passed through the Customs without examination, Humphrey's guide shaking hands with the officials, and they went into a sunny place where a large yellow car was standing.

"Are you going to drive me?" asked Carruthers.

"I'm her ladyship's chauffeur."

"Oh, I see. I didn't know."

He was not dressed like a chauffeur. He wore white duck trousers and espadrilles on his bare feet, a white tennis shirt, with no tie and open at the neck, and a straw hat. Carruthers frowned. Betty oughtn't to let her chauffeur drive the car like that. It was true that he had had to get up before daybreak and it looked like being a hot drive up to the villa. Perhaps under ordinary conditions he wore uniform. Though not so tall as Carruthers, who was six feet one in his socks, he was not short; but he was broad-shouldered and squarely built, so that he looked stocky. He was not fat, but plump rather; he looked as though he had a hearty appetite and ate well. Young still, thirty perhaps or thirty-one, he had already a massive look and one day would be very beefy. Now he was a hefty fellow. He had a broad face deeply sunburned, a short thickish nose and a somewhat sullen look. He wore a short fair moustache. Oddly enough Carruthers had a vague feeling that he had seen him before.

"Have you been with her ladyship long?" he asked.

"Well, I have, in a manner of speaking."

Carruthers became a trifle stiffer. He did not quite like the manner in which the chauffeur spoke. He wondered why he did not say 'sir' to him. He was afraid Betty had let him get a little above himself. It was like her to be a bit careless about such things. But it was a mistake. He'd give her a hint when he got a chance. Their eyes met for an instant and he could have sworn that there was a twinkle of amusement in the chauffeur's. Carruthers could not imagine why. He was not aware that there was anything amusing in him.

"That, I suppose, is the old city of the Knights," he said distantly, pointing to the battlemented walls.

"Yes. Her ladyship'll take you over. We get a rare lot of tourists here in the season."

Carruthers wished to be affable. He thought it would be nicer of him to offer to sit by the chauffeur rather than behind by himself and was just going to suggest it, when the matter was taken out of his hands. The chauffeur told the porters to put Carruthers' bags at the back, and settling himself at the wheel said:

"Now if you'll hop in we'll get along."

Carruthers sat down beside him and they set off along a white road that ran by the sea. In a few minutes they were in the open country. They drove in silence. Carruthers was a little on his dignity. He felt that the chauffeur was inclined to be familiar and he did not wish to give him occasion to be so. He flattered himself that he had a manner with him that put his inferiors in their place. He thought with sardonic grimness that it would not be long before the chauffeur would be calling him 'sir.' But the morning was lovely; the white road ran between olive groves, and the farmhouses they passed now and then, with their white walls and flat roofs, had an oriental look that took the fancy. And Betty was waiting for him. The love in his heart disposed him to kindliness towards all men, and lighting himself a cigarette he thought it would be a generous act to offer the chauffeur one too. After all, Rhodes was very far away from England and the age was democratic. The

chauffeur accepted the gift and stopped the car to light
up.

"Have you got the baccy?" he asked suddenly.

"Have I got what?"

The chauffeur's face fell.

"Her ladyship wired to you to bring two pounds of
Player's Navy Cut. That's why I fixed it up with the
Customs people not to open your luggage."

"I never got the wire."

"Damn!"

"What on earth does her ladyship want with two
pounds of Player's Navy Cut?"

He spoke with hauteur. He did not like the chauffeur's
exclamation. The fellow gave him a sidelong glance in
which Carruthers read a certain insolence.

"We can't get it here," he said briefly.

He threw away with what looked very like exasperation the Egyptian cigarette Carruthers had given him
and started off again. He looked sulky. He said nothing
more. Carruthers felt that his efforts at sociability had
been a mistake. For the rest of the journey he ignored
the chauffeur. He adopted the frigid manner that he
had used so successfully as secretary at the Embassy
when a member of the British public came to him for
assistance. For some time they had been running up hill,
and now they came to a long low wall and then to an
open gate. The chauffeur turned in.

"Have we arrived?" cried Carruthers.

"Sixty-five kilometres in fifty-seven minutes," said
the chauffeur, a smile suddenly showing his fine white
teeth. "Not so bad, considering the road."

He sounded his klaxon shrilly. Carruthers was
breathless with excitement. They drove up a narrow
road through an olive grove, and came to a low, white,
rambling house. Betty was standing at the door. He
jumped out of the car and kissed her on both cheeks.
For a moment he could not speak. But subconsciously
he noticed that at the door stood an elderly butler in
white ducks and a couple of footmen in the fustanellas
of their country. They were smart and picturesque.
Whatever Betty permitted her chauffeur, it was evident
that the house was run in the civilized style suited to
her station. She led him through the hall, a large apartment with whitewashed walls in which he was vaguely
conscious of handsome furniture, into the drawing-room.
This also was large and low, with the same whitewashed
walls, and he had immediately an impression of comfort
and luxury.

"The first thing you must do is to come and look at
my view," she said.

"The first thing I must do is to look at you."

She was dressed in white. Her arms, her face, her
neck, were deeply burned by the sun; her eyes were
bluer than he had ever seen them, and the whiteness of
her teeth was startling. She looked extremely well. She
was very trim and neat. Her hair was waved, her nails
were manicured; he had had a moment's anxiety that in
the easy life she led on this romantic isle she had let
herself go.

"Upon my word you look eighteen, Betty. How do
you manage it?"

"Happiness," she smiled.

It gave him a momentary pang to hear her say this.
He did not want her to be too happy. He wanted to give
her happiness. But now she insisted on taking him out
on the terrace. The drawing-room had five long windows
that led out to it and from the terrace the olive-clad hill
tumbled steeply to the sea. There was a tiny bay below
in which a white boat, mirrored on the calm water, lay
at anchor. On a farther hill, round the corner you saw
the white houses of a Greek village, and beyond it a
huge grey crag surmounted by the battlements of a
medieval castle.

"It was one of the strongholds of the Knights," she
said. "I'll take you up there this evening."

The scene was exquisitely lovely. It took your breath
away. It was peaceful and yet it had a strange air of life.
It moved you not to contemplation, but stirred you to
activity.

"You've got the tobacco all right, I suppose."

He started.

"I'm afraid I haven't. I never got your wire."

"But I wired to the Embassy and I wired to the
Excelsior."

"I stayed at the Plaza."

"What a bore! Albert'll be furious."

"Who is Albert?"

"He drove you out. Player's is the only tobacco he
likes and he can't get it here."

"Oh, the chauffeur." He pointed to the boat that lay
gleaming beneath them. "Is that the yacht I've heard
about?"

"Yes."

It was a large caïque that Betty had bought, fitted with a motor auxiliary and smartened up. In it she wandered about the Greek islands. She had been as far north as Athens and as far south as Alexandria.

"We'll take you for a trip if you can spare the time," she said. "You ought to see Cos while you're here."

"Who runs it for you?"

"Of course I have a crew, but Albert chiefly. He's very clever with motors and all that."

He did not know why it gave him a vague discomfort to hear her speak of the chauffeur again. Carruthers wondered if she did not leave too much in his hands. It was a mistake to give a servant too much leeway.

"You know, I couldn't help thinking I'd seen Albert before somewhere. But I can't place him."

She smiled brightly, her eyes shining, with that sudden gaiety of hers that gave her face its delightful frankness.

"You ought to remember him. He was the second footman at Aunt Louise's. He must have opened the door to you hundreds of times."

Aunt Louise was the aunt with whom Betty had lived before her marriage.

"Oh, is that who he is? I suppose I must have seen him there without noticing him. How does he happen to be here?"

"He comes from our place at home. When I married he wanted to come with me, so I took him. He was Jimmie's valet for some time and then I sent him to some motor works; he was mad about cars, and eventu-

ally I took him on as my chauffeur. I don't know what
I should do without him now."

"Don't you think it's rather a mistake to get too
dependent on a servant?"

"I don't know. It never occurred to me."

Betty showed him the rooms that had been got ready
for him, and when he had changed they strolled down
to the beach. A dinghy was waiting for them and they
rowed out to the caïque and bathed from there. The
water was warm and they sunned themselves on the
deck. The caïque was roomy, comfortable and luxurious.
Betty showed him over and they came upon Albert
tinkering with the engines. He was in filthy overalls, his
hands were black and his face was smeared with grease.

"What's the matter, Albert?" said Betty.

He raised himself and faced her respectfully.

"Nothing, m'lady. I was just 'aving a look round."

"There are only two things Albert loves in the world.
One is the car and the other's the yacht. Isn't that true,
Albert?"

She gave him a gay smile, and Albert's rather stolid
face lit up. He showed his beautiful white teeth.

"That's true, m'lady."

"He sleeps on board, you know. We rigged up a very
nice cabin for him aft."

Carruthers fell into the life very easily. Betty had
bought the estate from a Turkish pasha exiled to
Rhodes by Abdul Hamid, and she had added a wing to
the picturesque house. She had made a wild garden of
the olive grove that surrounded it. It was planted with

rosemary and lavender and asphodel, broom that she had had sent from England and the roses for which the island was famous. In the spring, she told him, the ground was carpeted with anemones. But when she showed him her property, telling him her plans and what alterations she had in mind, Carruthers could not help feeling a little uneasy.

"You talk as though you were going to live here all your life," he said.

"Perhaps I am," she smiled.

"What nonsense! At your age."

"I'm getting on for forty, old boy," she answered lightly.

He discovered with satisfaction that Betty had an excellent cook, and it gratified his sense of propriety to dine with her in the splendid dining-room, with its Italian furniture, and be waited on by the dignified Greek butler and the two handsome footmen in their flamboyant uniforms. The house was furnished with taste; the rooms contained nothing that was not essential, but every piece was exquisite. Betty lived in considerable state. When, the day after his arrival, the Governor with several members of his staff came over to dinner she displayed all the resources of the household. The Governor, entering the house, passed between a double row of flunkeys magnificent in their starched petticoats, embroidered jackets and velvet caps. It was almost a bodyguard. Carruthers liked the grand style. The dinner-party was very gay. Betty's Italian was fluent and Carruthers spoke it perfectly. The young officers in the Governor's suite were un-

commonly smart in their uniforms. They were very
attentive to Betty and she treated them with easy
cordiality. She chaffed them. After dinner the gramophone was turned on and they danced with her one
after the other.

When they were gone Carruthers asked her:

"Aren't they all madly in love with you?"

"I don't know about that. They hint occasionally at
alliances permanent or otherwise, but they take it very
good-naturedly when I decline with thanks."

They were not serious. The young ones were callow
and the not so young were fat and bald. Whatever they
might feel about her, Carruthers could not for a moment believe that Betty would make a fool of herself
with a middle-class Italian. But a day or two later a
curious thing happened. He was in his rooms dressing
for dinner; he heard a man's voice outside in the passage, he could not hear what was said or what language
was spoken, and then ringing out suddenly Betty's
laughter. It was a charming laugh, rippling and gay,
like a young girl's, and it had a joyous abandon that
was infectious. But whom could she be laughing with?
It was not the way you would laugh with a servant. It
had a curious intimacy. It may seem strange that Carruthers read all this into a peal of laughter, but it must
be remembered that Carruthers was very subtle. His
stories were remarkable for such touches.

When they met presently on the terrace and he was
shaking a cocktail he sought to gratify his curiosity.

"What were you laughing your head off over just
now? Has anyone been here?"

"No."

She looked at him with genuine surprise.

"I thought one of your Italian officers had come to pass the time of day."

"No."

Of course the passage of years had had its effect on Betty. She was beautiful, but her beauty was mature. She had always had assurance, but now she had repose; her serenity was a feature, like her blue eyes and her candid brow, that was part of her beauty. She seemed to be at peace with all the world; it rested you to be with her as it rested you to lie among the olives within sight of the wine-coloured sea. Though she was as gay and witty as ever, the seriousness which once he had been alone to know was now patent. No one could accuse her any longer of being scatter-brained; it was impossible not to perceive the fineness of her character. It had even nobility. That was not a trait it was usual to find in the modern woman, and Carruthers said to himself that she was a throw-back; she reminded him of the great ladies of the eighteenth century. She had always had a feeling for literature, the poems she wrote as a girl were graceful and melodious, and he was more interested than surprised when she told him that she had undertaken a solid historical work. She was getting materials together for an account of the Knights of St. John in Rhodes. It was a story of romantic incidents. She took Carruthers to the city and showed him the noble battlements, and together they wandered through austere and stately buildings. They strolled up the silent Street of the Knights with the lovely stone façades and the great coats of arms that recalled a dead chivalry. She had a surprise for him here. She had bought one of the old houses and with affectionate care had restored it to its old state. When you entered the little court-yard, with its carved stone stairway, you were taken back into the Middle Ages. It had a tiny walled garden in which a fig tree grew and roses. It was small and secret and silent. The old Knights had been in contact with the East long enough to have acquired oriental ideas of privacy.

"When I'm tired of the villa I come here for two or three days and picnic. It's a relief sometimes not to be surrounded by people."

"But you're not alone here?"

"Practically."

There was a little parlour austerely furnished.

"What is this?" said Carruthers, pointing with a smile to a copy of *The Sporting Times* that lay on a table.

"Oh, that's Albert's. I suppose he left it here when he came to meet you. He has *The Sporting Times* and *The News of the World* sent him every week. That is how he keeps abreast of the great world."

She smiled tolerantly. Next to the parlour was a bed-room with nothing much in it but a large bed.

"The house belonged to an Englishman. That's partly why I bought it. He was a Sir Giles Quern, and one of my ancestors married a Mary Quern who was a cousin of his. They were Cornish people."

Finding that she could not get on with her history without such a knowledge of Latin as would enable

her to read the medieval documents with ease, Betty
had set about learning the classical language. She
troubled to acquire only the elements of grammar and
then started, with a translation by her side, to read the
authors that interested her. It is a very good method of
learning a language and I have often wondered that it
is not used in schools. It saves all the endless turning
over of dictionaries and the fumbling search for meaning. After nine months Betty could read Latin as
fluently as most of us can read French. It seemed a trifle
ridiculous to Carruthers that this lovely, brilliant
creature should take her work so seriously and yet he
was moved; he would have liked to snatch her in his
arms and kiss her, not at that moment as a woman, but
as a precocious child whose cleverness suddenly en-
chants you. But later he reflected upon what she had
told him. He was of course a very clever man, otherwise
he could not have attained the position he held in the
Foreign Office, and it would be silly to claim that those
two books of his could have made so much stir without
some merit; if I have made him look a bit of a fool it is
only because I did not happen to like him, and if I have
derided his stories it is merely because stories of that
sort seem to me rather silly. He had tact and insight.
He had a conviction that there was but one way to win
her. She was in a groove and happy in it, her plans were
definite; but her life at Rhodes was so well-ordered,
so complete and satisfying, that for that very reason
its hold over her could be combated. His chance was to
arouse in her the restlessness that lies deep in the heart
of the English. So he talked to Betty of England and

London, their common friends and the painters, writers and musicians with whom his literary success had brought him acquaintance. He talked of the bohemian parties in Chelsea, and of the opera, of trips to Paris *en bande* for a fancy-dress ball or to Berlin to see the new plays. He recalled to her imagination a life rich and easy, varied, cultured, intelligent and highly civilized. He tried to make her feel that she was stagnating in a backwater. The world was hurrying on, from one new and interesting phase to another, and she was standing still. They were living in a thrilling age and she was missing it. Of course he did not tell her this; he left her to infer it. He was amusing and spirited, he had an excellent memory for a good story, he was whimsical and gay. I know I have not made Humphrey Carruthers witty any more than I have shown Lady Betty brilliant. The reader must take my word for it that they were. Carruthers was generally reckoned an entertaining companion, and that is half the battle; people were willing to find him amusing and they vowed the things he said were marvellous. Of course his wit was social. It needed a particular company, who understood his allusions and shared his exclusive sense of humour. There are a score of journalists in Fleet Street who could knock spots off the most famous of the society wits; it is their business to be witty and brilliance is in their day's work. There are few of the society beauties whose photographs appear in the papers who could get a job at three pounds a week in the chorus of a song-and-dance show. Amateurs must be judged with tolerance. Carruthers knew that Betty enjoyed his society. They laughed

a great deal together. The days passed in a flash.
"I shall miss you terribly when you go," she said
in her frank way. "It's been a treat having you here.
You are a sweet, Humphrey."

"Have you only just discovered it?"

He patted himself on the back. His tactics had been
right. It was interesting to see how well his simple plan
had worked. Like a charm. The vulgar might laugh
at the Foreign Office, but there was no doubt it taught
you how to deal with difficult people. Now he had but to
choose his opportunity. He felt that Betty had never
been more attached to him. He would wait till the end
of his visit. Betty was emotional. She would be sorry
that he was going. Rhodes would seem very dull without him. Whom would she have to talk to when he was
gone? After dinner they usually sat on the terrace looking at the starry sea; the air was warm and balmy and
vaguely scented: it was then he would ask her to marry
him, on the eve of his departure. He felt it in his bones
that she would accept him.

One morning when he had been in Rhodes a little
over a week, he happened to be coming upstairs as
Betty was walking along the passage.

"You've never shown me your room, Betty," he
said.

"Haven't I? Come in and have a look now. It's
rather nice."

She turned back and he followed her in. It was over
the drawing-room and nearly as large. It was furnished
in the Italian style, and as is the present way more like a

sitting-room than a bedroom. There were fine Paninis on the walls and one or two handsome cabinets. The bed was Venetian and beautifully painted.

"That's a couch of rather imposing dimensions for a widow lady," he said facetiously.

"It is enormous, isn't it? But it was so lovely, I had to buy it. It cost a fortune."

His eye took in the bed-table by the side. There were two or three books on it, a box of cigarettes, and on an ash-tray a briar pipe. Funny! What on earth had Betty got a pipe by her bed for?

"Do look at this *cassone*. Isn't the painting marvellous? I almost cried when I found it."

"I suppose that cost a fortune too."

"I daren't tell you what I paid."

When they were leaving the room he cast another glance at the bed-table. The pipe had vanished.

It was odd that Betty should have a pipe in her bedroom; she certainly didn't smoke one herself, and if she had would have made no secret of it; but of course there were a dozen reasonable explanations. It might be a present she was making to somebody, one of the Italians or even Albert—he had not been able to see if it was new or old—or it might be a pattern that she was going to ask him to take home to have others of the same sort sent out to her. After the moment's perplexity, not altogether unmingled with amusement, he put the matter out of his mind. They were going for a picnic that day, taking their luncheon with them, and Betty was driving him herself. They had arranged to go for a cruise of a couple of days before he left, so that he should see Patmos and Cos, and Albert was busy with the engines of the caïque. They had a wonderful day. They visited a ruined castle and climbed a mountain on which grew asphodel, hyacinth and narcissus, and returned dead beat. They separated not long after dinner and Carruthers went to bed. He read for a little while and then turned out his light. But he could not sleep. It was hot under his mosquito net. He turned and tossed. Presently he thought he would go down to the little beach at the foot of the hill and bathe. It was not more than three minutes' walk. He put on his espadrilles and took a towel. The moon was full and he saw it shining on the sea through the olive trees. But he was not alone to have thought that this radiant night would be lovely to bathe in, for just before he came out on to the beach sounds reached his ears. He muttered a little damn of vexation; some of Betty's servants were bathing, and he could not very well disturb them. The olive trees came almost to the water's edge and, undecided, he stood in their shelter. He heard a voice that gave him a sudden start.

"Where's my towel?"

English. A woman waded out of the water and stood for a moment at its edge. From the darkness a man came forward with nothing but a towel round his loins. The woman was Betty. She was stark naked. The man wrapped a bath-robe round her and began drying her vigorously. She leaned on him while she put on first one shoe and then the other, and to support her he placed his arm round her shoulders. The man was Albert.

Carruthers turned and fled up the hill. He stumbled blindly. Once he nearly fell. He was gasping like a wounded beast. When he got into his room he flung himself on the bed and clenched his fists, and the dry, painful sobs that tore his chest broke into tears. He evidently had a violent attack of hysterics. It was all clear to him, clear with the ghastly vividness with which on a stormy night a flash of lightning can disclose a ravaged landscape, clear, horribly clear. The way the man had dried her and the way she leaned against him pointed not to passion, but to a long continued intimacy, and the pipe by the bedside, the pipe had a hideously conjugal air. It suggested the pipe a man might smoke while he was reading in bed before going to sleep. *The Sporting Times!* That was why she had that little house in the Street of the Knights, so that they could spend two or three days together in domestic familiarity. They were like an old married couple. Humphrey asked himself how long the hateful thing had lasted and suddenly he knew the answer; for years. Ten, twelve, fourteen: it had started when the young footman first came to London—he was a boy then, and it was obvious enough that it was not he who had made the advances; all through those years when she was the idol of the British public, when everyone adored her and she could have married anyone she liked, she was living with the second footman at her aunt's house. She took him with her when she married. Why had she made that surprising marriage? And the still-born child that came before its time. Of course that was why she had married Jimmie Welldon-Burns, because she was going to have a child by Albert. Oh shameless, shameless! And then, when Jimmie's health broke down she had made him take Albert as his valet. And what had Jimmie known and what had he suspected? He drank, that was what had started his tuberculosis; but why had he started drinking? Perhaps it was to still a suspicion that was so ugly that he could not face it. And it was to live with Albert that she had left Jimmie, and it was to live with Albert that she had settled in Rhodes. Albert, his hands with their broken nails stained by his work on the motors, coarse of aspect and stocky, rather like a butcher with his high colour and clumsy strength, Albert not even very young any more and running to fat, uneducated and vulgar, with his common way of speaking. Albert, Albert, how could she?

Carruthers got up and drank some water. He threw himself into a chair. He could not bear his bed. He smoked cigarette after cigarette. He was a wreck in the morning. He had not slept at all. They brought him in his breakfast; he drank the coffee but could eat nothing. Presently there was a brisk knock on his door.

"Coming down to bathe, Humphrey?"

That cheerful voice sent the blood singing through his head. He braced himself and opened the door.

"I don't think I will to-day. I don't feel very well."

She gave him a look.

"Oh my dear, you look all in. What's the matter with you?"

"I don't know I think I must have got a touch of the sun."

His voice was dead and his eyes were tragic. She looked at him more closely. She did not say anything for a moment. He thought she went pale. *He knew.* Then a faintly mocking smile crossed her eyes; she thought the situation comic.

"Poor old boy, go and lie down. I'll send you in some aspirin. Perhaps you'll feel better at luncheon."

He lay in his darkened room. He would have given anything to get away then so that he need not set eyes on her again, but there was no means of that; the ship that was to take him back to Brindisi did not touch at Rhodes till the end of the week. He was a prisoner. And the next day they were to go to the islands. There was no escape from her there; in the caïque they would be in one another's pockets all day long. He couldn't face that. He was so ashamed. But she wasn't ashamed. At that moment when it had been plain to her that nothing was hidden from him any longer she had smiled. She was capable of telling him all about it. He could not bear that. That was too much. After all, she couldn't be certain that he knew, at best she could only suspect; if he behaved as if nothing had happened, if at luncheon and during the days that remained he was as gay and jolly as usual, she would think she had been mistaken. It was enough to know what he knew; he would not suffer the crowning humiliation of hearing from her own lips the disgraceful story. But at luncheon the first thing she said was:

"Isn't it a bore, Albert says something's gone wrong

with the motor, we shan't be able to go on our trip after all. I daren't trust to sail at this time of the year. We might be becalmed for a week."

She spoke lightly and he answered in the same casual fashion.

"Oh, I'm sorry, but still I don't really care. It's so lovely here, I really didn't much want to go."

He told her that the aspirin had done him good and he felt much better; to the Greek butler and the two footmen in fustanellas it must have seemed that they talked as vivaciously as usual. That night the British consul came to dinner, and the night after, some Italian officers. Carruthers counted the days, he counted the hours. Oh, if the moment would only come when he could step on the ship and be free from the horror that, every moment of the day, obsessed him! He was growing so tired. But Betty's manner was so self-possessed that sometimes he asked himself if she really knew that he was aware of her secret. Was it the truth that she had told about the caïque and not, as had at once struck him, an excuse; and was it an accident that a succession of visitors prevented them from ever being alone to-gether? The worst of having so much tact was that you never quite knew whether other people were acting naturally or being tactful too. When he looked at her, so easy and calm, so obviously happy, he could not believe the odious truth. And yet he had seen with his own eyes. And the future. What would her future be? It was horrible to think of. Sooner or later the truth must become notorious. And to think of Betty a mock and an outcast, in the power of a coarse and common man, growing older, losing her beauty; and the man was five years younger than she. One day he would take a mistress, one of her own maids, perhaps, with whom he would feel at home as he had never felt with the great lady, and what could she do then? What humiliation then must she be prepared to put up with! He might be cruel to her. He might beat her. Betty. Betty.

Carruthers wrung his hands. And on a sudden an idea came to him that filled him with a painful exultation; he put it away from him, but it returned; it would not let him be. He must save her; he had loved her ;too much and too long to let her sink, sink as she was sinking; a passion of self-sacrifice welled up in him. Notwithstanding everything, though his love now was dead and he felt for her an almost physical repulsion, he would marry her. He laughed mirthlessly. What would his life be? He couldn't help that. He didn't matter. It was the only thing to do. He felt wonderfully exalted, and yet very humble, for he was awed at the thought of the heights which the divine spirit of man could reach.

His ship was to sail on Saturday, and on Thursday, when the guests who had been dining left them, he said:

"I hope we're going to be alone to-morrow."

"As a matter of fact I've asked some Egyptians who spend the summer here. She's a sister of the ex-Khedive and very intelligent. I'm sure you'll like her."

"Well, it's my last evening. Couldn't we spend it alone?"

She gave him a glance. There was a faint amusement in her eyes, but his were grave.

"If you like. I can put them off."
"Then do."

He was to start early in the morning and his luggage was packed. Betty had told him not to dress, but he had answered that he preferred to. For the last time they sat down to dinner facing one another. The dining-room, with its shaded lights, was bare and formal, but the summer night flooding in through the great open windows gave it a sober richness. It had the effect of the private refectory in a convent to which a royal lady had retired in order to devote the remainder of her life to a piety not too austere. They had their coffee on the terrace. Carruthers drank a couple of liqueurs. He was feeling very nervous.

"Betty my dear, I've got something I want to say to you," he began.

"Have you? I wouldn't say it if I were you."

She answered gently. She remained perfectly calm, watching him shrewdly, but with the glimmer of a smile in her blue eyes.

"I must."

She shrugged her shoulders and was silent. He was conscious that his voice trembled a little and he was angry with himself.

"You know I've been madly in love with you for many years. I don't know how many times I've asked you to marry me. But after all, things change and people change too, don't they? We're neither of us so young as we were. Won't you marry me now, Betty?"

She gave him the smile that had always been such an attractive thing in her; it was so kindly, so frank and still, still so wonderfully innocent.

"You're very sweet, Humphrey. It's awfully nice of you to ask me again. I can't tell you how touched I am. But you know, I'm a creature of habit, I've got in the habit of saying no to you now, and I can't change it."

"Why not?"

There was something aggressive in his tone, something almost ominous, that made her give him a quick look. Her face blanched with sudden anger, but she immediately controlled herself.

"Because I don't want to," she smiled.

"Are you going to marry anyone else?"

"I? No. Of course not."

For a moment she seemed to draw herself up as though a wave of ancestral pride swept through her, and then she began to laugh. But whether she laughed at the thought that had passed through her mind or because something in Humphrey's proposal had amused her none but she could have told.

"Betty, I implore you to marry me."

"Never."

"You can't go on living this life."

He put into his voice all the anguish of his heart, and his face was drawn and tortured. She smiled affectionately.

"Why not? Don't be such a donkey. You know I adore you, Humphrey, but you are rather an old woman."

"Betty, Betty."

Did she not see that it was for her sake that he wanted it? It was not love that made him speak, but human pity and shame. She got up.

"Don't be tiresome, Humphrey. You'd better go to bed. You know you have to be up with the lark. I shan't see you in the morning. Good-bye and God bless you. It's been wonderful having you here."

She kissed him on both cheeks.

Next morning, early, for he had to be on board at eight, when Carruthers stepped out of the front door he found Albert waiting for him in the car. He wore a singlet, duck trousers and a beret basque. Carruthers' luggage was in the back. He turned to the butler.

"Put my bags beside the chauffeur," he said. "I'll sit behind."

Albert made no remark. Carruthers got in and they drove off. When they arrived at the harbour porters ran up. Albert got out of the car. Carruthers looked down at him from his greater height.

"You need not see me on board. I can manage perfectly well by myself. Here's a tip for you."

He gave him a five-pound note. Albert flushed. He was taken aback; he would have liked to refuse it, but did not know how to, and the servility of years asserted itself. Perhaps he did not know what he said.

"Thank you, sir."

Carruthers gave him a curt nod and walked away. He had forced Betty's lover to call him 'sir.' It was as though he had struck her a blow across that smiling mouth of hers and flung in her face an opprobrious word. It filled him with a bitter satisfaction.

He shrugged his shoulders and I could see that even this small triumph now seemed vain. For a little while we were silent. There was nothing for me to say. Then he began again.

"I daresay you think it's very strange that I should tell you all this. I don't care. You know, I feel as if nothing mattered any more. I feel as if decency no longer existed in the world. Heaven knows, I'm not jealous. You can't be jealous unless you love, and my love is dead. It was killed in a flash. After all those years. I can't think of her now without horror. What destroys me, what makes me so frightfully unhappy, is to think of her unspeakable degradation."

So it has been said that it was not jealousy that caused Othello to kill Desdemona, but an agony that the creature that he believed angelic should be proved impure and worthless. What broke his noble heart was that virtue should so fall.

"I thought there was no one like her. I admired her so much. I admired her courage and her frankness, her intelligence and her love of beauty. She's just a sham and she's never been anything else."

"I wonder if that's true. Do you think any of us are all of a piece? Do you know what strikes me? I should have said that Albert was only the instrument, her toll to the solid earth, so to speak, that left her soul at liberty to range the empyrean. Perhaps the mere fact that he was so far below her gave her a sense of freedom in her relations with him that she would have lacked with a man of her own class. The spirit is very strange; it never soars so high as when the body has wallowed for a period in the gutter."

"Oh, don't talk such rot," he answered angrily.

"I don't think it is rot. I don't put it very well, but the idea's sound."

"Much good it does me. I'm broken and done for. I'm finished."

"Oh, nonsense. Why don't you write a story about it?"

"I?"

"You know that's the great pull a writer has over other people. When something has made him terribly unhappy, and he's tortured and miserable, he can put it all into a story and it's astonishing what a comfort and relief it is."

"It would be monstrous. Betty was everything in the world to me. I couldn't do anything so caddish."

He paused for a little and I saw him reflect. I saw that notwithstanding the horror that my suggestion caused him he did for one minute look at the situation from the standpoint of the writer. He shook his head.

"Not for her sake, for mine. After all, I have some self-respect. Besides, there's no story there."

JANE

JANE

I REMEMBER very well the occasion on which I first saw Jane Fowler. It is indeed only because the details of the glimpse I had of her then are so clear that I trust my recollection at all, for, looking back, I must confess that I find it hard to believe that it has not played me a fantastic trick. I had lately returned to London from China and was drinking a dish of tea with Mrs. Tower. Mrs. Tower had been seized with the prevailing passion for decoration; and with the ruthlessness of her sex had sacrificed chairs in which she had comfortably sat for years, tables, cabinets, ornaments, on which her eyes had dwelt in peace since she was married, pictures that had been familiar to her for a generation; and delivered herself into the hands of an expert. Nothing remained in her drawing-room with which she had any association, or to which any sentiment was attached; and she had invited me that day to see the fashionable glory in which she now lived. Everything that could be pickled was pickled and what couldn't be pickled was painted. Nothing matched, but everything harmonized.

"Do you remember that ridiculous drawing-room suite that I used to have?" asked Mrs. Tower.

The curtains were sumptuous yet severe; the sofa

was covered with Italian brocade; the chair on which I sat was in *petit point*. The room was beautiful, opulent without garishness and original without affectation; yet to me it lacked something; and while I praised with my lips I asked myself why I so much preferred the rather shabby chintz of the despised suite, the Victorian water-colours that I had known so long, and the ridiculous Dresden china that had adorned the chimney-piece. I wondered what it was that I missed in all these rooms that the decorators were turning out with a profitable industry. Was it heart? But Mrs. Tower looked about her happily.

"Don't you like my alabaster lamps?" she said. "They give such a soft light."

"Personally I have a weakness for a light that you can see by," I smiled.

"It's so difficult to combine that with a light that you can't be too much seen by," laughed Mrs. Tower.

I had no notion what her age was. When I was quite a young man she was a married woman a good deal older than I, but now she treated me as her contemporary. She constantly said that she made no secret of her age, which was forty, and then added with a smile that all women took five years off. She never sought to conceal the fact that she dyed her hair (it was a very pretty brown with reddish tints), and she said she did this because hair was hideous while it was going grey; as soon as hers was white she would cease to dye it.

"Then they'll say what a young face I have."

Meanwhile it was painted, though with discretion, and her eyes owed not a little of their vivacity to art.

She was a handsome woman, exquisitely gowned, and in the sombre glow of the alabaster lamps did not look a day more than the forty she gave herself.

"It is only at my dressing-table that I can suffer the naked brightness of a thirty-two-candle electric bulb," she added with smiling cynicism. "There I need it to tell me first the hideous truth and then to enable me to take the necessary steps to correct it."

We gossiped pleasantly about our common friends and Mrs. Tower brought me up to date in the scandal of the day. After roughing it here and there it was very agreeable to sit in a comfortable chair, the fire burning brightly on the hearth, charming tea-things set out on a charming table, and talk with this amusing, attractive woman. She treated me as a prodigal returned from his husks and was disposed to make much of me. She prided herself on her dinner-parties; she took no less trouble to have her guests suitably assorted than to give them excellent food; and there were few persons who did not look upon it as a treat to be bidden to one of them. Now she fixed a date and asked me whom I would like to meet.

"There's only one thing I must tell you. If Jane Fowler is still here I shall have to put it off."

"Who is Jane Fowler?" I asked.

Mrs. Tower gave a rueful smile.

"Jane Fowler is my cross."

"Oh!"

"Do you remember a photograph that I used to have on the piano before I had my room done of a woman in a tight dress with tight sleeves and a gold locket, with her hair drawn back from a broad forehead and her ears showing and spectacles on a rather blunt nose? Well, that was Jane Fowler."

"You had so many photographs about the room in your unregenerate days," I said, vaguely.

"It makes me shudder to think of them. I've made them into a huge brown-paper parcel and hidden them in an attic."

"Well, who is Jane Fowler?" I asked again, smiling.

"She's my sister-in-law. She was my husband's sister and she married a manufacturer in the north. She's been a widow for many years, and she's very well-to-do."

"And why is she your cross?"

"She's worthy, she's dowdy, she's provincial. She looks twenty years older than I do and she's quite capable of telling anyone she meets that we were at school together. She has an overwhelming sense of family affection, and because I am her only living connection she's devoted to me. When she comes to London it never occurs to her that she should stay anywhere but here—she thinks it would hurt my feelings—and she'll pay me visits of three or four weeks. We sit here and she knits and reads. And sometimes she insists on taking me to dine at Claridge's and she looks like a funny old charwoman and everyone I particularly don't want to be seen by is sitting at the next table. When we are driving home she says she loves giving me a little treat. With her own hands she makes me tea-cozies that I am forced to use when she is here and doilies and centre-pieces for the dining-room table."

Mrs. Tower paused to take breath.

"I should have thought a woman of your tact would find a way to deal with a situation like that."

"Ah, but don't you see, I haven't a chance. She's so immeasurably kind. She has a heart of gold. She bores me to death, but I wouldn't for anything let her suspect it."

"And when does she arrive?"

"To-morrow."

But the answer was hardly out of Mrs. Tower's mouth when the bell rang. There were sounds in the hall of a slight commotion and in a minute or two the butler ushered in an elderly lady.

"Mrs. Fowler," he announced.

"Jane!" cried Mrs. Tower, springing to her feet. "I wasn't expecting you to-day."

"So your butler has just told me. I certainly said to-day in my letter."

Mrs. Tower recovered her wits.

"Well, it doesn't matter. I'm very glad to see you whenever you come. Fortunately I'm doing nothing this evening."

"You mustn't let me give you any trouble. If I can have a boiled egg for my dinner that's all I shall want."

A faint grimace for a moment distorted Mrs. Tower's handsome features. A boiled egg!

"Oh, I think we can do a little better than that."

I chuckled inwardly when I recollected that the two ladies were contemporaries. Mrs. Fowler looked a good fifty-five. She was a rather big woman; she wore a black straw hat with a wide brim, and from it a black lace veil hung over her shoulders, a cloak that oddly combined severity with fussiness, a long black dress, voluminous as though she wore several petticoats under it, and stout boots. She was evidently short-sighted, for she looked at you through large gold-rimmed spectacles.

"Won't you have a cup of tea?" asked Mrs. Tower.

"If it wouldn't be too much trouble. I'll take off my mantle."

She began by stripping her hands of the black gloves she wore, and then took off her cloak. Round her neck was a solid gold chain from which hung a large gold locket in which I felt certain was a photograph of her deceased husband. Then she took off her hat and placed it neatly with her gloves and cloak on the sofa corner. Mrs. Tower pursed her lips. Certainly those garments did not go very well with the austere but sumptuous beauty of Mrs. Tower's redecorated drawing-room. I wondered where on earth Mrs. Fowler had found the extraordinary clothes she wore. They were not old, and the materials were expensive. It was astounding to think that dressmakers still made things that had not been worn for a quarter of a century. Mrs. Fowler's grey hair was very plainly done, showing all her forehead and her ears, with a parting in the middle. It had evidently never known the tongs of Monsieur Marcel. Now her eyes fell on the tea-table with its teapot of Georgian silver and its cups in old Worcester.

"What have you done with the tea-cozy I gave you last time I came up, Marion?" she asked. "Don't you use it?"

"Yes, I use it every day, Jane," answered Mrs. Tower

glibly. "Unfortunately we had an accident with it a little while ago. It got burnt."

"But the last one I gave you got burnt."

"I'm afraid you'll think us very careless."

"It doesn't really matter," smiled Mrs. Fowler. "I shall enjoy making you another. I'll go to Liberty's to-morrow and buy some silks."

Mrs. Tower kept her face bravely.

"I don't deserve it, you know. Doesn't your vicar's wife need one?"

"Oh, I've just made her one," said Mrs. Fowler brightly.

I noticed that when she smiled she showed white, small and regular teeth. They were a real beauty. Her smile was certainly very sweet.

But I felt it high time for me to leave the two ladies to themselves, so I took my leave.

Early next morning Mrs. Tower rang me up, and I heard at once from her voice that she was in high spirits.

"I've got the most wonderful news for you," she said. "Jane is going to be married."

"Nonsense."

"Her fiancé is coming to dine here to-night to be introduced to me, and I want you to come too."

"Oh, but I shall be in the way."

"No, you won't. Jane suggested herself that I should ask you. Do come."

She was bubbling over with laughter.

"Who is he?"

"I don't know. She tells me he's an architect. Can you imagine the sort of man Jane would marry?"

I had nothing to do and I could trust Mrs. Tower to give me a good dinner.

When I arrived Mrs. Tower, very splendid in a tea-gown a little too young for her, was alone.

"Jane is putting the finishing touches to her appearance. I'm longing for you to see her. She's all in a flutter. She says he adores her. His name is Gilbert and when she speaks of him her voice gets all funny and tremulous. It makes me want to laugh."

"I wonder what he's like."

"Oh, I'm sure I know. Very big and massive, with a bald head and an immense gold chain across an immense tummy. A large, fat, clean-shaven, red face and a booming voice."

Mrs. Fowler came in. She wore a very stiff black silk dress with a wide skirt and a train. At the neck it was cut into a timid V and the sleeves came down to the elbows. She wore a necklace of diamonds set in silver. She carried in her hands a long pair of black gloves and a fan of black ostrich feathers. She managed (as so few people do) to look exactly what she was. You could never have thought her anything in the world but the respectable relict of a north-country manufacturer of ample means.

"You've really got quite a pretty neck, Jane," said Mrs. Tower with a kindly smile.

It was indeed astonishingly young when you compared it with her weather-beaten face. It was smooth and unlined and the skin was white. And I noticed then that her head was very well placed on her shoulders.

"Has Marion told you my news?" she said, turning

to me with that really charming smile of hers as if we
were already old friends.

"I must congratulate you," I said.

"Wait to do that till you've seen my young man."

"I think it's too sweet to hear you talk of your young
man," smiled Mrs. Tower.

Mrs. Fowler's eyes certainly twinkled behind her preposterous spectacles.

"Don't expect anyone too old. You wouldn't like me
to marry a decrepit old gentleman with one foot in
the grave, would you?"

This was the only warning she gave us. Indeed there
was no time for any further discussion, for the butler
flung open the door and in a loud voice announced:

"Mr. Gilbert Napier."

There entered a youth in a very well-cut dinner
jacket. He was slight, not very tall, with fair hair in
which there was a hint of a natural wave, clean-shaven
and blue-eyed. He was not particularly good-looking,
but he had a pleasant, amiable face. In ten years he
would probably be wizened and sallow; but now, in
extreme youth, he was fresh, and clean and blooming.
For he was certainly not more than twenty-four. My
first thought was that this was the son of Jane Fowler's
fiancé (I had not known he was a widower) come to say
that his father was prevented from dining by a sudden
attack of gout. But his eyes fell immediately on Mrs.
Fowler, his face lit up, and he went towards her with
both hands outstretched. Mrs. Fowler gave him hers,
a demure smile on her lips, and turned to her sister-in-
law.

"This is my young man, Marion," she said.
He held out his hand.
"I hope you'll like me, Mrs. Tower," he said. "Jane
tells me you're the only relation she has in the world."
Mrs. Tower's face was wonderful to behold. I saw
then to admiration how bravely good breeding and
social usage could combat the instincts of the natural
woman. For the astonishment and then the dismay that
for an instant she could not conceal were quickly driven
away, and her face assumed an expression of affable
welcome. But she was evidently at a loss for words.
It was not unnatural if Gilbert felt a certain embarrassment, and I was too busy preventing myself from
laughing to think of anything to say. Mrs. Fowler alone
kept perfectly calm.
"I know you'll like him, Marion. There's no one enjoys good food more than he does." She turned to the
young man. "Marion's dinners are famous."
"I know," he beamed.
Mrs. Tower made some quick rejoinder and we went
downstairs. I shall not soon forget the exquisite comedy
of that meal. Mrs. Tower could not make up her mind
whether the pair of them were playing a practical joke
on her or whether Jane by wilfully concealing her
fiancé's age had hoped to make her look foolish. But
then Jane never jested and she was incapable of doing
a malicious thing. Mrs. Tower was amazed, exasperated
and perplexed. But she had recovered her self-control,
and for nothing would she have forgotten that she was a
perfect hostess whose duty it was to make her party
go. She talked vivaciously; but I wondered if Gilbert

Napier saw how hard and vindictive was the expression
of her eyes behind the mask of friendliness that she
turned to him. She was measuring him. She was seeking
to delve into the secret of his soul. I could see that she
was in a passion, for under her rouge her cheeks glowed
with an angry red.

"You've got a very high colour, Marion," said Jane,
looking at her amiably through her great round spectacles.

"I dressed in a hurry. I daresay I put on too much
rouge."

"Oh, is it rouge? I thought it was natural. Otherwise
I shouldn't have mentioned it." She gave Gilbert a shy
little smile. "You know, Marion and I were at school
together. You would never think it to look at us now,
would you? But of course I've lived a very quiet life."

I do not know what she meant by these remarks;
it was almost incredible that she made them in complete
simplicity; but anyhow they goaded Mrs. Tower to such
a fury that she flung her own vanity to the winds. She
smiled brightly.

"We shall neither of us see fifty again, Jane," she said.

If the observation was meant to discomfit the widow
it failed.

"Gilbert says I mustn't acknowledge to more than
forty-nine for his sake," she answered blandly.

Mrs. Tower's hands trembled slightly, but she found
a retort.

"There is of course a certain disparity of age between you," she smiled.

"Twenty-seven years," said Jane. "Do you think

it's too much? Gilbert says I'm very young for my age.
I told you I shouldn't like to marry a man with one foot
in the grave."

I was really obliged to laugh, and Gilbert laughed too.
His laughter was frank and boyish. It looked as though
he were amused at everything Jane said. But Mrs.
Tower was almost at the end of her tether, and I was
afraid that unless relief came she would for once forget
that she was a woman of the world. I came to the rescue
as best I could.

"I suppose you're very busy buying your trousseau,"
I said.

"No. I wanted to get my things from the dressmaker
in Liverpool I've been to ever since I was first married.
But Gilbert won't let me. He's very masterful, and of
course he has wonderful taste."

She looked at him with a little affectionate smile,
demurely, as though she were a girl of seventeen.

Mrs. Tower went quite pale under her make-up.

"We're going to Italy for our honeymoon. Gilbert
has never had a chance of studying Renaissance architecture, and of course it's important for an architect
to see things for himself. And we shall stop in Paris on
the way and get my clothes there."

"Do you expect to be away long?"

"Gilbert has arranged with his office to stay away
for six months. It will be such a treat for him, won't it?
You see, he's never had more than a fortnight's holiday
before."

"Why not?" asked Mrs. Tower in a tone that no
effort of will could prevent from being icy.

"He's never been able to afford it, poor dear."

"Ah!" said Mrs. Tower, and into the exclamation put volumes.

Coffee was served and the ladies went upstairs. Gilbert and I began to talk in the desultory way in which men talk who have nothing whatever to say to one another; but in two minutes a note was brought in to me by the butler. It was from Mrs. Tower and ran as follows:

Come upstairs quickly and then go as soon as you can. Take him with you. Unless I have it out with Jane at once I shall have a fit.

I told a facile lie.

"Mrs. Tower has a headache and wants to go to bed. I think if you don't mind we'd better clear out."

"Certainly," he answered.

We went upstairs and five minutes later were on the doorstep. I called a taxi and offered the young man a lift.

"No, thanks," he answered. "I'll just walk to the corner and jump on a bus."

Mrs. Tower sprang to the fray as soon as she heard the front door close behind us.

"Are you crazy, Jane?" she cried.

"Not more than most people who don't habitually live in a lunatic asylum, I trust," Jane answered blandly.

"May I ask why you're going to marry this young man?" asked Mrs. Tower with formidable politeness.

"Partly because he won't take no for an answer. He's asked me five times. I grew positively tired of refusing him."

"And why do you think he's so anxious to marry you?"

"I amuse him."

Mrs. Tower gave an exclamation of annoyance.

"He's an unscrupulous rascal. I very nearly told him so to his face."

"You would have been wrong, and it wouldn't have been very polite."

"He's penniless and you're rich. You can't be such a besotted fool as not to see that he's marrying you for your money."

Jane remained perfectly composed. She observed her sister-in-law's agitation with detachment.

"I don't think he is, you know," she replied. "I think he's very fond of me."

"You're an old woman, Jane."

"I'm the same age as you are, Marion," she smiled.

"I've never let myself go. I'm very young for my age. No one would think I was more than forty. But even I wouldn't dream of marrying a boy twenty years younger than myself."

"Twenty-seven," corrected Jane.

"Do you mean to tell me that you can bring yourself to believe that it's possible for a young man to care for a woman old enough to be his mother?"

"I've lived very much in the country for many years. I daresay there's a great deal about human nature that

I don't know. They tell me there's a man called Freud,
an Austrian, I believe——"

But Mrs. Tower interrupted her without any politeness at all.

"Don't be ridiculous, Jane. It's so undignified. It's
so ungraceful. I always thought you were a sensible
woman. Really you're the last person I should ever have
thought likely to fall in love with a boy."

"But I'm not in love with him. I've told him that.
Of course I like him very much or I wouldn't think of
marrying him. I thought it only fair to tell him quite
plainly what my feelings were towards him."

Mrs. Tower gasped. The blood rushed to her head
and her breathing oppressed her. She had no fan, but
she seized the evening paper and vigorously fanned herself with it.

"If you're not in love with him why do you want to
marry him?"

"I've been a widow a very long time and I've led a
very quiet life. I thought I'd like a change."

"If you want to marry just to be married why don't
you marry a man of your own age?"

"No man of my own age has asked me five times.
In fact no man of my own age has asked me at all."

Jane chuckled as she answered. It drove Mrs. Tower
to the final pitch of frenzy.

"Don't laugh, Jane. I won't have it. I don't think
you can be right in your mind. It's dreadful."

It was altogether too much for her and she burst into
tears. She knew that at her age it was fatal to cry; her
eyes would be swollen for twenty-four hours and she

would look a sight. But there was no help for it. She wept. Jane remained perfectly calm. She looked at Marion through her large spectacles and reflectively smoothed the lap of her black silk dress.

"You're going to be so dreadfully unhappy," Mrs. Tower sobbed, dabbing her eyes cautiously in the hope that the black on her lashes would not smudge.

"I don't think so, you know," Jane answered in those equable, mild tones of hers, as if there were a little smile behind the words. "We've talked it over very thoroughly. I always think I'm a very easy person to live with. I think I shall make Gilbert very happy and comfortable. He's never had anyone to look after him properly. We're only marrying after mature consideration. And we've decided that if either of us wants his liberty the other will place no obstacles in the way of his getting it."

Mrs. Tower had by now recovered herself sufficiently to make a cutting remark.

"How much has he persuaded you to settle on him?"

"I wanted to settle a thousand a year on him, but he wouldn't hear of it. He was quite upset when I made the suggestion. He says he can earn quite enough for his own needs."

"He's more cunning than I thought," said Mrs. Tower acidly.

Jane paused a little and looked at her sister-in-law with kindly but resolute eyes.

"You see, my dear, it's different for you," she said. "You've never been so very much a widow, have you?"

Mrs. Tower looked at her. She blushed a little. She

even felt slightly uncomfortable. But of course Jane was much too simple to intend an innuendo. Mrs. Tower gathered herself together with dignity.

"I'm so upset that I really must go to bed," she said. "We'll resume the conservation to-morrow morning."

"I'm afraid that won't be very convenient, dear. Gilbert and I are going to get the license to-morrow morning."

Mrs. Tower threw up her hands in a gesture of dismay, but she found nothing more to say.

The marriage took place at a registrar's office. Mrs. Tower and I were the witnesses. Gilbert in a smart blue suit looked absurdly young, and he was obviously nervous. It is a trying moment for any man. But Jane kept her admirable composure. She might have been in the habit of marrying as frequently as a woman of fashion. Only a slight colour on her cheeks suggested that beneath her calm was some faint excitement. It is a thrilling moment for any woman. She wore a very full dress of silver grey velvet, in the cut of which I recognized the hand of the dressmaker in Liverpool (evidently a widow of unimpeachable character), who had made her gowns for so many years; but she had so far succumbed to the frivolity of the occasion as to wear a large picture hat covered with blue ostrich feathers. Her gold-rimmed spectacles made it extraordinarily grotesque. When the ceremony was over the registrar (somewhat taken aback, I thought, by the difference of age between the pair he was marrying) shook hands with her, tendering his strictly official congratulations;

and the bridegroom, blushing slightly, kissed her. Mrs. Tower, resigned but implacable, kissed her; and then the bride looked at me expectantly. It was evidently fitting that I should kiss her too. I did. I confess that I felt a little shy as we walked out of the registrar's office past loungers who waited cynically to see the bridal pairs, and it was with relief that I stepped into Mrs. Tower's car. We drove to Victoria Station, for the happy couple were to go over to Paris by the two o'clock train, and Jane had insisted that the wedding-breakfast should be eaten at the station restaurant. She said it always made her nervous not to be on the platform in good time. Mrs. Tower, present only from a strong sense of family duty, was able to do little to make the party go off well; she ate nothing (for which I could not blame her, since the food was execrable, and anyway I hate champagne at luncheon) and talked in a strained voice. But Jane went through the menu conscientiously.

"I always think one should make a hearty meal before starting out on a journey," she said.

We saw them off, and I drove Mrs. Tower back to her house.

"How long do you give it?" she said. "Six months?"

"Let's hope for the best," I smiled.

"Don't be so absurd. There can be no best. You don't think he's marrying her for anything but her money, do you? Of course it can't last. My only hope is that she won't have to go through as much suffering as she deserves."

I laughed. The charitable words were spoken in such

a tone as to leave me in small doubt of Mrs. Tower's
meaning.

"Well, if it doesn't last you'll have the consolation of
saying 'I told you so,'" I said.

"I promise you I'll never do that."

"Then you'll have the satisfaction of congratulating
yourself on your self-control in not saying 'I told you
so.'"

"She's old and dowdy and dull."

"Are you sure she's dull?" I said. "It's true she
doesn't say very much, but when she says anything it's
very much to the point."

"I've never heard her make a joke in my life."

I was once more in the Far East when Gilbert and
Jane returned from their honeymoon, and this time I
remained away for nearly two years. Mrs. Tower was
a bad correspondent and though I sent her an occasional
picture-postcard I received no news from her. But I
met her within a week of my return to London; I was
dining out and found that I was seated next to her. It
was an immense party—I think we were four-and-
twenty like the blackbirds in the pie—and, arriving
somewhat late, I was too confused by the crowd in
which I found myself to notice who was there. But when
we sat down, looking round the long table I saw that a
good many of my fellow-guests were well known to the
public from their photographs in the illustrated papers.
Our hostess had a weakness for the persons technically
known as celebrities, and this was an unusually brilliant
gathering. When Mrs. Tower and I had exchanged the

conventional remarks that two people make when they
have not seen one another for a couple of years I asked
about Jane.

"She's very well," said Mrs. Tower with a certain
dryness.

"How has the marriage turned out?"

Mrs. Tower paused a little and took a salted almond
from the dish in front of her.

"It appears to be quite a success."

"You were wrong, then?"

"I said it wouldn't last and I still say it won't last.
It's contrary to human nature."

"Is she happy?"

"They're both happy."

"I suppose you don't see very much of them."

"At first I saw quite a lot of them. But now . . ."
Mrs. Tower pursed her lips a little. "Jane is becoming
very grand."

"What *do* you mean?" I laughed.

"I think I should tell you that she's here to-night."

"Here?"

I was startled. I looked round the table again. Our
hostess was a delightful and an entertaining woman,
but I could not imagine that she would be likely to invite to a dinner such as this the elderly and dowdy wife
of an obscure architect. Mrs. Tower saw my perplexity
and was shrewd enough to see what was in my mind.
She smiled thinly.

"Look on the left of our host."

I looked. Oddly enough the woman who sat there had
by her fantastic appearance attracted my attention the

moment I was ushered into the crowded drawing-room. I thought I noticed a gleam of recognition in her eye, but to the best of my belief I had never seen her before. She was not a young woman, for her hair was iron-grey; it was cut very short and clustered thickly round her well-shaped head in tight curls. She made no attempt at youth, for she was conspicuous in that gathering by using neither lipstick, rouge nor powder. Her face, not a particularly handsome one, was red and weather-beaten; but because it owed nothing to artifice had a naturalness that was very pleasing. It contrasted oddly with the whiteness of her shoulders. They were really magnificent. A woman of thirty might have been proud of them. But her dress was extraordinary. I had not seen often anything more audacious. It was cut very low, with short skirts, which were then the fashion, in black and yellow; it had almost the effect of fancy-dress and yet so became her that though on anyone else it would have been outrageous, on her it had the inevitable simplicity of nature. And to complete the impression of an eccentricity in which there was no pose and of an extravagance in which there was no ostentation she wore, attached by a broad black ribbon, a single eye-glass.

"You're not going to tell me *that* is your sister-in-law," I gasped.

"That is Jane Napier," said Mrs. Tower icily.

At that moment she was speaking. Her host was turned towards her with an anticipatory smile. A bald-ish white-haired man, with a sharp, intelligent face, who sat on her left, was leaning forward eagerly, and the couple who sat opposite, ceasing to talk with one another, listened intently. She said her say and they all, with a sudden movement, threw themselves back in their chairs and burst into vociferous laughter. From the other side of the table a man addressed Mrs. Tower: I recognized a famous statesman.

"Your sister-in-law has made another joke, Mrs. Tower," he said.

Mrs. Tower smiled.

"She's priceless, isn't she?"

"Let me have a long drink of champagne and then for heaven's sake tell me all about it," I said.

Well, this is how I gathered it had all happened. At the beginning of their honeymoon Gilbert took Jane to various dressmakers in Paris and he made no objection to her choosing a number of 'gowns' after her own heart; but he persuaded her to have a 'frock' or two made according to his own design. It appeared that he had a knack for that kind of work. He engaged a smart French maid. Jane had never had such a thing before. She did her own mending and when she wanted 'doing up' was in the habit of ringing for the housemaid. The dresses Gilbert had devised were very different from anything she had worn before; but he had been careful not to go too far too quickly, and because it pleased him she persuaded herself, though not without misgivings, to wear them in preference to those she had chosen herself. Of course she could not wear them with the voluminous petticoats she had been in the habit of using, and these, though it cost her an anxious moment, she discarded.

"Now, if you please," said Mrs. Tower, with something very like a sniff of disapproval, "she wears nothing but thin silk tights. It's a wonder to me she doesn't catch her death of cold at her age."

Gilbert and the French maid taught her how to wear her clothes, and, unexpectedly enough, she was very quick at learning. The French maid was in raptures over Madame's arms and shoulders. It was a scandal not to show anything so fine.

"Wait a little, Alphonsine," said Gilbert. "The next lot of clothes I design for Madame we'll make the most of her."

The spectacles of course were dreadful. No one could look really well in gold-rimmed spectacles. Gilbert tried some with tortoise-shell rims. He shook his head.

"They'd look all right on a girl," he said. "You're too old to wear spectacles, Jane." Suddenly he had an inspiration. "By George, I've got it. You must wear an eyeglass."

"Oh, Gilbert, I couldn't."

She looked at him, and his excitement, the excitement of the artist, made her smile. He was so sweet to her she wanted to do what she could to please him.

"I'll try," she said.

When they went to an optician and, suited with the right size, she placed an eyeglass jauntily in her eye Gilbert clapped his hands. There and then, before the astonished shopman, he kissed her on both cheeks.

"You look wonderful," he cried.

So they went down to Italy and spent happy months studying Renaissance and Baroque architecture. Jane not only grew accustomed to her changed appearance but found she liked it. At first she was a little shy when she went into the dining-room of a hotel and people turned round to stare at her—no one had ever raised an eyelid to look at her before—but presently she found that the sensation was not disagreeable. Ladies came up to her and asked her where she got her dress.

"Do you like it?" she answered demurely. "My husband designed it for me."

"I should like to copy it if you don't mind."

Jane had certainly for many years lived a very quiet life, but she was by no means lacking in the normal instincts of her sex. She had her answer ready.

"I'm so sorry, but my husband's very particular and he won't hear of anyone copying my frocks. He wants me to be unique."

She had an idea that people would laugh when she said this, but they didn't; they merely answered:

"Oh, of course I quite understand. You *are* unique."

But she saw them making mental notes of what she wore, and for some reason this quite 'put her about.' For once in her life when she wasn't wearing what everybody else did, she reflected, she didn't see why everybody else should want to wear what she did.

"Gilbert," she said, quite sharply for her, "next time you're designing dresses for me I wish you'd design things that people *can't* copy."

"The only way to do that is to design things that only you can wear."

"Can't you do that?"

"Yes, if you'll do something for me."

"What is it?"

"Cut off your hair."

I think this was the first time that Jane jibbed. Her hair was long and thick, and as a girl she had been quite vain of it; to cut it off was a very drastic proceeding. This really was burning her boats behind her. In her case it was not the first step that cost so much, it was the last; but she took it ("I know Marion will think me a perfect fool, and I shall *never* be able to go to Liverpool again," she said), and when they passed through Paris on their way home Gilbert led her (she felt quite sick, her heart was beating so fast) to the best hairdresser in the world. She came out of his shop with a jaunty, saucy, impudent head of crisp grey curls. Pygmalion had finished his fantastic masterpiece: Galatea was come to life.

"Yes," I said, "but that isn't enough to explain why Jane is here to-night amid this crowd of duchesses, cabinet ministers and such like; nor why she is sitting on one side of her host with an admiral of the Fleet on the other."

"Jane is a humorist," said Mrs. Tower. "Didn't you see them all laughing at what she said?"

There was no doubt now of the bitterness in Mrs. Tower's heart.

"When Jane wrote and told me they were back from their honeymoon I thought I must ask them both to dinner. I didn't much like the idea, but I felt it had to be done. I knew the party would be deadly and I wasn't going to sacrifice any of the people who really mattered. On the other hand I didn't want Jane to think I hadn't any nice friends. You know I never have more than eight, but on this occasion I thought it would make things go better if I had twelve. I'd been too busy to see Jane until the evening of the party. She kept us all waiting a little—that was Gilbert's cleverness—and at last she sailed in. You could have knocked me down with a feather. She made the rest of the women look dowdy and provincial. She made me feel like a painted old trollop."

Mrs. Tower drank a little champagne.

"I wish I could describe the frock to you. It would have been quite impossible on anyone else; on her it was perfect. And the eyeglass! I'd known her for thirty-five years and I'd never seen her without spectacles."

"But you knew she had a good figure."

"How should I? I'd never seen her except in the clothes you first saw her in. Did *you* think she had a good figure? She seemed not to be unconscious of the sensation she made but to take it as a matter of course. I thought of my dinner and I heaved a sigh of relief. Even if she was a little heavy in hand, with that appearance it didn't so very much matter. She was sitting at the other end of the table and I heard a good deal of laughter; I was glad to think that the other people were playing up well; but after dinner I was a good deal taken aback when no less than three men came up to me and told me that my sister-in-law was priceless, and did I think she would allow them to call on her. I didn't quite know whether I was standing on my head or my heels. Twenty-four hours later our hostess of to-night rang me up and said she had heard my sister-in-law was in London and she was priceless and would I ask her to luncheon to meet her. She has an infallible instinct, that woman: in a month everyone was talking about Jane. I am here to-night, not because I've known our hostess for twenty years and have asked her to dinner a hundred times, but because I'm Jane's sister-in-law."

Poor Mrs. Tower. The position was galling, and though I could not help being amused, for the tables were turned on her with a vengeance, I felt that she deserved my sympathy.

"People never can resist those who make them laugh," I said, trying to console her.

"She never makes *me* laugh."

Once more from the top of the table I heard a guffaw and guessed that Jane had said another amusing thing.

"Do you mean to say that you are the only person who doesn't think her funny?" I asked, smiling.

"Had it struck *you* that she was a humorist?"

"I'm bound to say it hadn't."

"She says just the same things as she's said for the last thirty-five years. I laugh when I see everyone else does because I don't want to seem a perfect fool, but I am not amused."

"Like Queen Victoria," I said.

It was a foolish jest and Mrs. Tower was quite right sharply to tell me so. I tried another tack.

"Is Gilbert here?" I asked, looking down the table.

"Gilbert was asked because she won't go out without him, but to-night he's at a dinner of the Architects' Institute or whatever it's called."

"I'm dying to renew my acquaintance with her."

"Go and talk to her after dinner. She'll ask you to her Tuesdays."

"Her Tuesdays?"

"She's at home every Tuesday evening. You'll meet there everyone you ever heard of. They're the best parties in London. She's done in one year what I've failed to do in twenty."

"But what you tell me is really miraculous. How has it been done?"

Mrs. Tower shrugged her handsome but adipose shoulders.

"I shall be glad if you'll tell me," she replied.

After dinner I tried to make my way to the sofa on which Jane was sitting, but I was intercepted and it was not till a little later that my hostess came up to me and said:

"I must introduce you to the star of my party. Do you know Jane Napier? She's priceless. She's much more amusing than your comedies."

I was taken up to the sofa. The admiral who had been sitting beside her at dinner was with her still. He showed no sign of moving, and Jane, shaking hands with me, introduced me to him.

"Do you know Sir Reginald Frobisher?"

We began to chat. It was the same Jane as I had known before, perfectly simple, homely and unaffected, but her fantastic appearance certainly gave a peculiar savour to what she said. Suddenly I found myself shaking with laughter. She had made a remark, sensible and to the point, but not in the least witty, which her

manner of saying and the bland look she gave me
through her eyeglass made perfectly irresistible. I felt
light-hearted and buoyant. When I left her she said
to me:

"If you've got nothing better to do, come and see us
on Tuesday evening. Gilbert will be so glad to see you."

"When he's been a month in London he'll know that
he *can* have nothing better to do," said the admiral.

So, on Tuesday but rather late, I went to Jane's.
I confess I was a little surprised at the company. It was
quite a remarkable collection of writers, painters and
politicians, actors, great ladies and great beauties: Mrs.
Tower was right, it was a grand party; I had seen nothing like it in London since Stafford House was sold. No
particular entertainment was provided. The refresh-
ments were adequate without being luxurious. Jane in
her quiet way seemed to be enjoying herself; I could not
see that she took a great deal of trouble with her guests,
but they seemed to like being there, and the gay, pleasant party did not break up till two in the morning.
After that I saw much of her. I not only went often to
her house, but seldom went out to luncheon or to dinner
without meeting her. I am an amateur of humour and
I sought to discover in what lay her peculiar gift. It was
impossible to repeat anything she said, for the fun, like
certain wines, would not travel. She had no gift for
epigram. She never made a brilliant repartee. There was
no malice in her remarks nor sting in her rejoinders.
There are those who think that impropriety, rather than
brevity, is the soul of wit; but she never said a thing
that could have brought a blush to a Victorian cheek.

I think her humour was unconscious and I am sure it was unpremeditated. It flew like a butterfly from flower to flower, obedient only to its own caprice and pursuivant of neither method nor intention. It depended on the way she spoke and on the way she looked. Its subtlety gained by the flaunting and extravagant appearance that Gilbert had achieved for her; but her appearance was only an element in it. Now of course she was the fashion and people laughed if she but opened her mouth. They no longer wondered that Gilbert had married a wife so much older than himself. They saw that Jane was a woman with whom age did not count. They thought him a devilish lucky young fellow. The admiral quoted Shakespeare to me: "Age cannot wither her, nor custom stale her infinite variety." Gilbert was delighted with her success. As I came to know him better I grew to like him. It was quite evident that he was neither a rascal nor a fortune-hunter. He was not only immensely proud of Jane but genuinely devoted to her. His kindness to her was touching. He was a very unselfish and sweet-tempered young man.

"Well, what do you think of Jane now?" he said to me once, with boyish triumph.

"I don't know which of you is more wonderful," I said. "You or she."

"Oh, I'm nothing."

"Nonsense. You don't think I'm such a fool as not to see that it's you, and you only, who've made Jane what she is."

"My only merit is that I saw what was there when it wasn't obvious to the naked eye," he answered.

"I can understand your seeing that she had in her the possibility of that remarkable appearance, but how in the world have you made her into a humorist?"

"But I always thought the things she said a perfect scream. She was always a humorist."

"You're the only person who ever thought so."

Mrs. Tower, not without magnanimity, acknowledged that she had been mistaken in Gilbert. She grew quite attached to him. But notwithstanding appearances she never faltered in her opinion that the marriage could not last. I was obliged to laugh at her.

"Why, I've never seen such a devoted couple," I said.

"Gilbert is twenty-seven now. It's just the time for a pretty girl to come along. Did you notice the other evening at Jane's that pretty little niece of Sir Reginald's? I thought Jane was looking at them both with a good deal of attention, and I wondered to myself."

"I don't believe Jane fears the rivalry of any girl under the sun."

"Wait and see," said Mrs. Tower.

"You gave it six months."

"Well, now I give it three years."

When anyone is very positive in an opinion it is only human nature to wish him proved wrong. Mrs. Tower was really too cocksure. But such a satisfaction was not mine, for the end that she had always and confidently predicted to the ill-assorted match did in point of fact come. Still, the fates seldom give us what we want in the way we want it, and though Mrs. Tower could flatter herself that she had been right, I think after all she would sooner have been wrong. For things did not happen at all in the way she expected.

One day I received an urgent message from her and fortunately went to see her at once. When I was shown into the room Mrs. Tower rose from her chair and came towards me with the stealthy swiftness of a leopard stalking his prey. I saw that she was excited.

"Jane and Gilbert have separated," she said.

"Not really? Well, you were right after all."

Mrs. Tower looked at me with an expression I could not understand.

"Poor Jane," I muttered.

"Poor Jane!" she repeated, but in tones of such derision that I was dumbfounded.

She found some difficulty in telling me exactly what had occurred.

Gilbert had left her a moment before she leaped to the telephone to summon me. When he entered the room, pale and distraught, she saw at once that something terrible had happened. She knew what he was going to say before he said it.

"Marion, Jane has left me."

She gave him a little smile and took his hand.

"I knew you'd behave like a gentleman. It would have been dreadful for her for people to think that *you* had left her."

"I've come to you because I knew I could count on your sympathy."

"Oh, I don't blame you, Gilbert," said Mrs. Tower, very kindly. "It was bound to happen."

He sighed.

"I suppose so. I couldn't hope to keep her always. She was too wonderful and I'm a perfectly commonplace fellow."

Mrs. Tower patted his hand. He was really behaving beautifully.

"And what is going to happen now?"

"Well, she's going to divorce me."

"Jane always said she'd put no obstacle in your way if ever you wanted to marry a girl."

"You don't think it's likely I should ever be willing to marry anyone else after being Jane's husband," he answered.

Mrs. Tower was puzzled.

"Of course you mean that you've left Jane."

"I? That's the last thing I should ever do."

"Then why is she divorcing you?"

"She's going to marry Sir Reginald Frobisher as soon as the decree is made absolute."

Mrs. Tower positively screamed. Then she felt so faint that she had to get her smelling salts.

"After all you've done for her?"

"I've done nothing for her."

"Do you mean to say you're going to allow yourself to be made use of like that?"

"We arranged before we married that if either of us wanted his liberty the other should put no hindrance in the way."

"But that was done on your account. Because

you were twenty-seven years younger than she was."

"Well, it's come in very useful for her," he answered bitterly.

Mrs. Tower expostulated, argued, and reasoned; but Gilbert insisted that no rules applied to Jane, and he must do exactly what she wanted. He left Mrs. Tower prostrate. It relieved her a good deal to give me a full account of this interview. It pleased her to see that I was as surprised as herself, and if I was not so indignant with Jane as she was she ascribed that to the criminal lack of morality incident to my sex. She was still in a state of extreme agitation when the door was opened and the butler showed in—Jane herself. She was dressed in black and white as no doubt befitted her slightly ambiguous position, but in a dress so original and fantastic, in a hat so striking, that I positively gasped at the sight of her. But she was as ever bland and collected. She came forward to kiss Mrs. Tower, but Mrs. Tower withdrew herself with icy dignity.

"Gilbert has been here," she said.

"Yes, I know," smiled Jane. "I told him to come and see you. I'm going to Paris to-night and I want you to be very kind to him while I am away. I'm afraid just at first he'll be rather lonely and I shall feel more comfortable if I can count on your keeping an eye on him."

Mrs. Tower clasped her hands.

"Gilbert has just told me something that I can hardly bring myself to believe. He tells me that you're going to divorce him to marry Reginald Frobisher."

"Don't you remember, before I married Gilbert you

advised me to marry a man of my own age. The admiral is fifty-three."

"But, Jane, you owe everything to Gilbert," said Mrs. Tower indignantly. "You wouldn't exist without him. Without him to design your clothes, you'll be nothing."

"Oh, he's promised to go on designing my clothes," Jane answered blandly.

"No woman could want a better husband. He's always been kindness itself to you."

"Oh, I know he's been sweet."

"How *can* you be so heartless?"

"But I was never in love with Gilbert," said Jane. "I always told him that. I'm beginning to feel the need of the companionship of a man of my own age. I think I've probably been married to Gilbert long enough. The young have no conversation." She paused a little and gave us both a charming smile. "Of course I shan't lose sight of Gilbert. I've arranged that with Reginald. The admiral has a niece that would just suit him. As soon as we're married we'll ask them to stay with us at Malta—you know that the admiral is to have the Mediterranean Command—and I shouldn't be at all surprised if they fell in love with one another."

Mrs. Tower gave a little sniff.

"And have you arranged with the admiral that if you want your liberty neither should put any hindrance in the way of the other?"

"I suggested it," Jane answered with composure. "But the admiral says he knows a good thing when he sees it and he won't want to marry anyone else, and if anyone wants to marry me—he has eight twelve-inch guns on his flagship and he'll discuss the matter at short range." She gave us a look through her eyeglass which even the fear of Mrs. Tower's wrath could not prevent me from laughing at. "I think the admiral's a very passionate man."

Mrs. Tower indeed gave me an angry frown.

"I never thought you funny, Jane," she said, "I never understood why people laughed at the things you said."

"I never thought I was funny myself, Marion," smiled Jane, showing her bright, regular teeth. "I am glad to leave London before too many people come round to our opinion."

"I wish you'd tell me the secret of your astonishing success," I said.

She turned to me with that bland, homely look I knew so well.

"You know, when I married Gilbert and settled in London and people began to laugh at what I said no one was more surprised than I was. I'd said the same things for thirty years and no one ever saw anything to laugh at. I thought it must be my clothes or my bobbed hair or my eyeglass. Then I discovered it was because I spoke the truth. It was so unusual that people thought it humorous. One of these days someone else will discover the secret, and when people habitually tell the truth of course there'll be nothing funny in it."

"And why am I the only person not to think it funny?" asked Mrs. Tower.

Jane hesitated a little as though she were honestly searching for a satisfactory explanation.

"Perhaps you don't know the truth when you see it, Marion dear," she answered in her mild good-natured way.

It certainly gave her the last word. I felt that Jane would always have the last word. She *was* priceless.

THE ALIEN CORN

THE ALIEN CORN

I HAD known the Blands a long time before I discovered that they had any connection with Ferdy Rabenstein. Ferdy must have been nearly fifty when I first knew him, and at the time of which I write he was well over seventy. He had altered little. His hair, coarse but abundant and curly, was white, but he had kept his figure and held himself as gallantly as ever. It was not hard to believe that in youth he had been as beautiful as people said. He had still his fine Semitic profile and the lustrous black eyes that had caused havoc in so many a Gentile breast. He was very tall, lean, with an oval face and a clear skin. He wore his clothes very well, and in evening dress, even now, he was one of the handsomest men I had ever seen. He wore then large black pearls in his shirt front and platinum and sapphire rings on his fingers. Perhaps he was rather flashy, but you felt it was so much in character that it would have ill become him to be anything else.

"After all, I am an Oriental," he said. "I can carry a certain barbaric magnificence."

I have often thought that Ferdy Rabenstein would make an admirable subject for a biography. He was not a great man, but within the limits he set himself he made of his life a work of art. It was a masterpiece in little, like a Persian miniature, and derived its interest from its perfection. Unfortunately the materials are scanty. They would consist of letters that may very well have been destroyed and the recollections of people who are old now and will soon be dead. His memory is extraordinary, but he would never write his memoirs, for he looks upon his past as a source of purely private entertainment; and he is a man of the most perfect discretion. Nor do I know anyone who could do justice to the subject but Max Beerbohm. There is no one else in this hard world of to-day who can look upon the trivial with such tender sympathy and wring such a delicate pathos from futility. I wonder that Max, who must have known Ferdy much better than I, and long before, was never tempted to exercise his exquisite fancy on such a theme. He was born for Max to write about. And who should have illustrated the elegant book that I see in my mind's eye but Aubrey Beardsley? Thus would have been erected a monument of triple brass and the ephemera imprisoned to succeeding ages in the amber's exquisite translucency.

Ferdy's conquests were social and his venue was the great world. He was born in South Africa and did not come to England till he was twenty. For some time he was on the Stock Exchange, but on the death of his father he inherited a considerable fortune, and retiring from business devoted himself to the life of a man about town. At that period English society was still a closed body and it was not easy for a Jew to force its barriers, but to Ferdy they fell like the walls of Jericho. He was handsome, he was rich, he was a sportsman and he was good company. He had a house in Curzon Street, furnished with the most beautiful French furniture, and a French chef, and a brougham. It would be interesting to know the first steps in his wonderful career: they are lost in the dark abysm of time. When I first met him he had been long established as one of the smartest men in London: this was at a very grand house in Norfolk to which I had been asked as a promising young novelist by the hostess who took an interest in letters, but the company was very distinguished and I was overawed. We were sixteen, and I felt shy and alone among these cabinet ministers, great ladies and peers of the realm who talked of people and things of which I knew nothing. They were civil to me, but indifferent, and I was conscious that I was somewhat of a burden to my hostess. Ferdy saved me. He sat with me, walked with me and talked with me. He discovered that I was a writer and we discussed the drama and the novel; he learnt that I had lived much on the continent and he talked to me pleasantly of France, Germany and Spain. He seemed really to seek my society. He gave me the flattering impression that he and I stood apart from the other members of the company and by our conversation upon affairs of the spirit made that of the rest of them, the political situation, the scandal of somebody's divorce and the growing disinclination of pheasants to be killed, seem a little ridiculous. But if Ferdy had at the bottom of his heart a feeling of ever so faint a contempt for the hearty British gentry that surrounded us I am sure that it was only to me that he allowed an inkling of it to appear, and looking back I cannot but wonder whether it was not after all a suave and very delicate compliment that he paid me. I think of course that he liked to exercise his charm, and I daresay the obvious pleasure his conversation gave me gratified him, but he could have had no motive for taking so much trouble over an obscure novelist other than his real interest in art and letters. I felt that he and I at bottom were equally alien in that company, I because I was a writer and he because he was a Jew, but I envied the ease with which he bore himself. He was completely at home. Everyone called him Ferdy. He seemed to be always in good spirits. He was never at a loss for a quip, a jest or a repartee. They liked him in that house because he made them laugh but never made them uncomfortable by talking above their heads. He brought a faint savour of Oriental romance into their lives, but so cleverly that they only felt more English. You could never be dull when he was by and with him present you were safe from the fear of the devastating silences that sometimes overwhelm a British company. A pause looked inevitable and Ferdy Rabenstein had broken into a topic that interested everyone. An invaluable asset to any party. He had an inexhaustible fund of Jewish stories. He was a very good mimic and he assumed the Yiddish accent and reproduced the Jewish gestures to perfection; his head sank into his body, his face grew cunning, his voice oily, and he was a rabbi or an old-clothes merchant or a smart commercial traveller or a fat procuress in Frankfort. It was as good as a play. Because he was himself a Jew and insisted on it you laughed without reserve, but for my own part not without an undercurrent of discomfort. I was not quite sure of a sense of humour that made such cruel fun of his own race. I discovered afterwards that Jewish stories were his speciality, and I seldom met him anywhere without hearing him tell sooner or later the last he had heard.

But the best story he told me on this occasion was not a Jewish one. It struck me so that I have never forgotten it, but for one reason or another I have never had occasion to tell it again. I give it here because it is a curious little incident concerning persons whose names at least will live in the social history of the Victorian Era and I think it would be a pity if it were lost. He told me then that once when quite a young man he was staying in the country in a house where Mrs. Langtry, at that time at the height of her beauty and astounding reputation, was also a guest. It happened to be within driving distance of that in which lived the Duchess of Somerset, who had been Queen of Beauty at the Eglinton Tournament, and knowing her slightly, it occurred to him that it would be interesting to bring the two women together. He suggested it to Mrs. Langtry, who was willing, and forthwith wrote to the Duchess asking if he might bring the celebrated beauty to call on her. It was fitting, he said, that the loveliest woman of this generation (this was in the eighties) should pay her respects to the loveliest woman of the last. 'Bring her by all means,' answered the Duchess, 'but I warn you that it will be a shock to her.' They drove over in a carriage and pair, Mrs. Langtry in a close-fitting blue bonnet with long satin strings, which showed the ex-

quisite shape of her head and made her blue eyes even
bluer, and were received by a little ugly old hag who
looked with irony out of her beady eyes at the radiant
beauty who had come to see her. They had tea, they
talked and they drove home again. Mrs. Langtry was
very silent and when Ferdy looked at her he saw that
she was quietly weeping. When they got back to the
house she went to her room and would not come down
to dinner that night. For the first time she had realized
that beauty dies.

Ferdy asked me for my address and a few days after
I got back to London invited me to dinner. There were
only six of us, an American woman married to an
English peer, a Swedish painter, an actress and a well-
known critic. We ate very good food and drank excellent wine. The conversation was easy and intelligent.
After dinner Ferdy was persuaded to play the piano. He
only played Viennese waltzes—I discovered later that
they were his speciality—and the light, tuneful and
sensual music seemed to accord well with his discreet
flamboyance. He played without affectation, with a lilt,
and he had a graceful touch. This was the first of a good
many dinners I had with him; he would ask me two or
three times a year, and as time passed I met him more
and more frequently at other people's houses. I rose in
the world and perhaps he came down a little. Of late
years I had sometimes found him at parties where other
Jews were, and I fancied that I read in his shining liquid
eyes, resting for a moment on these members of his
race, a certain good-natured amusement at the thought

of what the world was coming to. There were people who said he was a snob, but I do not think he was; it just happened that in his early days he had never met any but the great. He had a real passion for art, and in his commerce with those that produced it was at his best. With them he had never that faint air of persiflage which when he was with very grand persons made you suspect that he was never quite the dupe of their grandeur. His taste was exquisite and many of his friends were glad to avail themselves of his knowledge. He was one of the first to value old furniture, and he rescued many an exquisite piece from the attics of ancestral mansions and gave it an honourable place in the drawing-room. It amused him to saunter round the auction rooms, and he was always willing to give his advice to great ladies who desired at once to acquire a beautiful thing and make a profitable investment. He was rich and good-natured. He liked to patronize the arts and would take a great deal of trouble to get commissions for some young painter whose talent he admired or an engagement to play at a rich man's house for a violinist who could in no other way get a hearing. But he never let his rich man down. His taste was too good to deceive, and civil though he might be to the mediocre he would not lift a finger to help them. His own musical parties, very small and carefully chosen, were a treat.

He never married.

"I am a man of the world," he said, "and I flatter myself that I have no prejudices, *tous les goûts sont dans la nature,* but I do not think I could bring myself to marry a Gentile. There's no harm in going to the opera in a dinner-jacket, but it just would never occur to me to do so."

"Then why didn't you marry a Jewess?"

(I did not hear this conversation, but the lively and audacious creature who thus tackled him told me of it.)

"Oh, my dear, our women are so prolific. I could not bear the thought of peopling the world with a little Ikey and a little Jacob and a little Rebecca and a little Leah and a little Rachel."

But he had had affairs of note and the glamour of past romance still clung to him. He was in his youth of an amorous complexion. I have met old ladies who told me that he was irresistible, and when in reminiscent mood they talked to me of this woman and that who had completely lost her head over him, I divined that, such was his beauty, they could not find it in their hearts to blame them. It was interesting to hear of great ladies that I had read of in the memoirs of the day or had met as respectable dowagers garrulous over their grandsons at Eton or making a mess of a hand at bridge and bethink myself that they had been consumed with sinful passion for the handsome Jew. Ferdy's most notorious amour was with the Duchess of Hereford, the loveliest, the most gallant and dashing of the beauties of the end of Queen Victoria's reign. It lasted for twenty years. He had doubtless flirtations meanwhile, but their relations were stable and recognized. It was proof of his marvellous tact that when at last they ended he exchanged an aging mistress for a loyal friend. I remember meeting the pair not so very long ago at luncheon.

She was an old woman, tall and of a commanding presence, but with a mask of paint on a ravaged face. We were lunching at the Carlton and Ferdy, our host, came a few minutes late. He offered us a cocktail and the Duchess told him we had already had one.

"Ah, I wondered why your eyes were so doubly bright," he said.

The old raddled woman flushed with pleasure.

My youth passed, I grew middle-aged, I wondered how soon I must begin to describe myself as elderly; I wrote books and plays, I travelled, I underwent experiences, I fell in love and out of it; and still I kept meeting Ferdy at parties. War broke out and was waged, millions of men were killed and the face of the world was changed. Ferdy did not like the war. He was too old to take part in it, and his German name was awkward, but he was discreet and took care not to expose himself to humiliation. His old friends were faithful to him, and he lived in a dignified but not too strict seclusion. But then peace came and with courage he set himself to making the best of changed conditions. Society was mixed now, parties were rowdy, but Ferdy fitted himself to the new life. He still told his funny Jewish stories, he still played charmingly the waltzes of Strauss, he still went round auction rooms and told the new rich what they ought to buy. I went to live abroad, but whenever I was in London I saw Ferdy, and now there was something a little uncanny in him. He did not give in. He had never known a day's illness. He seemed never to grow tired. He still dressed beautifully. He was interested in everybody. His mind was alert and people asked him to dinner, not for old times' sake, but because he was worth his salt. He still gave charming little concerts at his house in Curzon Street.

It was when he invited me to one of these that I made the discovery that started the recollections of him I have here set down. We were dining at a house in Hill Street, a large party, and the women having gone upstairs Ferdy and I found ourselves side by side. He told me that Lea Makart was coming to play for him on the following Friday evening and he would be glad if I would come.

"I'm awfully sorry," I said, "but I'm going down to the Blands."

"What Blands?"

"They live in Sussex at a place called Tilby."

"I didn't know you knew them."

He looked at me rather strangely. He smiled. I didn't know what amused him.

"Oh, yes, I've known them for years. It's a very nice house to stay at."

"Adolph is my nephew."

"Sir Adolphus?"

"It suggests one of the bucks of the Regency, doesn't it? But I will not conceal from you that he was named Adolph."

"Everyone I know calls him Freddy."

"I know, and I understand that Miriam, his wife, only answers to the name of Muriel."

"How does he happen to be your nephew?"

"Because Hannah Rabenstein, my sister, married

Alphonse Bleikogel, who ended life as Sir Alfred Bland, first baronet and Adolph, their only son, in due course became Sir Adolphus Bland, second baronet."

"Then Freddy Bland's mother, the Lady Bland who lives in Portland Place, is your sister?"

"Yes, my sister Hannah. She was the eldest of the family. She's eighty, but in full possession of her faculties and a remarkable woman."

"I've never met her."

"I think your friends the Blands would just as soon you didn't. She has never lost her German accent."

"Do you never see them?" I asked.

"I haven't spoken to them for twenty years. I am such a Jew and they are so English." He smiled. "I could never remember that their names were Freddy and Muriel. I used to come out with an Adolph or a Miriam at awkward moments. And they didn't like my stories. It was better that we should not meet. When the war broke out and I would not change my name it was the last straw. It was too late. I could never have accustomed my friends to think of me as anything but Ferdy Rabenstein. I was quite content. I was not ambitious to be a Smith, a Brown, or a Robinson."

Though he spoke facetiously, there was in his tone the faintest possible derision and I felt, hardly felt even, the sensation was so shadowy, that, as it had often vaguely seemed to me before, there was in the depth of his impenetrable heart a cynical contempt for the Gentiles he had conquered.

"Then you don't know the two boys?" I said.

"No."

"The eldest is called George, you know. I don't think he's so clever as Harry, the other one, but he's an engaging youth. I think you'd like him."

"Where is he now?"

"Well, he's just been sent down from Oxford. I suppose he's at home. Harry's still at Eton."

"Why don't you bring George to lunch with me?"

"I'll ask him. I should think he'd love to come."

"It has reached my ears that he's been a little troublesome."

"Oh, I don't know. He wouldn't go into the army, which is what they wanted. They rather fancied the Guards. And so he went to Oxford instead. He didn't work and he spent a great deal of money and he painted the town red. It was all quite normal."

"What was he sent down for?"

"I don't know. Nothing of any consequence."

At that moment our host rose and we went upstairs. When Ferdy bade me good-night he asked me not to forget about his great-nephew.

"Ring me up," he said. "Wednesday would suit me. Or Friday."

Next day I went down to Tilby. It was an Elizabethan mansion standing in a spacious park, in which roamed fallow dear, and from its windows you had wide views of rolling downs. It seemed to me that as far as the eye could reach the land belonged to the Blands. His tenants must have found Sir Adolphus a wonderful landlord, for I never saw farms kept in such order, the barns and cow-sheds were spick and span and the pig-

sties were a picture; the public-houses looked like old
English water-colours and the cottages he had built
on the estate combined admirably picturesqueness and
convenience. It must have cost him a pot of money to
run the place on these lines. Fortunately he had it. The
park with its grand old trees (and its nine-hole golf
course) was tended like a garden, and the wide-stretch-
ing gardens were the pride of the neighbourhood. The
magnificent house, with its steep roofs and mullioned
windows, had been restored by the most celebrated
architect in England and furnished by Lady Bland,
with taste and knowledge, in a style that perfectly
fitted it.

"Of course it's very simple," she said. "Just an
English house in the country."

The dining-room was adorned with old English sporting pictures, and the Chippendale chairs were of incredible value. In the drawing-room were portraits by
Reynolds and Gainsborough and landscapes by Old
Crome and Richard Wilson. Even in my bedroom with
its four-post bed were water-colours by Birket Foster.
It was very beautiful and a treat to stay there, but
though it would have distressed Muriel Bland beyond
anything to know it, it missed oddly enough entirely
the effect she had sought. It did not give you for a
moment the impression of an English house. You had
the feeling that every object had been bought with a
careful eye to the general scheme. You missed the dull
Academy portraits that hung in the dining-room beside
a Carlo Dolci that an ancestor had brought back from
the grand tour, and the water-colours painted by a

great-aunt that cluttered up the drawing-room so en-gagingly. There was no ugly Victorian sofa that had al-ways been there and that it never occurred to anybody to take away, and no needlework chairs that an un-married daughter had so painstakingly worked at about the time of the Great Exhibition. There was beauty but no sentiment.

And yet how comfortable it was and how well looked after you were! And what a cordial greeting the Blands gave you! They seemed really to like people. They were generous and kindly. They were never happier than when they were entertaining the county, and though they had not owned the property for more than twenty years they had established themselves firmly in the favour of their neighbours. Except perhaps in their splendour and the competent way in which the estate was run there was nothing to suggest that they had not been settled there for centuries.

Freddy had been at Eton and Oxford. He was now in the early fifties. He was quiet in manner, courtly, very clever, I imagine, but a trifle reserved. He had great elegance, but it was not an English elegance; he had grey hair and a short pointed grey beard, fine dark eyes and an aquiline nose. He was just above middle-height; I don't think you would have taken him for a Jew, but rather for a foreign diplomat of some distinction. He was a man of character, but gave you, strangely enough, notwithstanding the success he had had in life, an im-pression of faint melancholy. His successes had been financial and political; in the world of sport, for all his perseverance, he had never shone. For many years he had followed hounds, but he was a bad rider and I think it must have been a relief to him when he could persuade himself that middle-age and pressure of business forced him to give up hunting. He had excellent shooting and gave grand parties for it, but he was a poor shot; and despite the course in his park he never succeeded in being more than an indifferent golfer. He knew only too well how much these things meant in England, and his incapacity was a bitter disappointment to him. However, George would make up for it.

George was scratch at golf, and though tennis was not his game he played much better than the average; the Blands had had him taught to shoot as soon as he was old enough to hold a gun, and he was a fine shot; they had put him on a pony when he was two, and Freddy, watching him mount his horse, knew that out hunting when the boy came to a fence he felt exhilaration and not that sickening feeling in the pit of his stomach which, though he had chased the fox with such grim determination, had always made the sport a torture to him. George was so tall and slim, his curly hair, of a palish brown, was so fine, his eyes were so blue, he was the perfect type of the young Englishman. He had the engaging candour of the breed. His nose was straight, though perhaps a trifle fleshy, and his lips were perhaps a little full and sensual, but he had beautiful teeth, and his smooth skin was like ivory. George was the apple of his father's eye. He did not like Harry, his second son, so well. He was rather stocky, broad-shouldered and strong for his age, but his black eyes, shining with cleverness, his coarse dark hair and his big nose revealed his race. Freddy was severe with him, and often impatient, but with George he was all indulgence. Harry would go into the business, he had brains and push, but George was the heir. George would be an English gentleman.

George had offered to motor me down in the roadster his father had given him as a birthday present. He drove very fast and we arrived before the rest of the guests. The Blands were sitting on the lawn and tea was laid out under a magnificent cedar.

"By the way," I said presently, "I saw Ferdy Rabenstein the other day and he wants me to bring George to lunch with him."

I had not mentioned the invitation to George on the way because I thought that if there had been a family coldness I had better address his parents as well.

"Who in God's name is Ferdy Rabenstein?" said George.

How brief is human glory! A generation back such a question would have seemed grotesque.

"He's by way of being your great-uncle," I replied.

A glance had passed from father to mother when I first spoke.

"He's a horrid old man," said Muriel.

"I don't think it's in the least necessary for George to resume relationships that were definitely severed before he was born," said Freddy with decision.

"Anyhow I've delivered the message," said I, feeling somewhat snubbed.

"I don't want to see the old blighter," said George.

The conversation was broken off by the arrival of

other guests, and in a little while George went off to
play golf with one of his Oxford friends.

It was not till next day that the matter was referred
to again. I had played an indifferent round with Freddy
Bland in the morning, and several sets of what is known
as country-house tennis in the afternoon, and was sitting alone with Muriel on the terrace. In England we
have so much bad weather that it is only fair that a
beautiful day should be more beautiful than anywhere
in the world, and this June evening was perfect. The
blue sky was cloudless and the air was balmy; before us
stretched green rolling downs, and woods, and in the
distance you saw the red roofs of a little village and the
grey tower of the village church. It was a day when to be
alive was sufficient happiness. Detached lines of poetry
hovered vaguely in my memory. Muriel and I had been
chatting desultorily.

"I hope you didn't think it rather horrid of us to
refuse to let George lunch with Ferdy," she said
suddenly. "He's such a fearful snob, isn't he?"

"D'you think so? He's always been very nice to me."

"We haven't been on speaking terms for twenty
years. Freddy never forgave him for his behaviour during the war. So unpatriotic, I thought, and one really
must draw the line somewhere. You know, he absolutely
refused to drop his horrible German name. With Freddy
in Parliament and running munitions and all that sort of
thing it was quite impossible. I don't know why he
should want to see George. He can't mean anything to
him."

"He's an old man. George and Harry are his great-nephews. He must leave his money to some one."

"We'd rather not have his money," said Muriel coldly.

Of course I didn't care a row of pins whether George went to lunch with Ferdy Rabenstein, and I was quite willing to let the matter drop, but evidently the Blands had talked it over and Muriel felt that some explanation was due to me.

"Of course you know that Freddy has Jewish blood in him," she said.

She looked at me sharply. Muriel was rather a big blonde woman and she spent a great deal of time trying to keep down the corpulence to which she was predisposed. She had been very pretty when young and even now was a comely person; but her round blue eyes, slightly prominent, her fleshy nose, the shape of her face and the back of her neck, her exuberant manner, betrayed her race. No Englishwoman, however fair-haired, ever looked like that. And yet her observation was designed to make me take it for granted that she was a Gentile. I answered discreetly.

"So many people have nowadays."

"I know. But there's no reason to dwell on it, is there? After all, we're absolutely English; no one could be more English than George, in appearance and manner and everything; I mean, he's such a fine sportsman and all that sort of thing, I can't see any object in his knowing Jews just because they happen to be distant connections of his."

"It's very difficult in England now not to know Jews, isn't it?"

"Oh, I know, in London one does meet a good many, and I think some of them are very nice. They're so artistic. I don't go so far as to say that Freddy and I deliberately avoid them—of course I wouldn't do that—but it just happens that we don't really know any of them very well. And down here, there simply aren't any to know."

I could not but admire the convincing manner in which she spoke. It would not have surprised me to be told that she really believed every word she said.

"You say that Ferdy might leave George his money. Well, I don't believe it's so very much anyway; it was quite a comfortable fortune before the war, but that's nothing nowadays. Besides, we're hoping that George will go in for politics when he's a little older, and I don't think it would do him any good in the constituency to inherit money from a Mr. Rabenstein."

"Is George interested in politics?" I asked, to change the conversation.

"Oh, I do hope so. After all, there's the family constituency waiting for him. It's a safe Conservative seat and one can't expect Freddy to go on with the grind of the House of Commons indefinitely."

Muriel was grand. She talked already of the constituency as though twenty generations of Blands had sat for it. Her remark, however, was my first intimation that Freddy's ambition was not satisfied.

"I suppose Freddy would go to the House of Lords when George was old enough to stand."

"We've done a good deal for the party," said Muriel.

Muriel was a Catholic and she often told you that she had been educated in a convent—"Such sweet women, those nuns. I always said that if I had a daughter I should have sent her to a convent too"—but she liked her servants to be Church of England, and on Sunday evenings we had what was called supper because the fish was cold and there was ice cream, so that they could go to church, and we were waited on by two footmen instead of four. It was still light when we finished, and Freddy and I, smoking our cigars, walked up and down the terrace in the gloaming. I suppose Muriel had told him of her conversation with me, and it may be that his refusal to let George see his great-uncle still troubled him, but being subtler than she he attacked the question more indirectly. He told me that he had been very much worried about George. It had been a great disappointment that he had refused to go into the army.

"I should have thought he'd have loved the life," he said.

"And he would certainly have looked marvellous in his Guards' uniform."

"He would, wouldn't he?" returned Freddy, ingenuously. "I wonder he could resist that."

He had been completely idle at Oxford; although his father had given him a very large allowance, he had got monstrously into debt; and now he had been sent down. But though he spoke so tartly I could see that he was not a little proud of his scapegrace son, he loved him with, oh, such an un-English love, and in his heart it flattered him that George had cut such a dash.

"Why should you worry?" I said. "You don't really care if George has a degree or not."

Freddy chuckled.

"No, I don't suppose I do really. I always think the only important thing about Oxford is that people know you were there, and I daresay that George isn't any wilder than the other young men in his set. It's the future I'm thinking of. He's so damned idle. He doesn't seem to want to do anything but have a good time."

"He's young, you know."

"He's not interested in politics, and though he's so good at games he's not even very keen on sport. He seems to spend most of his time strumming the piano."

"That's a harmless amusement."

"Oh, yes, I don't mind that, but he can't go on loafing indefinitely. You see, all this will be his one day." Freddy gave a sweeping gesture that seemed to embrace the whole county, but I knew that he did not own it all yet. "I'm very anxious that he should be fit to assume his responsibilities. His mother is very ambitious for him, but I only want him to be an English gentleman."

Freddy gave me a sidelong glance as though he wanted to say something but hesitated in case I thought it ridiculous; but there is one advantage in being a writer, that, since people look upon you as of no account, they will often say things to you that they would not to their equals. He thought he would risk it.

"You know, I've got an idea that nowhere in the world now is the Greek ideal of life so perfectly culti-vated as by the English country gentleman living on his estates. I think his life has the beauty of a work of art."

I could not but smile when I reflected that it was impossible for the English country gentleman in these days to do anything of the sort without a packet of money safely invested in American bonds, but I smiled with sympathy. I thought it rather touching that this Jewish financier should cherish so romantic a dream.

"I want him to be a good landlord. I want him to take his part in the affairs of the country. I want him to be a thorough sportsman."

"Poor mutt," I thought, but said: "Well, what are your plans for George now?"

"I think he has a fancy for the diplomatic service. He's suggested going to Germany to learn the language."

"A very good idea, I should have thought."

"For some reason he's got it into his head that he wants to go to Munich."

"A nice place."

Next day I went back to London and shortly after my arrival rang up Ferdy.

"I'm sorry, but George isn't able to come to lunch on Wednesday."

"What about Friday?"

"Friday's no good either." I thought it useless to beat about the bush. "The fact is, his people aren't keen on his lunching with you."

There was a moment's silence. Then:

"I see. Well, will you come on Wednesday anyway?"

"Yes, I'd like to," I answered.

So on Wednesday at half-past one I strolled round to

Curzon Street. Ferdy received me with the somewhat elaborate graciousness that he cultivated. He made no reference to the Blands. We sat in the drawing-room and I could not help reflecting what an eye for beautiful objects that family had. The room was more crowded than the fashion of to-day approves and the gold snuff-boxes in vitrines, the French china, appealed to a taste that was not mine; but they were no doubt choice pieces; and the Louis XV suite, with its beautiful *petit point*, must have been worth an enormous lot of money. The pictures on the walls by Lancret, Pater and Watteau did not greatly interest me, but I recognized their intrinsic excellence. It was a proper setting for this aged man of the world. It fitted his period. Suddenly the door opened and George was announced. Ferdy saw my surprise and gave me a little smile of triumph.

"I'm very glad you were able to come after all," he said as he shook George's hand.

I saw him in a glance take in his great-nephew whom he saw to-day for the first time. George was very elegantly dressed. He wore a short black coat, striped trousers and the grey double-breasted waistcoat which at that time was the mode. You could only wear it with elegance if you were tall and thin and your belly was slightly concave. I felt sure that Ferdy knew exactly who George's tailor was and what haberdasher he went to, and approved of them. George, so smart and trim, wearing his clothes so beautifully, certainly looked very handsome. We went down to luncheon. Ferdy had the social graces at his fingers' ends and he put the boy at his ease, but I saw that he was carefully appraising him;

then, I do not know why, he began to tell some of his Jewish stories. He told them with gusto and with his wonderful mimicry. I saw George flush, and though he laughed at them, I could see that it was with embarrassment. I wondered what on earth had induced Ferdy to be so tactless. But he was watching George and he told story after story. It looked as though he would never stop. I wondered if for some reason I could not grasp he was taking a malicious pleasure in the boy's obvious discomfiture. At last we went upstairs, and to make things easier I asked Ferdy to play the piano. He played us three or four little waltzes. He had lost none of his exquisite lightness nor his sense of their lilting rhythm. Then he turned to George.

"Do you play?" he asked him.

"A little."

"Won't you play something?"

"I'm afraid I only play classical music. I don't think it would interest you."

Ferdy smiled slightly, but did not insist. I said it was time for me to go and George accompanied me.

"What a filthy old Jew," he said as soon as we were in the street. "I hated those stories of his."

"They're his great stunt. He always tells them."

"Would you if you were a Jew?"

I shrugged my shoulders.

"How is it you came to lunch after all?" I asked George.

He chuckled. He was a light-hearted creature, with a sense of humour, and he shook off the slight irritation his great-uncle had caused him.

"He went to see Granny. You don't know Granny, do you?"

"No."

"She treats Daddy like a kid in Etons. Granny said I was to go to lunch with great-uncle Ferdy, and what Granny says goes."

"I see."

A week or two later George went to Munich to learn German. I happened then to go on a journey, and it was not till the following spring that I was again in London. Soon after my arrival I found myself sitting next to Muriel Bland at dinner. I asked after George.

"He's still in Germany," she said.

"I see in the papers that you're going to have a great beano at Tilby for his coming of age."

"We're going to entertain the tenants and they're making George a presentation."

She was less exuberant than usual, but I did not pay much attention to the fact. She led a strenuous life and it might be that she was tired. I knew she liked to talk of her son, so I continued.

"I suppose George has been having a grand time in Germany," I said.

She did not answer for a moment and I gave her a glance. I was surprised to see that her eyes were filled with tears.

"I'm afraid George has gone mad," she said.

"What *do* you mean?"

"We've been so frightfully worried. Freddy's so

angry, he won't even discuss it. I don't know what we're going to do."

Of course it immediately occurred to me that George, who, I supposed, like most young Englishmen sent to learn the language, had been put with a German family, had fallen in love with the daughter of the house and wanted to marry her. I had a pretty strong suspicion that the Blands were intent on his making a very grand marriage.

"Why, what's happened?" I asked.

"He wants to become a pianist."

"A what?"

"A professional pianist."

"What on earth put that idea in his head?"

"Heaven knows. We didn't know anything about it. We thought he was working for his exam. I went out to see him. I thought I'd like to know that he was getting on all right. Oh, my dear. He looks like nothing on earth. And he used to be so smart; I could have cried. He told me he wasn't going in for the exam and had never had any intention of doing so; he'd only suggested the diplomatic service so that we'd let him go to Germany and he'd be able to study music."

"But has he any talent?"

"Oh, that's neither here nor there. Even if he had the genius of Paderewski we couldn't have George traipsing around the country playing at concerts. No one can deny that I'm very artistic, and so is Freddy—we love music and we've always known a lot of artists—but George will have a very great position; it's out of the question. We've set our hearts on his going into Parliament. He'll be very rich one day. There's nothing he can't aspire to."

"Did you point all that out to him?"

"Of course I did. He laughed at me. I told him he'd break his father's heart. He said his father could always fall back on Harry. Of course I'm devoted to Harry, and he's as clever as a monkey, but it was always understood that he was to go into the business; even though I am his mother I can see that he hasn't got the advantages that George has. Do you know what he said to me? He said that if his father would settle five pounds a week on him he would resign everything in Harry's favour and Harry could be his father's heir and succeed to the baronetcy and everything. It's too ridiculous. He said that if the Crown Prince of Roumania could abdicate a throne he didn't see why he couldn't abdicate a baronetcy. But you can't do that. Nothing can prevent him from being third baronet and, if Freddy should be granted a peerage, from succeeding to it at Freddy's death. Do you know, he even wants to drop the name of Bland and take some horrible German name."

I could not help asking what.

"Bleikogel or something like that," she answered.

That was a name I recognized. I remembered Ferdy telling me that Hannah Rabenstein had married Alphonse Bleikogel, who became eventually Sir Alfred Bland, first baronet. It was all very strange. I wondered what had happened to the charming and so typically English boy whom I had seen only a few months before.

"Of course when I came home and told Freddy he

was furious. I've never seen him so angry. He foamed
at the mouth. He wired to George to come back immediately, and George wired back to say he couldn't on
account of his work."

"Is he working?"

"From morning till night. That's the maddening
part of it. He never did a stroke of work in his life.
Freddy used to say he was born idle."

"H'm."

"Then Freddy wired to say that if he didn't come he'd
stop his allowance, and George wired back: 'Stop it.'
That put the lid on. You don't know what Freddy can
be when his back is up."

I knew that Freddy had inherited a large fortune, but
I knew also that he had immensely increased it, and I
could well imagine that behind the courteous and amiable Squire of Tilby there was a ruthless man of affairs.
He had been used to having his own way, and I could
believe that when crossed he would be hard and cruel.

"We'd been making George a very handsome allowance, but you know how frightfully extravagant he was.
We didn't think he'd be able to hold out long, and in
point of fact within a month he wrote to Ferdy and
asked him to lend him a hundred pounds. Ferdy went
to my mother-in-law—she's his sister, you know—and
asked her what it meant. Though they hadn't spoken
for twenty years Freddy went to see him and begged
him not to send George a penny, and he promised he
wouldn't. I don't know how George has been making
both ends meet. I'm sure Freddy's right, but I can't help
being rather worried. If I hadn't given Freddy my word

of honour that I wouldn't send him anything I think I'd
have slipped a few notes in a letter in case of accident.
I mean, it's awful to think that perhaps he hasn't got
enough to eat."

"It'll do him no harm to go short for a bit."

"We were in an awful hole, you know. We'd made all
sorts of preparations for his coming of age, and I'd issued
hundreds of invitations. Suddenly George said he
wouldn't come. I was simply frantic. I wrote and wired.
I would have gone over to Germany, only Freddy
wouldn't let me. I practically went down on my bended
knees to George. I begged him not to put us in such a
humiliating position. I mean, it's the sort of thing it's
so difficult to explain. Then my mother-in-law stepped
in. You don't know her, do you? She's an extraordinary
old woman. You'd never think she was Freddy's mother.
She was German originally but of very good family."

"Oh?"

"To tell you the truth I'm rather frightened of her.
She tackled Freddy and then she wrote to George herself. She said that if he'd come home for his twenty-
first birthday she'd pay any debts he had in Munich
and we'd all give a patient hearing to anything he had to
say. He agreed to that and we're expecting him one day
next week. But I'm not looking forward to it I can tell
you."

She gave a deep sigh. When we were walking upstairs
after dinner Freddy addressed me.

"I see Muriel has been telling you about George.
The damned fool! I have no patience with him. Fancy
wanting to be a pianist! It's so ungentlemanly."

"He's very young, you know," I said soothingly. "He's had things too easy for him. I've been much too indulgent. There's never been a thing he wanted that I haven't given him. I'll learn him."

The Blands had a discreet apprehension of the uses of advertisement, and I gathered from the papers that the celebrations at Tilby of George's twenty-first birthday were conducted in accordance with the usage of English county families. There were a dinner party and a ball for the gentry and a collation and a dance in marquees on the lawn for the tenants. Expensive bands were brought down from London. In the illustrated papers were pictures of George, surrounded by his family, being presented with a solid silver tea set by the tenantry. They had subscribed to have his portrait painted, but since his absence from the country had made it impossible for him to sit, the tea service had been substituted. I read in the columns of the gossip writers that his father had given him a hunter, his mother a gramophone that changed its own records, his grandmother the dowager Lady Bland an Encyclopædia Britannica and his great-uncle Ferdinand Rabenstein a Virgin and Child by Pellegrino da Modena. I could not help observing that these gifts were bulky and not readily convertible into cash. From Ferdy's presence at the festivities I concluded that George's unaccountable vagary had effected a reconciliation between uncle and nephew. I was right. Ferdy did not at all like the notion of his great-nephew becoming a professional pianist. At the first hint of danger to its prestige the family drew together and a united front was presented to oppose George's designs. Since I was not there I only know from hearsay what happened when the birthday celebrations were over. Ferdy told me something and so did Muriel, and later George gave me his version. The Blands had very much the impression that when George came home and found himself occupying the centre of the stage, when, surrounded by splendour, he saw for himself once more how much it meant to be the heir of a great estate, he would weaken. They surrounded him with love. They flattered him. They hung on his words. They counted on the goodness of his heart and thought that if they were very kind to him he would not have the courage to cause them pain. They seemed to take it for granted that he had no intention of going back to Germany, and in conversation included him in all their plans. George did not say very much. He seemed to be enjoying himself. He did not open a piano. Things looked as though they were going very well. Peace descended on the troubled house. Then one day at luncheon when they were discussing a garden party to which they had all been asked for one day of the following week, George said pleasantly:

"Don't count on me. I shan't be here."

"Oh, George, why not?" asked his mother.

"I must get back to my work. I'm leaving for Munich on Monday."

There was an awful pause. Everyone looked for something to say, but was afraid of saying the wrong thing, and at last it seemed impossible to break it.

Luncheon was finished in silence. Then George went into the garden and the others, old Lady Bland and Ferdy, Muriel and Sir Adolphus, into the morning-room. There was a family council. Muriel wept. Freddy flew into a temper. Presently from the drawing-room they heard the sound of someone playing a nocturne of Chopin. It was George. It was as though, now he had announced his decision, he had gone for comfort, rest and strength to the instrument he loved. Freddy sprang to his feet.

"Stop that noise," he cried. "I won't have him play the piano in my house."

Muriel rang for a servant and gave him a message.

"Will you tell Mr. Bland that her ladyship has a bad headache and would he mind not playing the piano."

Ferdy, the man of the world, was deputed to have a talk with George. He was authorized to make him certain promises if he would give up the idea of becoming a pianist. If he did not wish to go into the diplomatic service his father would not insist, but if he would stand for Parliament he was prepared to pay his election expenses, give him a flat in London and make him an allowance of five thousand a year. I must say it was a handsome offer. I do not know what Ferdy said to the boy. I suppose he painted to him the life that a young man could lead in London on such an income. I am sure he made it very alluring. It availed nothing. All George asked was five pounds a week to be able to continue his studies and to be left alone. He was indifferent to the position that he might some day enjoy. He didn't want to hunt. He didn't want to shoot. He didn't want to be a

Member of Parliament. He didn't want to be a million-aire. He didn't want to be a baronet. He didn't want to be a peer. Ferdy left him, defeated and in a state of considerable exasperation.

After dinner that evening there was a battle royal. Freddy was a quick-tempered man, unused to opposi-tion, and he gave George the rough side of his tongue. I gather that it was very rough indeed. The women who sought to restrain his violence were sternly silenced. Perhaps for the first time in his life Freddy would not listen to his mother. George was obstinate and sullen. He had made up his mind and if his father didn't like it he could lump it. Freddy was peremptory. He forbade George to go back to Germany. George answered that he was twenty-one and his own master. He would go where he chose. Freddy swore he would not give him a penny.

"All right, I'll earn money."

"You! You've never done a stroke of work in your life. What do you expect to do to earn money?"

"Sell old clothes," grinned George.

There was a gasp from all of them. Muriel was so taken aback that she said a stupid thing.

"Like a Jew?"

"Well, aren't I a Jew? And aren't you a Jewess and isn't Daddy a Jew? We're all Jews, the whole gang of us, and everyone knows it and what the hell's the good of pretending we're not?"

Then a very dreadful thing happened. Freddy burst suddenly into tears. I'm afraid he didn't behave very much like Sir Adolphus Bland, Bart., M.P., and the good old English gentleman he so much wanted to be,

but like an emotional Adolph Bleikogel who loved his
son and wept with mortification because the great
hopes he had set on him were brought to nothing and
the ambition of his life was frustrated. He cried noisily
with great loud sobs and pulled his beard and beat his
breast and rocked to and fro. Then they all began to
cry, old Lady Bland and Muriel, and Ferdy, who
sniffed and blew his nose and wiped the tears streaming
down his face, and even George cried. Of course it was
very painful, but to our rough Anglo-Saxon temperament I am afraid it must seem also a trifle ridiculous.
No one tried to console anybody else. They just sobbed
and sobbed. It broke up the party.

But it had no result on the situation. George remained
obdurate. His father would not speak to him. There
were more scenes. Muriel sought to excite his pity; he
was deaf to her piteous entreaties, he did not seem to
mind if he broke her heart, he did not care two hoots
if he killed his father. Ferdy appealed to him as a sportsman and a man of the world. George was flippant and
indeed personally offensive. Old Lady Bland with her
guttural German accent and strong common sense
argued with him, but he would not listen to reason. It
was she, however, who at last found a way out. She
made George acknowledge that it was no use to throw
away all the beautiful things the world laid at his feet
unless he had talent. Of course he thought he had, but he
might be mistaken. It was not worth while to be a
second-rate pianist. His only excuse, his only justification, was genius. If he had genius his family had no
right to stand in his way.

"You can't expect me to show genius already," said George. "I shall have to work for years."

"Are you sure you are prepared for that?"

"It's my only wish in the world. I'll work like a dog. I only want to be given my chance."

This was the proposition she made. His father was determined to give him nothing, and obviously they could not let the boy starve. He had mentioned five pounds a week. Well, she was willing to give him that herself. He could go back to Germany and study for two years. At the end of that time he must come back and they would get some competent and disinterested person to hear him play, and if then that person said he showed promise of becoming a first-rate pianist no further obstacles would be placed in his way. He would be given every advantage, help and encouragement. If on the other hand that person decided that his natural gifts were not such as to ensure ultimate success he must promise faithfully to give up all thoughts of making music his profession and in every way accede to his father's wishes. George could hardly believe his ears.

"Do you mean that, Granny?"

"I do."

"But will Daddy agree?"

"I vill see dat he does," she answered.

George seized her in his arms and impetuously kissed her on both cheeks.

"Darling," he cried.

"Ah, but de promise?"

He gave her his solemn word of honour that he would faithfully abide by the terms of the arrangement. Two

days later he went back to Germany. Though his father
consented unwillingly to his going, and indeed could
not help doing so, he would not be reconciled to him and
when he left refused to say good-bye to him. I imagine
that in no other manner could he have caused himself
such pain. I permit myself a trite remark. It is strange
that men, inhabitants for so short a while of an alien and
inhuman world, should go out of their way to cause
themselves so much unhappiness.

George had stipulated that during his two years
of study his family should not visit him, so that when
Muriel heard some months before he was due to come
home that I was passing through Munich on my way to
Vienna, whither business called me, it was not unnatural that she should ask me to look him up. She was
anxious to have first-hand information about him. She
gave me George's address and I wrote ahead, telling
him I was spending a day in Munich, and asked him to
lunch with me. His answer awaited me at the hotel. He
said he worked all day and could not spare the time to
lunch with me, but if I would come to his studio about
six he would like to show me that and if I had nothing
better to do would love to spend the evening with me.
So soon after six I went to the address he gave me. He
lived on the second floor of a large block of flats and
when I came to his door I heard the sound of piano-
playing. It stopped when I rang and George opened the
door for me. I hardly recognized him. He had grown
very fat. His hair was extremely long, it curled all over
his head in picturesque confusion; and he had certainly

not shaved for three days. He wore a grimy pair of Oxford bags, a tennis shirt and slippers. He was not very clean and his fingernails were rimmed with black. It was a startling change from the spruce, slim youth so elegantly dressed in such beautiful clothes that I had last seen. I could not but think it would be a shock to Ferdy to see him now. The studio was large and bare; on the walls were three or four unframed canvases of a highly cubist nature; there were several armchairs much the worse for wear, and a grand piano. Books were littered about and old newspapers and art magazines. It was dirty and untidy and there was a frousty smell of stale beer and stale smoke.

"Do you live here alone?" I asked.

"Yes, I have a woman who comes in twice a week and cleans up. But I make my own breakfast and lunch."

"Can you cook?"

"Oh, I only have bread and cheese and a bottle of beer for lunch. I dine at a *bier stube.*"

It was pleasant to discover that he was very glad to see me. He seemed in great spirits and extremely happy. He asked after his relations and we talked of one thing and another. He had a lesson twice a week and for the rest of the time practised. He told me that he worked ten hours a day.

"That's a change," I said.

He laughed.

"Daddy said I was born tired. I wasn't really lazy. I didn't see the use of working at things that bored me."

I asked him how he was getting on with the piano.

He seemed to be satisfied with his progress and I begged him to play to me.

"Oh, not now. I'm all in, I've been at it all day. Let's go out and dine and come back here later and then I'll play. I generally go to the same place; there are several students I know there, and it's rather fun."

Presently we set out. He put on socks and shoes and a very old golf coat, and we walked together through the wide quiet streets. It was a brisk cold day. His step was buoyant. He looked round him with a sigh of delight.

"I love Munich," he said. "It's the only city in the world where there's art in the very air you breathe. After all, art is the only thing that matters, isn't it? I loathe the idea of going home."

"All the same I'm afraid you'll have to."

"I know. I'll go all right, but I'm not going to think about it till the time comes."

"When you do, you might do worse than get a hair-cut. If you don't mind my saying so you look almost too artistic to be convincing."

"You English, you're such Philistines," he said.

He took me to a rather large restaurant in a side street, crowded even at that early hour with people dining and furnished heavily in the German medieval style. A table covered with a red cloth, well away from the air, was reserved for George and his friends, and when we went to it four or five youths were at it. There was a Pole studying Oriental languages, a student of philosophy, a painter—I suppose the author of George's cubist pictures—a Swede, and a young man who introduced himself to me, clicking his heels, as Hans

Reiting, *dichter*, namely Hans Reiting, poet. Not one of them was more than twenty-two and I felt a trifle out of it. They all addressed George as *du* and I noticed that his German was extremely fluent. I had not spoken it for some time and mine was rusty, so that I could not take much part in the lively conversation. But nevertheless I thoroughly enjoyed myself. They ate sparingly, but drank a good deal of beer. They talked of art and literature and life and ethics and motor-cars and women. They were very revolutionary, and though gay very much in earnest. They were contemptuous of everyone you had ever heard of, and the only point on which they all agreed was that in this topsy-turvy world only the vulgar could hope for success. They argued points of technique with animation, and contradicted one another, and shouted and were obscene. They had a grand time.

At about eleven George and I walked back to his studio. Munich is a city that frolics demurely, and except about the Marienplatz the streets were still and empty. When we got in he took off his coat and said:

"Now I'll play to you."

I sat in one of the dilapidated armchairs, and a broken spring stuck into my behind, but I made myself as comfortable as I could. George played Chopin. I know very little of music, and that is one of the reasons for which I have found this story difficult to write. When I go to a concert at the Queen's Hall and in the intervals read the programme it is all Greek to me. I know nothing of harmony and counterpoint. I shall never forget how humiliated I felt once when, having come to Munich for a

Wagner Festival, I went to a wonderful performance of *Tristan und Isolde* and never heard a note of it. The first few bars sent me off and I began to think of what I was writing, my characters leapt into life and I heard their long conversations, I suffered their pains and was a party to their joy; the years swept by and all sorts of things happened to me, the spring brought me its rapture and in the winter I was cold and hungry; and I loved and I hated and I died. I suppose there were intervals in which I walked round and round the garden and probably ate *schinken brödchen* and drank beer, but I have no recollection of them. The only thing I know is that when the curtain for the last time fell I woke with a start. I had had a wonderful time, but I could not help thinking it was very stupid of me to come such a long way and spend so much money if I couldn't pay attention to what I heard and saw.

I knew most of the things George played. They were the familiar pieces of concert programmes. He played with a great deal of dash. Then he played Beethoven's *Appassionata*. I used to play it myself when I played the piano (very badly) in my far distant youth and I still knew every note of it. Of course it is a classic and a great work, it would be foolish to deny it, but I confess that at this time of day it leaves me cold. It is like *Paradise Lost*, splendid, but a trifle stolid. This too George played with vigour. He sweated profusely. At first I could not make out what was the matter with his playing, something did not seem to me quite right, and then it struck me that the two hands did not exactly synchronize, so that there was ever so slight an interval between the bass and the treble; but I repeat, I am ignorant of these things; what disconcerted me might have been merely the effect of his having drunk a good deal of beer that evening, or indeed only my fancy. I said all I could think of to praise him.

"Of course I know I need a lot more work. I'm only a beginner, but I know I can do it. I feel it in my bones. It'll take me ten years, but then I shall be a pianist."

He was tired and came away from the piano. It was after midnight and I suggested going, but he would not hear of it. He opened a couple of bottles of beer and lit his pipe. He wanted to talk.

"Are you happy here?" I asked him.

"Very," he answered gravely. "I'd like to stay for ever. I've never had such fun in my life. This evening for instance. Wasn't it grand?"

"It was very jolly. But one can't go on leading the student's life. Your friends here will grow older and go away."

"Others'll come. There are always students here and people like that."

"Yes, but you'll grow older too. Is there anything more lamentable than the middle-aged man who tries to go on living the undergraduate's life? The old fellow who wants to be a boy among boys, and tries to persuade himself that they'll accept him as one of themselves— how ridiculous he is. It can't be done."

"I feel so at home here. My poor father wants me to be an English gentleman. It gives me gooseflesh. I'm not a sportsman. I don't care a damn for hunting and shooting and playing cricket. I was only acting."

"You gave a very natural performance."

"It wasn't till I came here that I knew it wasn't real. I loved Eton, and Oxford was a riot, but all the same I knew I didn't belong. I played the part all right, because acting's in my blood, but there was always something in me that wasn't satisfied. The house in Grosvenor Square is a freehold, and Daddy paid a hundred and eighty thousand pounds for Tilby; I don't know if you understand what I mean, I felt they were just furnished houses we'd taken for the season and one of these days we'd pack up and the real owners would come back."

I listened to him attentively, but I wondered how much he was describing what he had obscurely felt and how much he imagined now in his changed circumstances that he had felt.

"I used to hate hearing Great-uncle Ferdy tell his Jewish stories. I thought it so damned mean. I understand now; it was a safety valve. My God, the strain of being a man about town. It's easier for Daddy, he can play the old English squire at Tilby, but in the city he can be himself. He's all right. I've taken the make-up off and my stage clothes and at last I can be my real self too. What a relief! You know, I don't like English people. I never really know where I am with you. You're so dull and conventional. You never let yourselves go. There's no freedom in you, freedom of the soul, and you're such funks. There's nothing in the world you're so frightened of as doing the wrong thing."

"Don't forget that you're English yourself, George," I murmured.

He laughed.

"I? I'm not English. I haven't got a drop of English blood in me. I'm a Jew and you know it, and a German Jew into the bargain. I don't want to be English. I want to be a Jew. My friends are Jews. You don't know how much more easy I feel with them. I can be myself. We did everything we could to avoid Jews at home; Mummy because she was blonde thought she could get away with it and pretended she was a Gentile. What rot! D'you know, I have a lot of fun wandering about the Jewish parts of Munich and looking at the people. I went to Frankfort once—there are a lot of them there —and I walked about and looked at the frowsy old men with their hooked noses and the fat women with their false hair. I felt such a sympathy for them, I felt I belonged to them, I could have kissed them. When they looked at me I wondered if they knew that I was one of them. I wish to God I knew Yiddish. I'd like to become friends with them, and go into their houses and eat Kosher food and all that sort of thing. I wanted to go to a synagogue, but I was afraid I'd do the wrong thing and be kicked out. I like the smell of the Ghetto and the sense of life, and the mystery and the dust and the squalor and the romance. I shall never get the longing for it out of my head now. That's the real thing. All the rest is only pretence."

"You'll break your father's heart," I said.

"It's his or mine. Why can't he let me go? There's Harry. Harry would love to be squire of Tilby. He'd be an English gentleman all right. You know, Mummy's set her heart on my marrying a Christian. Harry would love to. He'll found the good old English family all right. After all, I ask so little. I only want five pounds a week, and they can keep the title and the park and the Gainsboroughs and the whole bag of tricks."

"Well, the fact remains that you gave your solemn word of honour to go back after two years."

"I'll go back all right," he said sullenly. "Lea Makart has promised to come and hear me play."

"What'll you do if she says you're no good?"

"Shoot myself," he said gaily.

"What nonsense," I answered in the same tone.

"Do *you* feel at home in England?"

"No," I said, "but then I don't feel at home any-where else."

But he was quite naturally not interested in me.

"I loathe the idea of going back. Now that I know what life has to offer I wouldn't be an English country gentleman for anything in the world. My God, the bore-dom of it!"

"Money's a very nice thing and I've always under-stood it's very pleasant to be an English peer."

"Money means nothing to me. I want none of the things it can buy, and I don't happen to be a snob."

It was growing very late and I had to get up early next day. It seemed unnecessary for me to pay too much attention to what George said. It was the sort of non-sense a young man might very well indulge in when thrown suddenly among painters and poets. Art is strong wine and needs a strong head to carry. The divine fire burns most efficiently in those who temper its fury with horse sense. After all, George was not twenty-three

yet. Time teaches. And when all was said and done his
future was no concern of mine. I bade him good-night
and walked back to my hotel. The stars were shining in
the indifferent sky. I left Munich in the morning.

I did not tell Muriel on my return to London what
George had said to me, or what he looked like, but con-
tented myself with assuring her that he was well and
happy, working very hard, and seemed to be leading a
virtuous and sober life. Six months later he came home.
Muriel asked me to go down to Tilby for the week-end:
Ferdy was bringing Lea Makart to hear George play
and he particularly wished me to be there. I accepted.
Muriel met me at the station.

"How did you find George?" I asked.

"He's very fat, but he seems in great spirits. I think
he's pleased to be back again. He's been very sweet to
his father."

"I'm glad of that."

"Oh, my dear, I do hope Lea Makart will say he's
no good. It'll be such a relief to all of us."

"I'm afraid it'll be a terrible disappointment to him."

"Life is full of disappointments," said Muriel crisply.
"But one learns to put up with them."

I gave her a smile of amusement. We were sitting in
a Rolls, and there was a footman as well as a chauffeur
on the box. She wore a string of pearls that had probably
cost forty thousand pounds. I recollected that in the
birthday honours Sir Adolphus Bland had not been one
of the three gentlemen on whom the King had been
pleased to confer a peerage.

Lea Makart was able to make only a flying visit. She was playing that evening at Brighton and would motor over to Tilby on the Sunday morning for luncheon. She was returning to London the same day because she had a concert in Manchester on the Monday. George was to play in the course of the afternoon.

"He's practising very hard," his mother told me. "That's why he didn't come with me to meet you."

We turned in at the park gates and drove up the imposing avenue of elms that led to the house. I found that there was no party.

I met the dowager Lady Bland for the first time. I had always been curious to see her. I had had in my mind's eye a somewhat sensational picture of an old, old Jewish woman who lived alone in her grand house in Portland Place and, with a finger in every pie, ruled her family with a despotic hand. She did not disappoint me. She was of a commanding presence, rather tall, and stout without being corpulent. Her countenance was markedly Hebraic. She wore a rather heavy moustache and a wig of a peculiarly metallic brown. Her dress was very grand, of black brocade, and she had a row of large diamond stars on her breast and round her neck a chain of diamonds. Diamond rings gleamed on her wrinkled hands. She spoke in a rather loud harsh voice and with a strong German accent. When I was introduced to her she fixed me with shining eyes. She summed me up with despatch and to my fancy at all events made no attempt to conceal from me that the judgment she formed was unfavourable.

"You have known my brother Ferdinand for many

years, is it not so?" she said, rolling a guttural *r*. "My
brother Ferdinand has always moved in very good society. Where is Sir Adolphus, Muriel? Does he know
your guest is arrived? And will you not send for George?
If he does not know his pieces by now he will not know
them by to-morrow."

Muriel explained that Freddy was finishing a round
of golf with his secretary and that she had had George
told I was there. Lady Bland looked as though she
thought Muriel's replies highly unsatisfactory and
turned again to me.

"My daughter tells me you have been in Italy?"

"Yes, I've only just come back."

"It is a beautiful country. How is the King?"

I said I did not know.

"I used to know him when he was a little boy. He
was not very strong then. His mother, Queen Margarita,
was a great friend of mine. They thought he would
never marry. The Duchess of Aosta was very angry
when he fell in love with that Princess of Montenegro."

She seemed to belong to some long past period of
history, but she was very alert and I imagine that little
escaped her beady eyes. Freddy, very spruce in plus
fours, presently came in. It was amusing and yet a little
touching to see this grey-bearded man, as a rule somewhat domineering, so obviously on his best behaviour
with the old lady. He called her Mamma. Then George
came in. He was as fat as ever, but he had taken my
advice and had his hair cut; he was losing his boyish
looks, but he was a powerful and well-set-up young
man. It was good to see the pleasure he took in his tea.

He ate quantities of sandwiches and great hunks of cake. He had still a boy's appetite. His father watched him with a tender smile, and as I looked at him I could not be surprised at the attachment which they all so obviously felt for him. He had an ingenuousness, a charm and an enthusiasm which were certainly very pleasant. There was about him a generosity of demeanour, a frankness and a natural cordiality which could not but make people take to him. I do not know whether it was owing to a hint from his grandmother or merely of his own good nature, but it was plain that he was going out of his way to be nice to his father; and in his father's soft eyes, in the way he hung upon the boy's words, in his pleased, proud and happy look, you felt how bitterly the estrangement of the last two years had weighed on him. He adored George.

We played golf in the morning, a three-ball match, since Muriel, having to go to Mass, could not join us, and at one Ferdy arrived in Lea Makart's car. We sat down to luncheon. Of course Lea Makart's reputation was well-known to me. She was acknowledged to be the greatest woman pianist in Europe. She was a very old friend of Ferdy's, who with his interest and patronage had greatly helped her at the beginning of her career, and it was he who had arranged for her to come and give her opinion of George's chances. At one time I went as often as I could to hear her play. She had no affectations; she played as a bird sings, without any appearance of effort, very naturally, and the silvery notes dripped from her light fingers in a curiously spontaneous manner, so that it gave you the impression that she was improvising those complicated rhythms. They used to tell me that her technique was wonderful. I could never make up my mind how much the delight her playing gave me was due to her person. In those days she was the most ethereal thing you could imagine, and it was surprising that a creature so sylphlike should be capable of so much power. She was very slight, pale, with enormous eyes and magnificent black hair, and at the piano she had a childlike wistfulness that was most appealing. She was very beautiful in a hardly human way, and when she played, a little smile on her closed lips, she seemed to be remembering things she had heard in another world. Now, however, a woman in the early forties, she was sylphlike no more; she was stout and her face had broadened; she had no longer that lovely remoteness, but the authority of her long succession of triumphs. She was brisk, businesslike and somewhat overwhelming. Her vitality lit her with a natural spotlight as his sanctity surrounds the saint with a halo. She was not interested in anything very much but her own affairs, but since she had humour and knew the world she was able to invest them with gaiety. She held the conversation, but did not absorb it. George talked little. Every now and then she gave him a glance, but did not try to draw him in. I was the only Gentile at the table. All but old Lady Bland spoke perfect English, yet I could not help feeling that they did not speak like English people; I think they rounded their vowels more than we do, they certainly spoke louder, and the words seemed not to fall, but to gush from their lips. I think if I had been in another room where I could hear the tone but not the words of their speech I should have thought it was in a foreign language that they were conversing. The effect was slightly disconcerting.

Lea Makart wished to set out for London at about six, so it was arranged that George should play at four. Whatever the result of the audition, I felt that I, a stranger in the circle which her departure must render exclusively domestic, would be in the way and so, pretexting an early engagement in town next morning, I asked her if she would take me with her in her car.

At a little before four we all wandered into the drawing-room. Old Lady Bland sat on a sofa with Ferdy; Freddy, Muriel and I made ourselves comfortable in armchairs; and Lea Makart sat by herself. She chose instinctively a high-backed Jacobean chair that had somewhat the air of a throne, and in a yellow dress, with her olive skin, she looked very handsome. She had magnificent eyes. She was very much made up and her mouth was scarlet.

George gave no sign of nervousness. He was already seated at the piano when I went in with his father and mother, and he watched us quietly settling ourselves down. He gave me the shadow of a smile. When he saw that we were all at our ease he began to play. He played Chopin. He played two waltzes that were familiar to me, a polonaise and an *étude*. He played with a great deal of *brio*. I wish I knew music well enough to give an exact description of his playing. It had strength and a youthful exuberance, but I felt that he missed what to me is the peculiar charm of Chopin, the tenderness, the nervous melancholy, the wistful gaiety and the slightly faded romance that reminds me always of an early Victorian keepsake. And again I had the vague sensation, so slight that it almost escaped me, that the two hands did not quite synchronize. I looked at Ferdy and saw him give his sister a look of faint surprise. Muriel's eyes were fixed on the pianist, but presently she dropped them and for the rest of the time stared at the floor. His father looked at him too, and his eyes were steadfast, but unless I was much mistaken he went pale and his face betrayed something like dismay. Music was in the blood of all of them, all their lives they had heard the greatest pianists in the world, and they judged with instinctive precision. The only person whose face betrayed no emotion was Lea Makart. She listened very attentively. She was as still as an image in a niche.

At last he stopped and turning round on his seat faced her. He did not speak.

"What is it you want me to tell you?" she asked.

They looked into one another's eyes.

"I want you to tell me whether I have any chance of becoming in time a pianist in the first rank."

"Not in a thousand years."

For a moment there was a dead silence. Freddy's head sank and he looked down at the carpet at his feet. His wife put out her hand and took his. But George continued to look steadily at Lea Makart.

"Ferdy has told me the circumstances," she said at last. "Don't think I'm influenced by them. Nothing of this is very important." She made a great sweeping gesture that took in the magnificent room with the beautiful things it contained and all of us. "If I thought you had in you the makings of an artist I shouldn't hesitate to beseech you to give up everything for art's sake. Art is the only thing that matters. In comparison with art, wealth and rank and power are not worth a row of pins." She gave us a look so sincere that it was void of insolence. "We are the only people who count. We give the world significance. You are only our raw material."

I was not too pleased to be included with the rest under that heading, but that is neither here nor there.

"Of course I can see that you've worked very hard. Don't think it's been wasted. It will always be a pleasure to you to be able to play the piano, and it will enable you to appreciate great playing as no ordinary person can hope to do. Look at your hands. They're not a pianist's hands."

Involuntarily I glanced at George's hands. I had never noticed them before. I was astounded to see how podgy they were and how short and stumpy the fingers.

"Your ear is not quite perfect. I don't think you can ever hope to be more than a very competent amateur. In art the difference between the amateur and the professional is immeasurable."

George did not reply. Except for his pallor no one would have known that he was listening to the blasting of all his hopes. The silence that fell was quite awful. Lea Makart's eyes suddenly filled with tears.

"But don't take my opinion alone," she said. "After all, I'm not infallible. Ask somebody else. You know how good and generous Paderewski is. I'll write to him about you and you can go down and play to him. I'm sure he'll hear you."

George now gave a little smile. He had very good manners and, whatever he was feeling, did not want to make the situation too difficult for others.

"I don't think that's necessary. I am content to accept your verdict. To tell you the truth it's not so very different from my master's in Munich."

He got up from the piano and lit a cigarette. It eased the strain. The others moved a little in their chairs. Lea Makart smiled at George.

"Shall I play to you?" she said.

"Yes, do."

She got up and went to the piano. She took off the rings with which her fingers were laden. She played Bach. I do not know the names of the pieces, but I recognized the stiff ceremonial of the frenchified little German courts and the sober, thrifty comfort of the burghers, and the dancing on the village green, the green trees that looked like Christmas trees, and the sunlight on the wide German country, and a tender coziness; and in my nostrils there was a warm scent of the soil and I was conscious of a sturdy strength that seemed to have its roots deep in mother earth, and of an elemental power that was timeless and had no home in space. She played exquisitely, with a soft brilliance that made you think of the full moon shining at dusk in the summer sky. With another part of me I watched the others and I saw how intensely they were conscious of the experience. They were rapt. I wished with all my heart that I could get from music the wonderful exaltation that possessed them. She stopped, a smile hovered on her lips, and she put on her rings. George gave a little chuckle.

"That clinches it, I fancy," he said.

The servants brought in tea, and after tea Lea Makart and I bade the company farewell and got into the car. We drove up to London. She talked all the way, if not brilliantly at all events with immense gusto, she told me of her early years in Manchester and of the struggle of her beginnings. She was very interesting. She never even mentioned George; the episode was of no consequence; it was finished and she thought of it no more.

We little knew what was happening at Tilby. When we left, George went out on the terrace and presently his father joined him. Freddy had won the day, but he was not happy. With his more than feminine sensitiveness he felt all that George was feeling, and George's anguish simply broke his heart. He had never loved his son more than then. When he appeared George greeted him with a little smile. Freddy's voice broke. In a sudden and overwhelming emotion he found it in him to surrender the fruits of his victory.

"Look here, old boy," he said, "I can't bear to think that you've had such a disappointment. Would you like to go back to Munich for another year and then see?"

George shook his head.

"No, it wouldn't be any good. I've had my chance. Let's call it a day."

"Try not to take it too hard."

"You see, the only thing in the world I want is to be
a pianist. And there's nothing doing. It's a bit thick
if you come to think of it."

George, trying so hard to be brave, smiled wanly.

"Would you like to go round the world? You can get
one of your Oxford pals to go with you and I'll pay all
the expenses. You've been working very hard for a long
time."

"Thanks awfully, Daddy, we'll talk about it. I'm just
going for a stroll now."

"Shall I come with you?"

"I'd rather go alone."

Then George did a strange thing. He put his arm
round his father's neck and kissed him on the lips. He
gave a funny little moved laugh and walked away.
Freddy went back to the drawing-room. His mother,
Ferdy and Muriel were sitting there.

"Freddy, why don't you marry the boy?" said the old
lady. "He is twenty-three. It would take his mind off
his troubles and when he is married and has a baby he
will soon settle down like everybody else."

"Who is he to marry, Mamma?" asked Sir Adolphus,
smiling.

"That's not so difficult. Lady Frielinghausen came
to see me the other day with her daughter Violet. She
is a very nice maiden and she will have money of her
own. Lady Frielinghausen gave me to understand that
her Sir Jacob would come down very handsome if Violet
made a good match."

Muriel flushed.

"I hate Lady Frielinghausen. George is much too

young to marry. He can afford to marry anyone he likes."

Old Lady Bland gave her daughter a strange look. "You are a very foolish girl, Miriam," she said, using the name Muriel had long discarded. "As long as I am here I shall not allow you to commit a foolishness."

She knew as well as if Muriel had said it in so many words that she wanted George to marry a Gentile, but she knew also that so long as she was alive neither Freddy nor his wife would dare to suggest it.

But George did not go for a walk. Perhaps because the shooting season was about to open he took it into his head to go into the gun-room. He began to clean the gun that his mother had given him on his twentieth birthday. No one had used it since he went to Germany. Suddenly the servants were startled by a report. When they went into the gun-room they found George lying on the floor shot through the heart. Apparently the gun had been loaded and George while playing about with it had accidentally shot himself. One reads of such accidents in the paper often.

THE CREATIVE IMPULSE

THE CREATIVE IMPULSE

I SUPPOSE that very few people know how Mrs. Albert Forrester came to write *The Achilles Statue;* and since it has been acclaimed as one of the great novels of our time I cannot but think that a brief account of the circumstances that gave it birth must be of interest to all serious students of literature; and indeed, if, as the critics say, this is a book that will live, the following narrative, serving a better purpose than to divert an idle hour, may be regarded by the historian of the future as a curious footnote to the literary annals of our day.

Everyone of course remembers the success that attended the publication of *The Achilles Statue*. Month after month printers were kept busy printing, binders were kept busy binding, edition after edition; and the publishers, both in England and America, were hard put to it to fulfil the pressing orders of the booksellers. It was promptly translated into every European tongue and it has been recently announced that it will soon be possible to read it in Japanese and in Urdu. But it had previously appeared serially in magazines on both sides of the Atlantic and from the editors of these Mrs. Albert Forrester's agent had wrung a sum that can only be described as thumping. A dramatization of the work was made, which ran for a season in New York, and there is little doubt that when the play is produced in London it will have an equal success. The film rights have been sold at a great price. Though the amount that Mrs. Albert Forrester is reputed (in literary circles) to have made is probably exaggerated, there can be no doubt that she will have earned enough money from this one book to save her for the rest of her life from any financial anxiety.

It is not often that a book meets with equal favour from the public and the critics, and that she, of all persons, had (if I may so put it) squared the circle must have proved the more gratifying to Mrs. Albert Forrester, since, though she had received the commendation of the critics in no grudging terms (and indeed had come to look upon it as her due) the public had always remained strangely insensible to her merit. Each work she published, a slender volume beautifully printed and bound in white buckram, was hailed as a masterpiece, always to the length of a column, and, in the weekly reviews which you see only in the dusty library of a very long-established club, even to the extent of a page; and all well-read persons read and praised it. But well-read persons apparently do not buy books, and she did not sell. It was indeed a scandal that so distinguished an author, with an imagination so delicate and a style so exquisite, should remain neglected of the vulgar. In America she was almost completely unknown; and though Mr. Carl Van Vechten had written an article berating the public for its obtuseness, the public remained callous. Her agent, a warm admirer of her genius, had blackmailed an American publisher into taking two of her books by refusing, unless he did so, to let him have others (trashy novels, doubtless) that he badly wanted, and they had been duly published. The reception they received from the press was flattering and showed that in America the best minds were sensitive to her talent; but when it came to the third book the American publisher (in the coarse way publishers have) told the agent that any money he had to spare he preferred to spend on synthetic gin.

Since *The Achilles Statue* Mrs. Albert Forrester's previous books have been republished (and Mr. Carl Van Vechten has written another article pointing out sadly, but firmly, that he had drawn the attention of the reading world to the merits of this exceptional writer fully fifteen years ago), and they have been so widely advertised that they can scarcely have escaped the cultured reader's attention. It is unnecessary, therefore, for me to give an account of them; and it would certainly be no more than cold potatoes after those two subtle articles by Mr. Carl Van Vechten. Mrs. Albert Forrester began to write early. Her first work (a volume of elegies) appeared when she was a maiden of eighteen; and published, every two or three years, for she had too exalted a conception of her art to hurry her production, a volume either of verse or prose. When *The Achilles Statue* was written she had reached the respectable age of fifty-seven, so that it will be readily surmised that the number of her works was considerable. She had given the world half a dozen volumes of verse, published under Latin titles, such as *Felicitas, Pax Maris* and *Aes Triplex*, all of the graver kind, for her muse, disinclined to skip on a light, fantastic toe, trod a somewhat solemn measure. She remained faithful to the Elegy, and the Sonnet claimed much of her attention; but her chief distinction was to revive the Ode, a form of poetry that the poets of the present day somewhat neglect; and it may be asserted with confidence that her *Ode to President Fallières* will find a place in every anthology of English verse. It is admirable not only for the noble sonority of its rhythms, but also for its felicitous description of the pleasant land of France. Mrs. Albert Forrester wrote of the valley of the Loire with its memories of Du Bellay, of Chartres and the jewelled windows of its cathedral, of the sun-swept cities of Provence, with a sympathy all the more remarkable since she had never penetrated farther into France than Boulogne, which she visited shortly after her marriage on an excursion steamer from Margate. But the physical mortification of being extremely seasick and the intellectual humiliation of discovering that the inhabitants of that popular seaside resort could not understand her fluent and idiomatic French made her determine not to expose herself a second time to experiences which were at once undignified and unpleasant; and she never again embarked on the treacherous element which she however sang (*Pax Maris*) in numbers both grave and sweet.

There are some fine passages too in the *Ode to Woodrow Wilson*, and I regret that, owing to a change in her sentiments towards that no doubt excellent man, the author decided not to reprint it. But I think it must be admitted that Mrs. Albert Forrester's most distinguished work was in prose. She wrote several volumes of brief but perfectly constructed essays on such subjects as Autumn in Sussex, Queen Victoria, Death, Spring in Norfolk, Georgian Architecture, Monsieur de Diaghileff and Dante; she also wrote works, both erudite and whimsical, on the Jesuit Architecture of the XVIIth Century, and on the Literary Aspect of the Hundred Years' War. It was her prose that gained her that body of devoted admirers, fit though few, as with her rare gift of phrase she herself put it, that proclaimed her the greatest master of the English language that this century has seen. She admitted herself that it was her style, sonorous yet racy, polished yet eloquent, that was her strong point; and it was only in her prose that she had occasion to exhibit the delicious but restrained humour that her readers found so irresistible. It was not a humour of ideas, nor even a humour of words; it was much more subtle than that, it was a humour of punctuation: in a flash of inspiration she had discovered the comic possibilities of the semicolon, and of this she had made abundant and exquisite use. She was able to place it in such a way that if you were a person of culture with a keen sense of humour, you did not exactly laugh through a horse-collar, but you giggled delightedly, and the greater your culture the more delightedly you giggled. Her friends said that it made every other form of humour coarse and exaggerated. Several writers had tried to imitate her; but in vain: whatever else you might say about Mrs. Albert

Forrester you were bound to admit that she was able to get every ounce of humour out of the semicolon and no one else could get within a mile of her.

Mrs. Albert Forrester lived in a flat not far from the Marble Arch, which combined the advantage of a good address and a moderate rent. It had a handsome drawing-room on the street and a large bedroom for Mrs. Albert Forrester, a darkish dining-room at the back and a small poky bedroom, next door to the kitchen, for Mr. Albert Forrester, who paid the rent. It was in the handsome drawing-room that Mrs. Albert Forrester every Tuesday afternoon received her friends. It was a severe and chaste apartment. On the walls was a paper designed by William Morris himself and on this, in plain black frames, mezzotints collected before mezzotints grew expensive; the furniture was of the Chippendale period, but for the roll-top desk, vaguely Louis XVI in character, at which Mrs. Albert Forrester wrote her works. This was pointed out to visitors the first time they came to see her, and there were few who looked at it without emotion. The carpet was thick and the lights discreet. Mrs. Albert Forrester sat in a straight-backed grandfather's chair covered with red damask. There was nothing ostentatious about it, but since it was the only comfortable chair in the room it set her apart as it were and above her guests. Tea was dispensed by a female of uncertain age, silent and colourless, who was never introduced to anyone but who was known to look upon it as a privilege to be allowed to save Mrs. Albert Forrester from the irksome duty of pouring out tea. She was thus able to devote herself

entirely to conversation, and it must be admitted that
her conversation was excellent. It was not sprightly;
and since it is difficult to indicate punctuation in speech
it may have seemed to some slightly lacking in humour,
but it was of wide range, solid, instructive and interesting. Mrs. Albert Forrester was well acquainted with
social science, jurisprudence and theology. She had
read much and her memory was retentive. She had
a pretty gift for quotation, which is a serviceable
substitute for wit, and having for thirty years known
more or less intimately a great many distinguished
people, she had a great many interesting anecdotes to
tell, which she placed with tact and which she did not
repeat more than was pardonable. Mrs. Albert Forrester had the gift of attracting the most varied persons,
and you were liable at one and the same time to meet
in her drawing-room an ex-prime minister, a newspaper
proprietor and the ambassador of a First Class Power.
I always imagined that these great people came because
they thought that here they rubbed shoulders with
Bohemia, but with a Bohemia sufficiently neat and
clean for them to be in no danger that the dirt would
come off on them. Mrs. Albert Forrester was deeply
interested in politics and I myself heard a cabinet
minister tell her frankly that she had a masculine
intelligence. She had been opposed to female suffrage,
but when it was at last granted to women she began to
dally with the idea of going into Parliament. Her difficulty was that she did not know which party to choose.

"After all," she said, with a playful shrug of her somewhat massive shoulders, "I cannot form a party of one."

Like many serious patriots, in her inability to know for certain which way the cat would jump she held her political opinions in suspense; but of late she had been definitely turning towards Labour as the best hope of the country, and if a safe seat were offered her it was felt fairly certain that she would not hesitate to come out into the open as a champion of the oppressed proletariat.

Her drawing-room was always open to foreigners, to Czecho-Slovaks, Italians and Frenchmen if they were distinguished and to Americans even if they were obscure. But she was not a snob and you seldom met there a duke unless he was of a peculiarly serious turn and a peeress only if in addition to her rank she had the passport of some small social solecism such as having been divorced, written a novel or forged a check, which might give her claim on Mrs. Albert Forrester's Catholic Sympathies. She did not much care for painters, who were shy and silent; and musicians did not interest her: even if they consented to play—and if they were celebrated they were too often reluctant—their music was a hindrance to conversation: if people wanted to hear music they could go to a concert; for her part she preferred the more subtle music of the soul. But her hospitality to writers, especially if they were promising and little known, was warm and constant. She had an eye for budding talent and there were few of the famous writers who from time to time drank a dish of tea with her whose first efforts she had not encouraged and whose early steps she had not guided. Her own position was too well assured for her to be capable of envy, and she had heard the word genius attached to her name too often to feel a trace of jealousy because the talents of others brought them a material success that was denied to her.

Mrs. Albert Forrester, confident in the judgment of posterity, could afford to be disinterested. With these elements then it is no wonder that she had succeeded in creating something as near the French salon of the eighteenth century as our barbarous nation has ever reached. To be invited to 'eat a bun and drink a cup of tea on Tuesday' was a privilege that few failed to recognize; and when you sat on your Chippendale chair in the discreetly lit but austere room, you could not but feel that you were living literary history. The American ambassador once said to Mrs. Albert Forrester:

"A cup of tea with you, Mrs. Forrester, is one of the richest intellectual treats which it has ever been my lot to enjoy."

It was indeed on occasion a trifle overwhelming. Mrs. Albert Forrester's taste was so perfect, she so inevitably admired the right thing and made the just observation about it, that sometimes you almost gasped for air. For my part I found it prudent to fortify myself with a cocktail or two before I exposed myself to the rarefied atmosphere of her society. Indeed, I very nearly found myself for ever excluded from it, for one afternoon, presenting myself at the door, instead of asking the maid who opened it: "Is Mrs. Forrester at home?" I asked: "Is there Divine Service to-day?"

Of course it was said in pure inadvertence, but it was unfortunate that the maid sniggered and one of Mrs.

Albert Forrester's most devoted admirers, Ellen Hanna-
way, happened to be at the moment in the hall taking
off her galoshes. She told my hostess what I had said
before I got into the drawing-room, and as I entered
Mrs. Albert Forrester fixed me with an eagle eye.

"Why did you ask if there was Divine Service to-
day?" she inquired.

I explained that I was absent-minded, but Mrs.
Albert Forrester held me with a gaze that I can only
describe as compelling.

"Do you mean to suggest that my parties are . . ."
She searched for a word. "Sacramental?"

I did not know what she meant, but did not like to
show my ignorance before so many clever people, and I
decided that the only thing was to seize my trowel and
the butter.

"Your parties are like you, dear lady, perfectly
beautiful and perfectly divine."

A little tremor passed through Mrs. Albert Forrester's
substantial frame. She was like a man who enters suddenly a room filled with hyacinths; the perfume is so
intoxicating that he almost staggers. But she relented.

"If you were trying to be facetious," she said, "I
should prefer you to exercise your facetiousness on my
guests rather than on my maids. . . . Miss Warren will
give you some tea."

Mrs. Albert Forrester dismissed me with a wave of
the hand, but she did not dismiss the subject, since for
the next two or three years whenever she introduced
me to someone she never failed to add:

"You must make the most of him, he only comes here

as a penance. When he comes to the door he always asks: 'Is there Divine Service to-day?' So amusing, isn't he?"

But Mrs. Albert Forrester did not confine herself to weekly tea-parties: every Saturday she gave a luncheon of eight persons; this according to her opinion being the perfect number for general conversation and her dining-room conveniently holding no more. If Mrs. Albert Forrester flattered herself upon anything it was not that her knowledge of English prosody was unique, but that her luncheons were celebrated. She chose her guests with care and an invitation to one of them was more than a compliment, it was a consecration. Over the luncheon-table it was possible to keep the conversation on a higher level than in the mixed company of a tea-party, and few can have left her dining-room without taking away with them an enhanced belief in Mrs. Albert Forrester's ability and a brighter faith in human nature. She only asked men, since, stout enthusiast for her sex as she was and glad to see women on other occasions, she could not but realize that they were inclined at table to talk exclusively to their next-door neighbours and thus hinder the general exchange of ideas that made her own parties an entertainment not only of the body but of the soul. For it must be said that Mrs. Albert Forrester gave you uncommonly good food, excellent wine and a first-rate cigar. Now to any-one who has partaken of literary hospitality this must appear very remarkable, since literary persons for the most part think highly and live plainly; their minds are occupied with the things of the spirit and they do not notice that the roast mutton is underdone and the potatoes cold: the beer is all right, but the wine has a sobering effect, and it is unwise to touch the coffee. Mrs. Albert Forrester was pleased enough to receive compliments on the fare she provided.

"If people do me the honour to break bread with me," she said, "it is only fair that I should give them as good food as they can get at home."

But if the flattery was excessive she deprecated it.

"You really embarrass me when you give me a meed of praise which is not my due. You must praise Mrs. Bulfinch."

"Who is Mrs. Bulfinch?"

"My cook."

"She's a treasure then, but you're not going to ask me to believe that she's responsible for the wine."

"Is it good? I'm terribly ignorant of such things; I put myself entirely in the hands of my wine-merchant."

But if mention was made of the cigars Mrs. Albert Forrester beamed.

"Ah, for them you must compliment Albert. It is Albert who chooses the cigars and I am given to understand that no one knows more about a cigar than Albert."

She looked at her husband, who sat at the end of the table, with the proud bright eyes of a pedigree hen (a Buff Orpington for choice) looking at her only chick. Then there was a quick flutter of conversation as the guests, anxious to be civil to their host and relieved at length to find an occasion, expressed their appreciation of his peculiar merit.

"You're very kind," he said. "I'm glad you like them."

Then he would give a little discourse on cigars, explaining the excellences he sought and regretting the deterioration in quality which had followed on the commercialization of the industry. Mrs. Albert Forrester listened to him with a complacent smile, and it was plain that she enjoyed this little triumph of his. Of course you cannot go on talking of cigars indefinitely, and as soon as she perceived that her guests were growing restive she broached a topic of more general, and it may be of more significant, interest. Albert subsided into silence. But he had had his moment.

It was Albert who made Mrs. Forrester's luncheons to some less attractive than her tea-parties, for Albert was a bore; but though without doubt perfectly conscious of the fact, she made a point that he should come to them and in fact had fixed upon Saturdays (for the rest of the week he was busy) in order that he should be able to. Mrs. Albert Forrester felt that her husband's presence on these festive occasions was an unavoidable debt that she paid to her own self-respect. She would never by a negligence admit to the world that she had married a man who was not spiritually her equal, and it may be that in the silent watches of the night she asked herself where indeed such could have been found. Mrs. Albert Forrester's friends were troubled by no such reticence and they said it was dreadful that such a woman should be burdened with such a man. They asked one another how she had ever come to marry him and (being most celibate) answered despairingly that no one ever knew why anybody married anybody else.

It was not that Albert was a verbose and aggressive bore; he did not buttonhole you with interminable stories or pester you with pointless jokes; he did not crucify you on a platitude or hamstring you with a commonplace; he was just dull. A cipher. Clifford Boyleston, for whom the French Romantics had no secrets and who was himself a writer of merit, had said that when you looked into a room into which Albert had just gone there was nobody there. This was thought very clever by Mrs. Albert Forrester's friends, and Rose Waterford, the well-known novelist and the most fearless of women, had ventured to repeat it to Mrs. Albert Forrester. Though she pretended to be annoyed, she had not been able to prevent the smile that rose to her lips. Her behaviour towards Albert could not but increase the respect in which her friends held her. She insisted that whatever in their secret hearts they thought of him, they should treat him with the decorum that was due to her husband. Her own demeanour was admirable. If he chanced to make an observation she listened to him with a pleasant expression, and when he fetched her a book that she wanted or gave her his pencil to make a note of an idea that had occurred to her, she always thanked him. Nor would she allow her friends pointedly to neglect him, and though, being a woman of tact, she saw that it would be asking too much of the world if she took him about with her always, and she went out much alone, yet her friends knew that she expected them to ask him to dinner at least once a year. He always accompanied her to public banquets when she was going to make a speech, and if she delivered a lecture she took care that he should have a seat on the platform.

Albert was, I believe, of average height, but perhaps because you never thought of him except in connection with his wife (of imposing dimensions) you only thought of him as a little man. He was spare and frail and looked older than his age. This was the same as his wife's. His hair, which he kept very short, was white and meagre, and he wore a stubby white moustache; his was a face, thin and lined, without a noticeable feature; and his blue eyes, which once might have been attractive, were now pale and tired. He was always very neatly dressed in pepper-and-salt trousers, which he chose always of the same pattern, a black coat and a grey tie with a small pearl pin in it. He was perfectly unobtrusive, and when he stood in Mrs. Albert Forrester's drawing-room to receive the guests whom she had asked to luncheon you noticed him as little as you noticed the quiet and gentlemanly furniture. He was well-mannered and it was with a pleasant, courteous smile that he shook hands with them.

"How do you do? I'm very glad to see you," he said if they were friends of some standing. "Keeping well, I hope?"

But if they were strangers of distinction coming for the first time to the house, he went to the door as they entered the drawing-room, and said:

"I am Mrs. Albert Forrester's husband. I will introduce you to my wife."

Then he led the visitor to where Mrs. Albert Forrester stood, with her back to the light, and she with a
glad and eager gesture advanced to make the stranger
welcome.

It was agreeable to see the demure pride he took in
his wife's literary reputation and the self-effacement
with which he furthered her interests. He was always
there when he was wanted and never when he wasn't.
His tact, if not deliberate, was instinctive. Mrs. Albert
Forrester was the first to acknowledge his merits.

"I really don't know what I should do without him,"
she said. "He's invaluable to me. I read him everything
I write and his criticisms are often very useful."

"Molière and his cook," said Miss Waterford.

"Is that funny, dear Rose?" asked Mrs. Forrester,
somewhat acidly.

When Mrs. Albert Forrester did not approve of a
remark, she had a way, that put many persons to confusion, of asking you whether it was a joke which she
was too dense to see. But it was impossible to embarrass Miss Waterford. She was a lady who in
the course of a long life had had many affairs, but
only one passion, and this was for printer's ink.
Mrs. Albert Forrester tolerated rather than approved
her.

"Come, come, my dear," she replied, "you know
very well that he wouldn't exist without you. He
wouldn't know us. It must be wonderful to him to come
in contact with all the best brains and the most distinguished people of our day."

"It may be that the bee would perish without the

hive which shelters it, but the bee nevertheless has a significance of its own."

And since Mrs. Albert Forrester's friends, though they knew all about art and literature, knew little about natural history, they had no reply to this observation. She went on:

"He doesn't interfere with me. He knows subconsciously when I don't want to be disturbed and, indeed, when I am following out a train of thought I find his presence in the room a comfort rather than a hindrance to me."

"Like a Persian cat," said Miss Waterford.

"But like a very well-trained, well-bred, and well-mannered Persian cat," answered Mrs. Forrester severely, thus putting Miss Waterford in her place.

But Mrs. Albert Forrester had not finished with her husband.

"We who belong to the intelligentsia," she said, "are apt to live in a world too exclusively our own. We are interested in the abstract rather than in the concrete, and sometimes I think that we survey the bustling world of human affairs in too detached a manner and from too serene a height. Do you not think that we stand in danger of becoming a little inhuman? I shall always be grateful to Albert because he keeps me in contact with the man in the street."

It was on account of this remark, to which none of her friends could deny the rare insight and subtlety that characterized so many of her utterances, that for some time Albert was known in her immediate circle as The Man in the Street. But this was only for a while, and it

was forgotten. He then became known as The Philatelist. It was Clifford Boyleston, with his wicked wit, who
invented the name. One day, his poor brain exhausted
by the effort to sustain a conversation with Albert, he
had asked in desperation:

"Do you collect stamps?"

"No," answered Albert mildly. "I'm afraid I don't."

But Clifford Boyleston had no sooner asked the
question than he saw its possibilities. He had written a
book on Baudelaire's aunt by marriage, which had
attracted the attention of all who were interested in
French literature, and was well known in his exhaustive
studies of the French spirit to have absorbed a goodly
share of the Gallic quickness and the Gallic brilliancy.
He paid no attention to Albert's disclaimer, but at the
first opportunity informed Mrs. Albert Forrester's
friends that he had at last discovered Albert's secret.
He collected stamps. He never met him afterwards
without asking him:

"Well, Mr. Forrester, how is the stamp collection?"
Or: "Have you been buying any stamps since I saw
you last?"

It mattered little that Albert continued to deny
that he collected stamps, the invention was too apt not
to be made the most of; Mrs. Albert Forrester's friends
insisted that he did, and they seldom spoke to him
without asking him how he was getting on. Even Mrs.
Albert Forrester, when she was in a specially gay
humour, would sometimes speak of her husband as
The Philatelist. The name really did seem to fit Albert
like a glove. Sometimes they spoke of him thus to his

face and they could not but appreciate the good nature with which he took it; he smiled unresentfully and presently did not even protest that they were mistaken.

Of course Mrs. Albert Forrester had too keen a social sense to jeopardize the success of her luncheons by allowing her more distinguished guests to sit on either side of Albert. She took care that only her older and more intimate friends should do this, and when the appointed victims came in she would say to them:

"I know you won't mind sitting by Albert, will you?"

They could only say that they would be delighted, but if their faces too plainly expressed their dismay she would pat their hands playfully and add:

"Next time you shall sit by me. Albert is so shy with strangers and you know so well how to deal with him."

They did: they simply ignored him. So far as they were concerned the chair in which he sat might as well have been empty. There was no sign that it annoyed him to be taken no notice of by persons who after all were eating food he paid for, since the earnings of Mrs. Forrester could certainly not have provided her guests with spring salmon and forced asparagus. He sat quiet and silent, and if he opened his mouth it was only to give a direction to one of the maids. If a guest were new to him he would let his eyes rest on him in a stare that would have been embarrassing if it had not been so childlike. He seemed to be asking himself what this strange creature was; but what answer his mild scrutiny gave him he never revealed. When the conversation grew animated he would look from one speaker to the other, but again you could not tell from his thin, lined face what he thought of the fantastic notions that were bandied across the table.

Clifford Boyleston said that all the wit and wisdom he heard passed over his head like water over a duck's back. He had given up trying to understand and now only made a semblance of listening. But Harry Oakland, the versatile critic, said that Albert was taking it all in; he found it all too, too marvellous, and with his poor, muddled brain he was trying desperately to make head or tail of the wonderful things he heard. Of course in the city he must boast of the distinguished persons he knew; perhaps there he was a light of learning and letters, an authority on the ideal; it would be perfectly divine to hear what he made of it all. Harry Oakland was one of Mrs. Albert Forrester's staunchest admirers, and had written a brilliant and subtle essay on her style. With his refined and even beautiful features he looked like a San Sebastian who had had an accident with a hair restorer; for he was uncommonly hirsute. He was a very young man, not thirty, but he had been in turn a dramatic critic, and a critic of fiction, a musical critic and a critic of painting. But he was getting a little tired of art and threatened to devote his talents in future to the criticism of sport.

Albert, I should explain, was in the city and it was a misfortune that Mrs. Forrester's friends thought she bore with meritorious fortitude that he was not even rich. There would have been something romantic in it if he had been a merchant prince who held the fate of nations in his hand or sent argosies, laden with rare spices, to those ports of the Levant the names of which have provided many a poet with so rich and rare a rhyme. But Albert was only a currant-merchant and was supposed to make no more than just enabled Mrs. Albert Forrester to conduct her life with distinction and even with liberality. Since his occupation kept him in his office till six o'clock he never managed to get to Mrs. Albert Forrester's Tuesdays till the most important visitors were gone. By the time he arrived, there were seldom more than three or four of her more intimate friends in the drawing-room, discussing with freedom and humour the guests who had departed, and when they heard Albert's key in the front-door they realized with one accord that it was late. In a moment he opened the door in his hesitating way and looked mildly in. Mrs. Albert Forrester greeted him with a bright smile.

"Come in, Albert, come in. I think you know everybody here."

Albert entered and shook hands with his wife's friends.

"Have you just come from the city?" she asked eagerly, though she knew there was nowhere else he could have come from. "Would you like a cup of tea?"

"No, thank you, my dear. I had tea in my office."

Mrs. Albert Forrester smiled still more brightly and the rest of the company thought she was perfectly wonderful with him.

"Ah, but I know you like a second cup. I will pour it out for you myself."

She went to the tea-table and, forgetting that the tea had been stewing for an hour and a half and was stone cold, poured him out a cup and added milk and sugar. Albert took it with a word of thanks, and meekly stirred it, but when Mrs. Forrester resumed the conversation which his appearance had interrupted, without tasting it he put it quietly down. His arrival was the signal for the party finally to break up, and one by one the remaining guests took their departure. On one occasion, however, the conversation was so absorbing and the point at issue so important that Mrs. Albert Forrester would not hear of their going.

"It must be settled once for all. And after all," she remarked in a manner that for her was almost arch, "this is a matter on which Albert may have something to say. Let us have the benefit of his opinion."

It was when women were beginning to cut their hair and the subject of discussion was whether Mrs. Albert Forrester should or should not shingle. Mrs. Albert Forrester was a woman of authoritative presence. She was large-boned and her bones were well covered; had she not been so tall and strong it might have suggested itself to you that she was corpulent. But she carried her weight gallantly. Her features were a little larger than life-size, and it was this that gave her face doubtless the look of virile intellectuality that it certainly possessed. Her skin was dark and you might have thought that she had in her veins some trace of Levantine blood: she admitted that she could not but think there was in her a gypsy strain and that would account, she felt, for the wild and lawless passion that sometimes characterized her poetry. Her eyes were large and black and bright, her nose like the great Duke of Wellington's, but more fleshy, and her chin square and determined. She had a big mouth, with full red lips, which owed nothing to cosmetics, for of these Mrs. Albert Forrester had never deigned to make use; and her hair, thick, solid and grey, was piled on the top of her head in such a manner as to increase her already commanding height. She was in appearance an imposing, not to say an alarming, female.

She was always very suitably dressed in rich materials of sombre hue and she looked every inch a woman of letters; but in her discreet way (being after all human and susceptible to vanity) she followed the fashions, and the cut of her gowns was modish. I think for some time she had hankered to shingle her hair, but she thought it more becoming to do it at the solicitation of her friends than on her own initiative.

"Oh, you must, you must," said Harry Oakland, in his eager, boyish way. "You'd look too, too wonderful."

Clifford Boyleston, who was now writing a book on Madame de Maintenon, was doubtful. He thought it a dangerous experiment.

"I think," he said, wiping his eyeglasses with a cambric handkerchief, "I think when one has made a type one should stick to it. What would Louis XIV have been without his wig?"

"I'm hesitating," said Mrs. Forrester. "After all, we must move with the times. I am of my day and I do not wish to lag behind. America, as Wilhelm Meister said, is here and now." She turned brightly to Albert. "What does my lord and master say about it? What is your opinion, Albert? To shingle or not to shingle, that is the question."

"I'm afraid my opinion is not of great importance, my dear," he answered mildly.

"To me it is of the greatest importance," answered Mrs. Albert Forrester, flatteringly.

She could not but see how beautifully her friends thought she treated The Philatelist.

"I insist," she proceeded, "I insist. No one knows me as you do, Albert. Will it suit me?"

"It might," he answered. "My only fear is that with your—statuesque appearance short hair would perhaps suggest, well, shall we say, the Isle of Greece where burning Sapho loved and sung."

There was a moment's embarrassed pause. Rose Waterford smothered a giggle, but the others preserved a stony silence. Mrs. Forrester's smile froze on her lips. Albert had dropped a brick.

"I always thought Byron a very mediocre poet," said Mrs. Albert Forrester at last.

The company broke up. Mrs. Albert Forrester did not shingle, nor indeed was the matter ever again referred to.

It was towards the end of another of Mrs. Albert Forrester's Tuesdays that the event occurred that had so great an influence on her literary career.

It had been one of her most successful parties. The

leader of the Labour Party had been there and Mrs.
Albert Forrester had gone as far as she could without
definitely committing herself to intimate to him that she
was prepared to throw in her lot with Labour. The time
was ripe and if she was ever to adopt a political career
she must come to a decision. A member of the French
Academy had been brought by Clifford Boyleston and,
though she knew he was wholly unacquainted with
English, it had gratified her to receive his affable compliment on her ornate and yet pellucid style. The American ambassador had been there and a young Russian
prince whose authentic Romanoff blood alone prevented him from looking a gigolo. A duchess who had
recently divorced her duke and married a jockey had
been very gracious; and her strawberry leaves, albeit
sere and yellow, undoubtedly added tone to the as-
sembly. There had been quite a galaxy of literary lights.
But now all, all were gone but Clifford Boyleston, Harry
Oakland, Rose Waterford, Oscar Charles and Simmons.
Oscar Charles was a little, gnome-like creature, young
but with the wizened face of a cunning monkey, with
gold spectacles, who earned his living in a government
office but spent his leisure in the pursuit of literature.
He wrote little articles for the sixpenny weeklies and
had a spirited contempt for the world in general. Mrs.
Albert Forrester liked him, thinking he had talent, but
though he always expressed the keenest admiration for
her style (it was indeed he who had named her the
mistress of the semicolon), his acerbity was so general
that she also somewhat feared him. Simmons was her

agent; a round-faced man who wore glasses so strong
that his eyes behind them looked strange and mis-
shapen. They reminded you of the eyes of some un-
couth crustacean that you had seen in an aquarium. He
came regularly to Mrs. Albert Forrester's parties, partly
because he had the greatest admiration for her genius
and partly because it was convenient for him to meet
prospective clients in her drawing-room.

Mrs. Albert Forrester, for whom he had long laboured
with but a trifling recompense, was not sorry to put
him in the way of earning an honest penny, and she
took care to introduce him, with warm expressions of
gratitude, to anyone who might be supposed to have
literary wares to sell. It was not without pride that she
remembered that the notorious and vastly lucrative
memoirs of Lady St. Swithin had been first mooted
in her drawing-room.

They sat in a circle of which Mrs. Albert Forrester
was the centre and discussed brightly, and, it must
be confessed, somewhat maliciously the various persons
who had been that day present. Miss Warren, the pallid
female who had stood for two hours at the tea-table,
was walking silently round the room collecting cups
that had been left here and there. She had some vague
employment, but was always able to get off in order to
pour out tea for Mrs. Albert Forrester, and in the
evening she typed Mrs. Albert Forrester's manuscripts.
Mrs. Albert Forrester did not pay her for this, thinking
quite rightly that as it was she did a great deal for the
poor thing; but she gave her the seats for the cinema
that were sent her for nothing and often presented her

with articles of clothing for which she had no further
use.

Mrs. Albert Forrester in her rather deep, full voice
was talking in a steady flow and the rest were listening
to her with attention. She was in good form and the
words that poured from her lips could have gone
straight down on paper without alteration. Suddenly
there was a noise in the passage as though something
heavy had fallen, and then the sound of an altercation.

Mrs. Albert Forrester stopped and a slight frown
darkened her really noble brow.

"I should have thought they knew by now that I will
not have this devastating racket in the flat. Would
you mind ringing the bell, Miss Warren, and asking
what is the reason of this tumult?"

Miss Warren rang the bell and in a moment the maid
appeared. Miss Warren at the door, in order not to
interrupt Mrs. Albert Forrester, spoke to her in under-
tones. But Mrs. Albert Forrester somewhat irritably
interrupted herself.

"Well, Carter, what is it? Is the house falling down or
has the Red Revolution at last broken out?"

"If you please, ma'am, it's the new cook's box,"
answered the maid. "The porter dropped it as he
was bringing it in and the cook got all upset about
it."

"What do you mean by the new cook?"

"Mrs. Bulfinch went away this afternoon, ma'am,"
said the maid.

Mrs. Albert Forrester stared at her.

"This is the first I've heard of it. Had Mrs. Bulfinch

given notice? The moment Mr. Forrester comes in tell him that I wish to speak to him."

"Very good, ma'am."

The maid went out and Miss Warren slowly returned to the tea-table. Mechanically, though nobody wanted them, she poured out several cups of tea.

"What a catastrophe!" cried Miss Waterford.

"You must get her back," said Clifford Boyleston. "She's a treasure, that woman, a remarkable cook, and she gets better and better every day."

But at that moment the maid came in again with a letter on a small plated salver and handed it to her mistress.

"What is this?" said Mrs. Albert Forrester.

"Mr. Forrester said I was to give you this letter when you asked for him, ma'am," said the maid.

"Where is Mr. Forrester then?"

"Mr. Forrester's gone, ma'am," answered the maid as though the question surprised her.

"Gone? That'll do. You can go."

The maid left the room and Mrs. Albert Forrester, with a look of perplexity on her large face, opened the letter. Rose Waterford has told me that her first thought was that Albert, fearful of his wife's displeasure at the departure of Mrs. Bulfinch, had thrown himself in the Thames. Mrs. Albert Forrester read the letter and a look of consternation crossed her face.

"Oh, monstrous," she cried. "Monstrous! Monstrous!"

"What is it, Mrs. Forrester?"

Mrs. Albert Forrester pawed the carpet with her foot like a restive, high-spirited horse pawing the ground, and crossing her arms with a gesture that is indescribable (but that you sometimes see in a fishwife who is going to make the very devil of a scene) bent her looks upon her curious and excessively startled friends.

"Albert has eloped with the cook."

There was a gasp of dismay. Then something terrible happened. Miss Warren, who was standing behind the tea-table, suddenly choked. Miss Warren, who never opened her mouth and whom no one ever spoke to, Miss Warren, whom not one of them, though he had seen her every week for three years, would have recognized in the street, Miss Warren suddenly burst into uncontrollable laughter. With one accord, aghast, they turned and stared at her. They felt as Balaam must have felt when his ass broke into speech. She positively shrieked with laughter. There was a nameless horror about the sight, as though something had on a sudden gone wrong with a natural phenomenon, and you were just as startled as though the chairs and tables without warning began to skip about the floor in an antic dance. Miss Warren tried to contain herself, but the more she tried the more pitilessly the laughter shook her, and seizing a handkerchief she stuffed it in her mouth and hurried from the room. The door slammed behind her.

"Hysteria," said Clifford Boyleston.

"Pure hysteria, of course," said Harry Oakland.

But Mrs. Albert Forrester said nothing.

The letter had dropped at her feet and Simmons, the agent, picked it up and handed it to her. She would not take it.

"Read it," she said. "Read it aloud."

Mr. Simmons pushed his spectacles up on his forehead and holding the letter very close to his eyes read as follows:

"MY DEAR,

"*Mrs. Bulfinch is in need of a change and has decided to leave, and as I do not feel inclined to stay on here without her I am going too. I have had all the literature I can stand and I am fed up with art.*

"*Mrs. Bulfinch does not care about marriage, but if you care to divorce me she is willing to marry me. I hope you will find the new cook satisfactory. She has excellent references. It may save you trouble if I inform you that Mrs. Bulfinch and I are living at 411, Kennington Road, S. E.*

"ALBERT."

No one spoke. Mr. Simmons slipped his spectacles back onto the bridge of his nose. The fact was that none of them, brilliant as they were and accustomed to find topics of conversation to suit every occasion, could think of an appropriate remark. Mrs. Albert Forrester was not the kind of woman to whom you could offer condolences, and each was too much afraid of the other's ridicule to venture upon the obvious. At last Clifford Boyleston came bravely to the rescue.

"One doesn't know what to say," he observed.

There was another silence and then Rose Waterford spoke.

"What does Mrs. Bulfinch look like?" she asked.

"How should I know?" answered Mrs. Albert Forrester, somewhat peevishly. "I have never looked at her. Albert always engaged the servants. She just came in for a moment so that I could see if her aura was satisfactory."

"But you must have seen her every morning when you did the housekeeping."

"Albert did the housekeeping. It was his own wish, so that I might be free to devote myself to my work. In this life one has to limit oneself."

"Did Albert order your luncheons?" asked Clifford Boyleston.

"Naturally. It was his province."

Clifford Boyleston slightly raised his eyebrows. What a fool he had been never to guess that it was Albert who was responsible for Mrs. Forrester's beautiful food! And of course it was owing to him that the excellent Chablis was always just sufficiently chilled to run coolly over the tongue, but never so cold as to lose its bouquet and its savour.

"He certainly knew good food and good wine."

"I always told you he had his points," answered Mrs. Albert Forrester, as though he were reproaching her. "You all laughed at him. You would not believe me when I told you that I owed a great deal to him."

There was no answer to this and once more silence, heavy and ominous, fell on the party. Suddenly Mr. Simmons flung a bombshell.

"You must get him back."

So great was her surprise that if Mrs. Albert Forrester had not been standing against the chimney-piece she would undoubtedly have staggered two paces to the rear.

"What on earth do you mean?" she cried. "I will never see him again as long as I live. Take him back? Never. Not even if he came and begged me on his bended knees."

"I didn't say take him back; I said get him back."

But Mrs. Albert Forrester paid no attention to the misplaced interruption.

"I have done everything for him. What would he be without me? I ask you. I have given him a position which never in his remotest dreams could he have aspired to."

None could deny that there was something magnificent in the indignation of Mrs. Albert Forrester, but it appeared to have little effect on Mr. Simmons.

"What are you going to live on?"

Mrs. Albert Forrester flung him a glance totally devoid of amiability.

"God will provide," she answered in freezing tones.

"I think it very unlikely," he returned.

Mrs. Albert Forrester shrugged her shoulders. She wore an outraged expression. But Mr. Simmons made himself as comfortable as he could on his chair and lit a cigarette.

"You know you have no warmer admirer of your art than me," he said.

"Than I," corrected Clifford Boyleston.

"Or than you," went on Mr. Simmons blandly. "We all agree that there is no one writing now who you need fear comparison with. Both in prose and verse you are absolutely first class. And your style—well, everyone knows your style."

"The opulence of Sir Thomas Browne with the lim-pidity of Cardinal Newman," said Clifford Boyleston. "The raciness of John Dryden with the precision of Jonathan Swift."

The only sign that Mrs. Albert Forrester heard was the smile that hesitated for a brief moment at the corners of her tragic mouth.

"And you have humour."

"Is there anyone in the world," cried Miss Waterford, "who can put such a wealth of wit and satire and comic observation into a semicolon?"

"But the fact remains that you don't sell," pursued Mr. Simmons imperturbably. "I've handled your work for twenty years and I tell you frankly that I shouldn't have grown fat on my commission, but I've handled it because now and again I like to do what I can for good work. I've always believed in you and I've hoped that sooner or later we might get the public to swallow you. But if you think you can make your living by writing the sort of stuff you do I'm bound to tell you that you haven't a chance."

"I have come into the world too late," said Mrs. Albert Forrester. "I should have lived in the eighteenth century when the wealthy patron rewarded a dedication with a hundred guineas."

"What do you suppose the currant business brings in?"

Mrs. Albert Forrester gave a little sigh.

"A pittance. Albert always told me he made about twelve hundred a year."

"He must be a very good manager. But you couldn't

expect him on that income to allow you very much. Take my word for it, there's only one thing for you to do and that's to get him back."

"I would rather live in a garret. Do you think I'm going to submit to the affront he has put upon me? Would you have me battle for his affections with my cook? Do not forget that there is one thing which is more valuable to a woman like me than her ease and that is her dignity."

"I was just coming to that," said Mr. Simmons coldly.

He glanced at the others and those strange, lopsided eyes of his looked more than ever monstrous and fish-like.

"There is no doubt in my mind," he went on, "that you have a very distinguished and almost unique position in the world of letters. You stand for something quite apart. You never prostituted your genius for filthy lucre and you have held high the banner of pure art. You're thinking of going into Parliament. I don't think much of politics myself, but there's no denying that it would be a good advertisement, and if you get in I daresay we could get you a lecture tour in America on the strength of it. You have ideals and this I can say, that even the people who've never read a word you've written respect you. But in your position there's one thing you can't afford to be and that's a joke."

Mrs. Albert Forrester gave a distinct start.

"What on earth do you mean by that?"

"I know nothing about Mrs. Bulfinch and for all I know she's a very respectable woman, but the fact remains that a man doesn't run away with his cook without making his wife ridiculous. If it had been a dancer or a lady of title I daresay it wouldn't have done you any harm, but a cook would finish you. In a week you'd have all London laughing at you, and if there's one thing that kills an author or a politician it is ridicule. You must get your husband back and you must get him back pretty damned quick."

A dark flush settled on Mrs. Albert Forrester's face, but she did not immediately reply. In her ears there rang on a sudden the outrageous and unaccountable laughter that had sent Miss Warren flying from the room.

"We're all friends here and you can count on our discretion."

Mrs. Forrester looked at her friends and she thought that in Rose Waterford's eyes there was already a malicious gleam. On the wizened face of Oscar Charles was a whimsical look. She wished that in a moment of abandon she had not betrayed her secret. Mr. Simmons, however, knew the literary world and allowed his eyes to rest on the company.

"After all, you are the centre and head of their set. Your husband has not only run away from you but also from them. It's not too good for them either. The fact is that Albert Forrester has made you all look a lot of damned fools."

"All," said Clifford Boyleston. "We're all in the same boat. He's quite right, Mrs. Forrester, The Philatelist must come back."

"*Et tu, Brute.*"

Mr. Simmons did not understand Latin and if he

had would probably not have been moved by Mrs. Albert Forrester's exclamation. He cleared his throat.

"My suggestion is that Mrs. Albert Forrester should go and see him to-morrow—fortunately we have his address—and beg him to reconsider his decision. I don't know what sort of things a woman says on these occasions, but Mrs. Forrester has tact and imagination and she must say them. If Mr. Forrester makes any conditions she must accept them. She must leave no stone unturned."

"If you play your cards well there is no reason why you shouldn't bring him back here with you to-morrow evening," said Rose Waterford lightly.

"Will you do it, Mrs. Forrester?"

For two minutes, at least, turned away from them, she stared at the empty fireplace; then, drawing herself to her full height, she faced them.

"For my art's sake, not for mine. I will not allow the ribald laughter of the Philistine to besmirch all that I hold good and true and beautiful."

"Capital," said Mr. Simmons, rising to his feet, "I'll look in on my way home to-morrow and I hope to find you and Mr. Forrester billing and cooing side by side like a pair of turtledoves."

He took his leave, and the others, anxious not to be left alone with Mrs. Albert Forrester and her agitation, in a body followed his example.

It was latish in the afternoon next day when Mrs. Albert Forrester, imposing in black silk and a velvet toque, set out from her flat in order to get a bus from the Marble Arch that would take her to Victoria Station. Mr. Simmons had explained to her by telephone how to reach the Kennington Road with expedition and economy. She neither felt nor looked like Delilah. At Victoria she took the tram that runs down the Vauxhall Bridge Road. When she crossed the river she found herself in a part of London more noisy, sordid and bustling than that to which she was accustomed, but she was too much occupied with her thoughts to notice the varied scene. She was relieved to find that the tram went along the Kennington Road, and asked the conductor to put her down a few doors from the house she sought. When it did and rumbled on, leaving her alone in the busy street, she felt strangely lost, like a traveller in an Eastern tale set down by a djinn in an unknown city. She walked slowly, looking to right and left, and notwithstanding the emotions of indignation and embarrassment that fought for the possession of her somewhat opulent bosom she could not but reflect that here was the material for a very pretty piece of prose. The little houses held about them the feeling of a bygone age when here it was still almost country, and Mrs. Albert Forrester registered in her retentive memory a note that she must look into the literary associations of the Kennington Road. Number 411 was one of a row of shabby houses that stood some way back from the street; in front of it was a narrow strip of shabby grass, and a paved way led up to a latticed wooden porch that badly needed a coat of paint. This and the straggling, stunted creeper that grew over the front of the house gave it a falsely rural air which was strange and even sinister in that road down which thundered a tumultuous traffic. There was something equivocal about the house that suggested that here lived women to whom a life of pleasure had brought an inadequate reward.

The door was opened by a scraggy girl of fifteen with long legs and a tousled head.

"Does Mrs. Bulfinch live here, do you know?"

"You've rung the wrong bell. Second floor." The girl pointed to the stairs and at the same time screamed shrilly: "Mrs. Bulfinch, a party to see you. Mrs. Bulfinch."

Mrs. Albert Forrester walked up the dingy stairs. They were covered with torn carpet. She walked slowly, for she did not wish to get out of breath. A door opened as she reached the second floor, and she recognized her cook.

"Good-afternoon, Bulfinch," said Mrs. Albert Forrester, with dignity. "I wish to see your master."

Mrs. Bulfinch hesitated for the shadow of a second, then held the door wide open.

"Come in, ma'am." She turned her head. "Albert, here's Mrs. Forrester to see you."

Mrs. Forrester stepped by quickly and there was Albert sitting by the fire in a leather-covered but rather shabby armchair, with his feet in slippers, and in shirt sleeves. He was reading the evening paper and smoking a cigar. He rose to his feet as Mrs. Albert Forrester came in. Mrs. Bulfinch followed her visitor into the room and closed the door.

"How are you, my dear?" said Albert cheerfully. "Keeping well, I hope."

THE CREATIVE IMPULSE   287

"You'd better put on your coat, Albert," said Mrs. Bulfinch. "What *will* Mrs. Forrester think of you, finding you like that? I never."

She took the coat, which was hanging on a peg, and helped him into it; and, like a woman familiar with the peculiarities of masculine dress, pulled down his waistcoat so that it should not ride over his collar.

"I received your letter, Albert," said Mrs. Forrester.

"I supposed you had, or you wouldn't have known my address, would you?"

"Won't you sit down, ma'am?" said Mrs. Bulfinch, deftly dusting a chair, part of a suite covered in plum-coloured velvet, and pushing it forwards.

Mrs. Albert Forrester with a slight bow seated herself.

"I should have preferred to see you alone, Albert," she said.

His eyes twinkled.

"Since anything you have to say concerns Mrs. Bulfinch as much as it concerns me I think it much better that she should be present."

"As you wish."

Mrs. Bulfinch drew up a chair and sat down. Mrs. Albert Forrester had never seen her before but with a large apron over a print dress. She was wearing now an open-work blouse of white silk, a black skirt, and high-heeled, patent-leather shoes with silver buckles. She was a woman of about five-and-forty, with reddish hair and a reddish face, not pretty, but with a good-natured look, and buxom. She reminded Mrs. Albert Forrester of a serving-wench, somewhat overblown, in a jolly picture by an old Dutch master.

"Well, my dear, what have you to say to me?" asked Albert.

Mrs. Albert Forrester gave him her brightest and most affable smile. Her great black eyes shone with tolerant good-humour.

"Of course you know that this is perfectly absurd, Albert. I think you must be out of your mind."

"Do you, my dear? Fancy that."

"I'm not angry with you, I'm only amused, but a joke's a joke and should not be carried too far. I've come to take you home."

"Was my letter not quite clear?"

"Perfectly. I ask no questions and I will make no reproaches. We will look upon this as a momentary aberration and say no more about it."

"Nothing will induce me ever to live with you again, my dear," said Albert in, however, a perfectly friendly fashion.

"You're not serious?"

"Quite."

"Do you love this woman?"

Mrs. Albert Forrester still smiled with an eager and somewhat metallic brightness. She was determined to take the matter lightly. With her intimate sense of values she realized that the scene was comic. Albert looked at Mrs. Bulfinch and a smile broke out on his withered face.

"We get on very well together, don't we, old girl?"

"Not so bad," said Mrs. Bulfinch.

Mrs. Albert Forrester raised her eyebrows; her husband had never in all their married life called *her* 'old girl': nor indeed would she have wished it.

"If Bulfinch has any regard or respect for you she must know that the thing is impossible. After the life you've led and the society you've moved in she can hardly expect to make you permanently happy in miserable furnished lodging."

"They're not furnished lodgin's, ma'am," said Mrs. Bulfinch. "It's all me own furniture. You see, I'm very independent like and I've always liked to have a home of me own. So I keep these rooms on whether I'm in a situation or whether I'm not, and so I always have some place to go back to."

"And a very nice cozy little place it is," said Albert.

Mrs. Albert Forrester looked about her. There was a kitchen range in the fireplace on which a kettle was simmering, and on the mantelshelf was a black marble clock flanked by black marble candelabra. There was a large table covered with a red cloth, a dresser, and a sewing-machine. On the walls were photographs and framed pictures from Christmas supplements. A door at the back, covered with a red plush portière, led into what, considering the size of the house, Mrs. Albert Forrester (who in her leisure moments had made a somewhat extensive study of architecture) could not but conclude was the only bedroom. Mrs. Bulfinch and Albert lived in a contiguity that allowed no doubt about their relations.

"Have you not been happy with me, Albert?" asked Mrs. Forrester in a deeper tone.

"We've been married for thirty-five years, my dear.

It's too long. It's a great deal too long. You're a good woman in your way, but you don't suit me. You're literary and I'm not. You're artistic and I'm not."

"I've always taken care to make you share in all my interests. I've taken great pains that you shouldn't be overshadowed by my success. You can't say that I've ever left you out of things."

"You're a wonderful writer, I don't deny it for a moment, but the truth is I don't like the books you write."

"That, if I may be permitted to say so, merely shows that you have very bad taste. All the best critics admit their power and their charm."

"And I don't like your friends. Let me tell you a secret, my dear. Often at your parties I've had an almost irresistible impulse to take off all my clothes just to see what would happen."

"Nothing would have happened," said Mrs. Albert Forrester with a slight frown. "I should merely have sent for the doctor."

"Besides, you haven't the figure for that, Albert," said Mrs. Bulfinch.

Mr. Simmons had hinted to Mrs. Albert Forrester that if the need arose she must not hesitate to use the allurements of her sex in order to bring back her erring husband to the conjugal roof, but she did not in the least know how to do this. It would have been easier, she could not but reflect, had she been in evening dress.

"Does the fidelity of five-and-thirty years count for nothing? I have never looked at another man, Albert. I'm used to you. I shall be lost without you."

"I've left all my menus with the new cook, ma'am. You've only got to tell her how many to luncheon and she'll manage," said Mrs. Bulfinch. "She's very reliable and she has as light a hand with pastry as anyone I ever knew."

Mrs. Albert Forrester began to be discouraged. Mrs. Bulfinch's remark, well-meant no doubt, made it difficult to bring the conversation onto the plane on which emotion could be natural.

"I'm afraid you're only wasting your time, my dear," said Albert. "My decision is irrevocable. I'm not very young any more and I want someone to take care of me. I shall of course make you as good an allowance as I can. Corinne wants me to retire."

"Who is Corinne?" asked Mrs. Forrester with the utmost surprise.

"It's my name," said Mrs. Bulfinch. "My mother was half French."

"That explains a great deal," replied Mrs. Forrester, pursing her lips, for though she admired the literature of the French she knew that their morals left much to be desired.

"What I say is, Albert's worked long enough, and it's about time he started enjoying himself. I've got a little bit of property at Clacton-on-Sea. It's a very healthy neighbourhood and the air is wonderful. We could live there very comfortable. And what with the beach and the pier there's always something to do. They're a very nice lot of people down there. If you don't interfere with nobody, nobody'll interfere with you."

"I discussed the matter with my partners to-day and they're willing to buy me out. It means a certain sacrifice. When everything is settled I shall have an income of nine hundred pounds a year. There are three of us, so it gives us just three hundred a year apiece."

"How am I to live on that?" cried Mrs. Albert Forrester. "I have my position to keep up."

"You have a fluent, a fertile and a distinguished pen, my dear."

Mrs. Albert Forrester impatiently shrugged her shoulders.

"You know very well that my books don't bring me in anything but reputation. The publishers always say that they lose by them and in fact they only publish them because it gives them prestige."

It was then that Mrs. Bulfinch had the idea that was to have consequences of such magnitude.

"Why don't you write a good thrilling detective story?" she asked.

"Me?" exclaimed Mrs. Albert Forrester, for the first time in her life regardless of grammar.

"It's not a bad idea," said Albert. "It's not a bad idea at all."

"I should have the critics down on me like a thousand of bricks."

"I'm not so sure of that. Give the highbrow the chance of being lowbrow without demeaning himself and he'll be so grateful to you, he won't know what to do."

"For this relief much thanks," murmured Mrs. Albert Forrester reflectively.

"My dear, the critics'll eat it. And written in your

beautiful English they won't be afraid to call it a masterpiece."

"The idea is preposterous. It's absolutely foreign to my genius. I could never hope to please the masses."

"Why not? The masses want to read good stuff, but they dislike being bored. They all know your name, but they don't read you, because you bore them. The fact is, my dear, you're dull."

"I don't know how you can say that, Albert," replied Mrs. Albert Forrester, with as little resentment as the equator might feel if someone called it chilly. "Everyone knows and acknowledges that I have an exquisite sense of humour and there is nobody who can extract so much good wholesome fun from a semicolon as I can."

"If you can give the masses a good thrilling story and let them think at the same time that they are improving their minds you'll make a fortune."

"I've never read a detective story in my life," said Mrs. Albert Forrester. "I once heard of a Mr. Barnes of New York and I was told that he had written a book called *The Mystery of a Hansom Cab*. But I never read it."

"Of course you have to have the knack," said Mrs. Bulfinch. "The first thing to remember is that you don't want any love-making—it's out of place in a detective story; what you want is murder, and sleuth-hounds, and you don't want to be able to guess who done it till the last page."

"But you must play fair with your reader, my dear," said Albert. "It always annoys me when suspicion has been thrown on the secretary or the lady of title and it turns out to be the second footman who's never done more than say, 'The carriage is at the door.' Puzzle your reader as much as you can, but don't make a fool of him."

"I love a good detective story," said Mrs. Bulfinch. "Give me a lady in evening dress, just streaming with diamonds, lying on the library floor with a dagger in her heart and I know I'm going to have a treat."

"There's no accounting for tastes," said Albert. "Personally, I prefer a respectable family solicitor, with side-whiskers, gold watch chain, and a benign appearance, lying dead in Hyde Park."

"With his throat cut?" asked Mrs. Bulfinch eagerly.

"No, stabbed in the back. There's something peculiarly attractive to the reader in the murder of a middle-aged gentleman of spotless reputation. It is pleasant to think that the most apparently blameless of us have a mystery in our lives."

"I see what you mean, Albert," said Mrs. Bulfinch. "He was the repository of a fatal secret."

"We can give you all the tips, my dear," said Albert, smiling mildly at Mrs. Albert Forrester. "I've read hundreds of detective stories."

"You!"

"That's what first brought Corinne and me together. I used to pass them on to her when I'd finished them."

"Many's the time I've heard him switch off the electric light as the dawn was creeping through the window and I couldn't help smiling to myself as I said: 'There, he's finished it at last, now he can have a good sleep.'"

Mrs. Albert Forrester rose to her feet. She drew herself up.

"Now I see what a gulf separates us," she said, and her fine contralto shook a little. "You have been surrounded for thirty years with all that was best in English literature and you read hundreds of detective novels."

"Hundreds and hundreds," interrupted Albert with a smile of satisfaction.

"I came here willing to make any reasonable concession so that you should come back to your home, but now I wish it no longer. You have shown me that we have nothing in common and never had. There is an abyss between us."

"Very well, my dear," said Albert gently, "I will submit to your decision. But you think over the detective story."

"I will arise and go now," she murmured, "and go to Innisfree."

"I'll just show you downstairs," said Mrs. Bulfinch. "One has to be careful of the carpet if one doesn't exactly know where the holes are."

With dignity, but not without circumspection, Mrs. Albert Forrester walked downstairs, and when Mrs. Bulfinch opened the door and asked her if she would like a taxi she shook her head.

"I shall take the tram."

"You need not be afraid that I won't take good care of Mr. Forrester, ma'am," said Mrs. Bulfinch pleasantly. "He shall have every comfort. I nursed Mr. Bulfinch for three years during his last illness and there's very little I don't know about invalids. Not that Mr.

Forrester isn't very strong and active for his years. And of course he'll have a hobby. I always think a man should have a hobby. He's going to collect postage-stamps."

Mrs. Albert Forrester gave a little start of surprise. But just then a tram came in sight and, as a woman (even the greatest of them) will, she hurried at the risk of her life into the middle of the road and waved frantically. It stopped and she climbed in. She did not know how she was going to face Mr. Simmons. He would be waiting for her when she got home. Clifford Boyleston would probably be there too. They would all be there and she would have to tell them that she had miserably failed. At that moment she had no warm feeling of friendship towards her little group of devoted admirers. Wondering what the time was, she looked up at the man sitting opposite her to see whether he was the kind of person she could modestly ask, and suddenly started; for sitting there was a middle-aged gentleman of the most respectable appearance, with side-whiskers, a benign expression and a gold watch chain. It was the very man whom Albert had described lying dead in Hyde Park and she could not but jump to the conclusion that he was a family solicitor. The coincidence was extraordinary and really it looked as though the hand of fate were beckoning to her. He wore a silk hat, a black coat and pepper-and-salt trousers, he was somewhat corpulent, of a powerful build, and by his side was a despatch-case. When the tram was halfway down the Vauxhall Bridge Road he asked the conductor to stop and she saw him go down a small, mean street. Why?

Ah, why? When it reached Victoria, so deeply immersed in thought was she, until the conductor somewhat roughly told her where she was, she did not move. Edgar Allan Poe had written detective stories. She took a bus. She sat inside, buried in reflection, but when it arrived at Hyde Park Corner she suddenly made up her mind to get out. She couldn't sit still any longer. She felt she must walk. She entered the gates, walking slowly, and looked about her with an air that was at once intent and abstracted. Yes, there was Edgar Allan Poe; no one could deny that. After all, he had invented the genre, and everyone knew how great his influence had been on the Parnassians. Or was it the Symbolists? Never mind. Baudelaire and all that. As she passed the Achilles Statue she stopped for a minute and looked at it with raised eyebrows.

At length she reached her flat and, opening the door, saw several hats in the hall. They were all there. She went into the drawing-room.

"Here she is at last," cried Miss Waterford.

Mrs. Albert Forrester advanced, smiling with animation, and shook the proffered hands. Mr. Simmons and Clifford Boyleston were there, Harry Oakland and Oscar Charles.

"Oh, you poor things, have you had no tea?" she cried brightly. "I haven't an idea what the time is, but I know I'm fearfully late."

"Well?" they said. "Well?"

"My dears, I've got something quite wonderful to tell you. I've had an inspiration. Why should the devil have all the best tunes?"

"What *do* you mean?"

She paused in order to give full effect to the surprise she was going to spring upon them. Then she flung it at them without preamble:

"I'M GOING TO WRITE A DETECTIVE STORY."

They stared at her with open mouths. She held up her hand to prevent them from interrupting her, but indeed no one had the smallest intention of doing so.

"I am going to raise the detective story to the dignity of Art. It came to me suddenly in Hyde Park. It's a murder story and I shall give the solution on the very last page. I shall write it in an impeccable English, and since it's occurred to me lately that perhaps I've exhausted the possibilities of the semicolon, I am going to take up the colon. No one yet has explored its potentialities. Humour and mystery are what I aim at. I shall call it *The Achilles Statue*."

"What a title!" cried Mr. Simmons, recovering himself before any of the others. "I can sell the serial rights on the title and your name alone."

"But what about Albert?" asked Clifford Boyleston.

"Albert?" echoed Mrs. Forrester. "Albert?"

She looked at him as though for the life of her she could not think what he was talking about. Then she gave a little cry as if she had suddenly remembered.

"Albert! I knew I'd gone out on some errand and it absolutely slipped my memory. I was walking through Hyde Park and I had this inspiration. What a fool you'll all think me!"

"Then you haven't seen Albert?"

"My dear, I forgot all about him." She gave an amused laugh. "Let Albert keep his cook. I can't bother about Albert now. Albert belongs to the semicolon period. I am going to write a detective story."

"My dear, you're too, too wonderful," said Harry Oakland.